Devil's Cave

Devil's Cave

The Treasure Lost—Circa, 1600

A Novel by

John Nuzzolese

Library of Congress Control Number: 2008905804
ISBN: Hardcover   978-1-4363-5287-1
                   Softcover   978-1-4363-5286-4

To order additional copies of this book, contact:
Xlibris Corporation
1-888-795-4274
www.Xlibris.com
Orders@Xlibris.com
50602

Contents

Dedication

*

For those who passed away in wonderment to whether there is a heaven or a hell standing in the wings to embrace them for all eternity. May enough good have been instilled in their lives, that the compassionate Savior's redemptive love will grant them an endless abode of everlasting happiness.

Acknowledgments

Gratitude and thanks to

The Child of Bethlehem, Lord and Savior, Jesus Christ

*you were born to die and enlighten, so that we may have eternal life.

My family and friends

*who encouraged me along the way.

The staff of the Centennial Park Library, Holiday, Florida

*for your cooperation and assistance in the research process.

Susie Kruse

*for being you.

John Brough

*for your promotional support.

Editors, mentors, and collaborators

*in making this publication a reality.

Introduction

Since the beginning of time, nature ranks supreme among the great artists. She ceaselessly scrawls her signature upon earth's incessant changing surface. Picasso and Rembrandt humbly acknowledge the matchless strokes of universal splendor reflected in each approaching dawn and every setting sun. Monet applauds nature's enriched blends of harmony and texture, as seen in white-covered mountains and painted deserts, greenish seas and tinctured skies. Michelangelo's finest sculpture graciously genuflects to the magnificent craftsmanship keenly etched in the far reaches of heaven's endless, glorious rapture.

It was during the age of ice when retreating glaciers and melting snowcaps gave form and grandeur to one of creation's most coveted treasures, a vast meandering coastline that stretches from the steep evading cliffs of Nova Scotia to the glistening emerald lakes of sunny Florida. Along the northern sector of this shoreline is one of nature's remarkable blunders, a geological indignity, an errant chromosome of sorts.

Amid the countless folds and ocean inlets that saturate Maine's rugged coast is a peculiar hollow or indentation. This ominous cavity looms menacingly at the base of a huge granite precipice that juts into the sea. There are numerous blowing caves and spouting rocks indigenous to this particular region, but none is more beguiling to the eye than Devil's Cave. The hellish manifestation looks quite beastly, almost alive, as it were.

Devil's Cave. To describe this underwater catacomb would be utter folly. The hollow stretches far beneath the bedrock from which it was formed. When the tide crests beneath the craggy buttress where this watery sanctuary abides, its aperture disappears from view. After the current is spent and ripples to a low ebb, the cave with a reproachful sneering stare reappears again. Treacherous rocks protrude from its surrounding depths. Crashing tons of saltwater seesaw in and out of the cave's entrance. Beleaguered by tempestuous waves, its cavernous jaws rhythmically cough up a foamy backwash. Bubbling eddies and lurid whirlpools monotonously lap at the imposing sight. Years of erosion etched a hideous toothy grimace upon the mouth of the granite face. Many wayfarers who had encountered Devil's Cave vouched to anyone who would hear their tale of woe that they had seen the devil himself.

According to legend, like the serpent of Genesis, there exists a foreboding enmity between the cave and all living things. It imprints an indelible mark in the consciousness of those whose paths have unavoidably clashed with this monolithic creature. Many are the lives it has claimed. Countless are the souls it has shattered. Devil's Cave is the pivotal fulcrum upon which several characters realize an insufferable fate. This is their compelling tale, one that speaks of a common nemesis, a rakish hellhole they have encountered and come to loath.

Devil's Cave is a place where strength and determination intermingle with perils of adventure. Daring and courage interlope with deceit and murder. Romance jousts with lust, and good collides with evil. It is here too that avarice and revenge entwine, and strange twists of fate unlock deep dark secrets of years long since remembered. After all is said and done, several people's lives, past and present, will have been ensnared in the gripping wake of Devil's Cave. This is their saga, as difficult it may seem to believe or even imagine. First, however, there is the beginning.

The Caribbean

Prologue

According to legend, a hastily etched map discloses the proximity of the richest contraband deposit ever concealed in history. The scroll managed to thread its way through the centuries where it currently lays obscurely veiled in an old Key West antique emporium. How it ended up there is an enigma in itself. All this time the exact location of the treasure map remained a mystery, as did its curious inscriptions. Determined to possess the centuries-old papyrus and fathom the secrets it contained, countless fortune hunters fell into the hands of iniquity and lost their ill-fated lives.

Ironically, the buried hoard of riches was thought to have been deliberately amassed to bait a delinquent statesman who turned to piracy and sought refuge in the Caribbean. Wanted more than any other buccaneer to have combed the high seas, Captain Marquis Jacques Lafitte, former French secretary of the Treasury, had been accused of betraying his king by fleeing Versailles with the newly constructed and unprecedented five-mast brigantine, a gift Her Majesty intended to present to her husband on the anniversary of his coronation.

Captain Lafitte and his small argosy of stolen merchant ships dodged naval fleets and bounty hunters seeking their capture. The band of rogue pirates fortified their hijacked brigantines with long-range cannons to defend themselves against anyone who dared to engage them in battle. Whenever Lafitte's renegades sighted a flotilla of enemy ships that outnumbered them, they sought sanctuary among the many protective lagoons that provided adequate shelter from their predators.

Ile de la Tortue was the perfect haven for such buccaneers. Situated off the coast of Hispaniola, it gave suitable refuge to Lafitte and his clique of ex-patriots who had a vendetta for the French government in connection to the many injustices sanctioned against them. Its steep cliffs and towering shoreline trees provided an umbrella of camouflage for Lafitte's tall-mast ship from being detected by vigilant spy watchers who incessantly canvassed island shores from atop their crow's nests.

Jacques and his unrelenting band of corsairs were desperately wanted for the havoc they incurred upon the various entrepreneurs who had established lucrative shipping lanes connecting Europe to the New World. Any merchant ship in alliance with France was targeted by Captain Lafitte and his bold marauders. Because this was very costly to the reigning sovereigns whose financial interests were entwined with greedy French capitalists who extorted commoners of what little possessions they had, a handsome reward was collectively offered to anyone for the capture of the delinquent ship, *Dantes's Revenge*.

In lieu of all this, the Crowns of Europe declared a general amnesty for all pirates in the Caribbean who would willingly quit their illegal plundering. This forgiving absolution guaranteed a full pardon for all sea rovers who surrendered peacefully to any lawful authority on either side of the ocean. Jacques Lafitte and his crew of convicts who had fallen from grace scoffed at the notion of capitulation. They continued to plunder and ease seafarers of their personal treasures. When a merchant ship refused to give up its cargo and attempted to elude the bandits, it was only then that unavoidable bloodshed took its toll.

Life was to be respected at all costs. Amid a rally on the forecastle of the *Dantes's Revenge*, the name given to the king's hijacked ship by Jacques Lafitte (in memory of his father who had been dishonored and murdered by an unscrupulous state official), the flamboyant captain endorsed these words of solidarity to his crew. "Mateys, if we value a single human life, we value that which is greater than gold or trinket. And I promise you, my brethren, in the end God Almighty will not chastise us for what we have done or will continue to do in the name of justice. Until our quarrel is consummated, we will remain united and steadfast in our purpose. Let us honor in our hearts the brotherhood we have sworn to uphold until our last dying breath. Long live *Dantes's Revenge*!"

So it was. Captain Lafitte and his fellowship of buccaneers were as one. The disenchanted pirates deemed the amnesty promised by the Crowns of

Europe insincere rhetoric. With a purpose in mind, they continued menacing cargo ships. Unbeknown to Jacques Lafitte, an ill-conceived plan had been contrived to draw him into the open, a plan that would go awry and cost the English, Spanish, and French monarchs the loss of the largest combined treasure ever amassed. Fortune hunters would overwhelmingly concede that the countless hidden treasure chests of contraband buried somewhere in the wake of Captain Lafitte's spine-chilling adventure is the largest cache ever to have disappeared in the annals of history.

"I, Charles, Sovereign King of France, do take thee, Catherine, daughter of King Edward of England, to be my wedded wife, to have and to hold, from this day forward, for better, for worse, for richer, for poorer, in sickness and in health, to love and to cherish, till death do us part, according to God's holy ordinance, and thereto I pledge thee my troth."

"In the name of God, I, Catherine, daughter of King Edward of England, take you, Charles, Sovereign King of France, to be my husband, to have and to hold from this day forward, for better for worse, for richer for poorer, in sickness and in health, to love and to cherish, until we are parted by death. This is my solemn promise."

"What God hath joined together, let no man put asunder. I now pronounce you man and wife."

With the two of them duly married by the Bishop of Canterbury, our tale begins where an abundance of adventurous twists and turns unravel their secrets.

For what she was about to do, Catherine, the Queen of France, knelt before a crucifix in her private chapel and thusly prayed:

Forgive me my sins, O Lord,

*forgive me my sins; the sins of my youth,
the sins of my age, the sins of my soul,
the sins of my body; my idle sins,
my serious voluntary sins, the sins I know,
the sins I have concealed so long, and
which are now hidden from my memory.*

*I am truly sorry for every sin, mortal
and venial, for all the sins of my childhood
up to the present hour.*

*I know my sins have wounded Thy tender
Heart, O my Savior, let me be freed from
the bonds of evil through the most bitter
passion of my Redeemer.*

*O my Jesus, forget and forgive what I
have been. Amen.*

Her Majesty's Dilemma

The queen sat primly in an elegant silk threaded chair. Her slender fingers were fidgeting with the lace handkerchief she kept tucked away in the cuff of an embroidered sleeve. It would be difficult for Catherine to hold her tongue, but common sense prompted Her Majesty not to speak. She made this decision even before the conclave came to order. Whatever transpired here was secondary to her personal agenda which she forthwith planned to unleash. Since the crown jewels belonged to the throne, and their destiny was on the verge of being disclosed, the queen needed to know precisely how the council intended to use them in the scheme of things about to unfold.

Catherine felt distraught and alone. How could matters have unraveled so chaotically? Unanswered questions continuously raced through her mind. Conflicting thoughts shrouded her thinking, as would the dazzling jewel-studded tiara she donned impair her vision upon looking in a sun-laden mirror. Did Jacques still love her? It had been almost eight months since she last saw him. Would she ever see him again? she wondered.

If Catherine were someone else, not the Queen of France, perhaps her emotions would help her to see things more arbitrarily. Maybe then the pain would subside. Her heart needed to calm itself; think rationally. She'd give anything right now to have a moment's peace. The more she thought about him, the deeper Catherine felt entangled in her quandary. Though the queen was an exceptionally handsome woman, at the present she felt nothing of beauty or contentment.

The meeting came to order in an anteroom adjacent to the royal stately quarters that reflected late fifteenth-century baroque grandeur. A display of antique furnishings gave the chamber a distinguished appearance in a grotesque sort of way. Lord Governor Jean Dupree, who had been influential in establishing a cluster of recently acquired French colonies in the Caribbean, remained seated as he addressed King Charles and a small assembly of loyal officials who listened attentively to the corpulent speaker.

"Contrary to those who'd rather proceed with caution, Your Majesty, after conferring with various astute commercial advisors, my colleagues and I see fit to endorse Monsieur Fuquay's proposal. Martinique's inaugural occasion justifies the minimal risk his meticulous plan suggests. Displaying the crown jewels abroad can do nothing less than enhance France's prestige in the New World."

Dupree stood up and removed a chiffon cloth that covered a map resting on an easel. "If we pool our resources here"—he was pointing to a chain of islands located in the Caribbean—"the result will surely give France a decisive edge in establishing her presence and sovereign rule in the West Indies. Countless islands are overflowing with lush, natural treasures just waiting to be plucked."

"Like plump barnyard chickens being readied for a feast, Monsieur Dupree?" The king's aloof remark extracted a smattering of courteous laughter from the assembled dignitaries.

Acknowledging His Majesty's usual dry sense of humor, the speaker dignified Charles's witticism with a slight bow of the head. Dupree continued. "We can no longer procrastinate asserting ourselves in the West. Not only will an elaborate display of the crown jewels confirm France's eminent domain abroad, but the occasion will ratify her eagerness to share a touch of royal splendor with her newly acquired alliances. Anyone opposing France's interests in the West Indies, according to your latest proclamation, will do so under the severest reprisals."

"At the moment, Monsieur Dupree, I am more interested in listening to what you have to say concerning your report on Lafitte," retorted Charles. Upon hearing his name, Catherine's heart skipped a beat. She was aware of the council's plan to capture him. It had been gone over and rehashed several times. The crown jewels, among other things, would serve as bait to entice the dishonorable statesman into the open. Jacques Lafitte had a number of charges against him including high treason, grand theft, and piracy.

Charles was none too happy when news reached his ears that Jacques Lafitte, former Treasury minister to the king's court, had hijacked and absconded with His Majesty's newly constructed royal brigantine, a ship Catherine endorsed him to build in honor of her husband's fifteenth anniversary coronation ceremony. Its unprecedented five masts and one hundred twenty cannons simply vanished from the port of Versailles's naval shipyard. The indignation was so contemptuous Charles ordered, under the penalty of imprisonment, that the incident be stricken from public discourse.

"If I may, Your Majesty," interrupted Pierre Fuquay, who had filled the ministerial position vacated by Lafitte. Taking the pointer from Dupree, he said, "The plan to capture Monsieur Lafitte is in readiness. With your approval, Your Grace, dozens of combat vessels will escort the primary convoy carrying the crown jewels to Martinique. The heavily laden treasure ships will sail under the protection of twenty of Your Majesty's elite French brigantines. They will form an arc here, safeguarding the bow and starboard positions of the cargo ships for the duration of the journey. Furthermore, ten Spanish galleons will flank the portside here, and another twenty British naval schooners will form a protective shield to the rear in the event Lafitte circumvents the escort and tries to forge an attack from the east. As you can see, we have taken the precaution that his small fleet might emerge from one of the numerous lagoons that populate the island waters."

"Monsieur Fuquay, do you think Lafitte is the ordinary fool you take him to be?" Charles spoke with a resonance of impatience. "The web you have spun for him may very well ensure the shipment's safety, but only a mad dog would attempt a skirmish on the high seas against such odds. I hate to disappoint you, Pierre, but Lafitte will not jeopardize his meager handful of rogue ships to engage an attack that seems so futile. Though the prize is tempting enough, he'll most certainly bide his time and wait for a more opportune moment in securing a loophole in your plan of using plunder to capture him." The king's apparent lack of faith prompted Fuquay to retaliate quickly.

"Not exactly, Your Majesty. Monsieur Lafitte, as you say, may not be an ordinary fool, but nonetheless he is a fool. You see, his personal vendetta against me, which is no secret to anyone, will, shall we say, encourage him to make an unannounced call."

"And just how, may I inquire, does that have any significance here, Fuquay?" Before Pierre could answer, Charles continued to say, "Might, I remind you, that while you are in France, Lafitte at the moment is undoubtedly commandeering another one of my cargo ships almost halfway round the world." Somewhat sarcastically Charles added, "Under the circumstances one would think my Treasury minister might find it somewhat comforting in keeping it that way."

Ignoring the king's facetious remark, Fuquay continued. "What if Lafitte was to somehow learn that I, Monsieur Fuquay, will be accompanying the transport to Martinique? Do you suppose he would find it amusing? After all, has he not accused me of his father's death and vowed his vengeance? My presence in the Caribbean would seem, don't you think, reason enough for him to come out of hiding? You see, Your Highness, as each of us here can attest, Lafitte is a treacherous liar."

When he spoke those last few words, Fuquay gave Catherine a quizzical glance. How else could the statesman who turned pirate have sailed off with the king's own ship? The queen was obviously duped into believing the flamboyant young politician was a man of honor. To safeguard what really transpired during that fateful occasion, Catherine had to maintain her silence. She chose not to dignify Fuquay's remark with the remotest expression of acknowledgment.

"Continue, Fuquay. What is it you have in mind?" The king's voice noticeably softened.

"Your Majesty, Lafitte is vulnerable. He too has an Achilles' heel."

"Don't we all?" the king injected amusingly. A soft chuckle emanated from the gathered listeners. Charles smiled wryly. The audience was obviously entertained by his frivolous remark. "Go on, Monsieur Fuquay, I'm listening. We're all ears." Pausing for a sip of water, Pierre Fuquay continued in a more relaxed tone of voice.

"Lafitte and his infamous marauders stalk the shipping lanes looking for prey. Surely, by now, he has secured enough gold and trinkets to last a hundred years. So then, why does he continue his charades regarding what he intends to do next? I've researched this quite thoroughly, Your Highness. Nearly everyone of Lafitte's band of cutthroats, according to reliable sources from abroad, is a French expatriate. The rogues primarily attack ships whose sails bear the fleur-de-lis. I tell you, he's playing a game, Your Highness. His intent is to make a mockery of France."

"A game?" It was Lord Dupree who questioned Fuquay's perplexing remark. Ignoring the interruption, Fuquay remained focused on his train of thought.

"His motivation, as I see it, is revenge. Ever since he—" Catherine, upon hearing enough, spoke compellingly, but in a controlled voice.

"Monsieur Fuquay, we have been over this many times. Can you give His Majesty the intricate details of your proposal? I think right now that's what he wants to hear."

"Of course, Your Highness, I was just getting to that." Addressing the king once again, Fuquay added, "Your Majesty, as everyone here is aware, Monsieur Lafitte has publicly accused me of having something to do with his father's death and has promised an oath of vengeance against me. My presence at the inaugural colonization of Martinique will hardly dissuade the dastardly coward from inviting himself to the celebration."

Catherine had to restrain herself from showing any emotion. She knew full well that Fuquay would never have spoken those words to Jacques's face. "At the opportune moment"—Pierre's voice heightened dramatically—"when he thinks it's safe to act, Lafitte will come out of hiding. And that's when we'll get him."

"You've aroused my curiosity, Fuquay, what precisely do you plan to do?"

"Please forgive me, Your Liege, due to certain sensitive issues still to be finalized, if you permit me, I would like to divulge the intricacies of my proposal to you in private."

"Very well, Fuquay. It's extraordinary for my Treasury minister to venture abroad, but of late, that particular seat in my cabinet seems to have captivated all Europe's attention, much more than I could ever hope to achieve, if I lived for a millennium. Are we nearly finished here?"

"Yes, Your Eminence. Rest assured, in the end, France will control the West Indian shipping lanes, and Lafitte will no longer be a thorn in your crown. As you have stated earlier, he will undoubtedly avoid making his presence felt in open waters. If my plan comes to fruition, as I believe it will, the maverick will seal his doom on the isle of Martinique. And that's where we'll hang him." In a more subtle voice, he added, "Unless, Your Majesty, you'd rather we capture him and bring Captain Lafitte back to France so the people will see, firsthand, the exacting fate that befits anyone who has the audacity to oppose the crown."

Cringing at his words, the queen was convinced that whatever malevolent trickery Pierre Fuquay had contrived for Lafitte, she somehow had to intercede. Though clouds of confusion raced through her mind, Catherine knew in her heart that she still loved him. Fuquay's innuendoes were undoubtedly fabricated lies. His accusations were obviously garnished with falsified shreds of information purposely designed to mislead her husband. Though she knew Lafitte could easily outwit Fuquay, the unscrupulous magistrate could not be trusted. Catherine needed to learn the exact details of his nefarious plan before it was too late.

Failing to elicit a response from the king at his last words, Fuquay said, "If then, everything is to your satisfaction, a required signature or two on a few prepared documents will conclude these proceedings. All will be in readiness to set sail for Martinique this very afternoon, Your Highness." As an afterthought, he added, "Rest assured, Your Majesty, the plan I have devised to end Captain Lafitte's tyrannical acts of treason against the state is nothing more than a mere formality."

Charles replied with a blank stare, "Your reassurance is most convincing, Pierre."

While Fuquay verified the contents of the enormous treasure chest filled with a fortune of bullion in gold and silver, the king scrawled his name on several official documents set before him. The queen's encased tiara was the final piece to be carefully placed in the shipment. Every last item had been documented in a ledger and duly signed by Fuquay and Philippe De Villefort, the captain of the transport, *Vera Cruz*. Before the huge lid was closed and sealed, Catherine turned her head away. She truly believed the lovely crown she had come to cherish would never again adorn her noble head.

It disheartened the king to see a tear drift down the side of her disenchanted face. Since his prearranged marriage to the daughter of England's Crown, King Edward, it elated Charles that his beautiful young bride, upon inheriting the throne of France, often filled the palace with continuous gaiety and abundant cheer. It tantalized the maturing king when his young and beautiful, lighthearted Catherine amused him with coquettish bantering and humorous witticisms. He hoped that whatever transpired between his wife and the tyrant who commandeered his ship was nothing more than much of the same.

Reviving himself from his revelry, King Charles motioned to a gendarme standing next to one of the upper chamber windows to draw the curtains. Perhaps the early afternoon sun might shed a hint of light on what otherwise turned out to be a dismal occasion. Repeated shouts of "God save the queen!" resounded from the courtyard below. Instinctively, Catherine sashayed to the casement where the hoopla reverberated. The assembled crowd continued its chant, louder and louder.

"See to it, Fuquay," uttered Charles, somewhat perturbed. "What's this din I hear?"

"Certainly, Your Majesty," replied the Treasure secretary. Pierre went to the window where he eyed the situation carefully. Catherine peered over his shoulder and ceremoniously acknowledged the crowd with a slight wave of her handkerchief. She noticed several placards among the rowdy dissidents. One read *Despot*. Another hailed the word *Taxes* with a bloodstained sword precariously sticking through it. Fuquay returned to where Charles had reclined himself and said, "It's the usual peasantry doing its thing, nothing more, Your Majesty."

"And now, if you will," Governor Jean Dupree, minister of Foreign Affairs, spoke importantly, "the chest, as you can see, Your Majesty, has been officially processed. With your permission—" Charles nodded before Dupree finished his sentence. The governor signaled two courtiers to close the great lid and lock it shut. "If you please, Your Majesty, the imprint of your royal seal on this envelope containing the manifest will conclude these proceedings."

Charles limply motioned to a clerk who humbly approached the king with a bowl containing freshly prepared wax. Jean Dupree took it upon himself to generously spill the crimson paraffin on a portion of the document. With the imprint of the sovereign seal in place, the transfer of the precious cargo proceeded on schedule. Several courtiers hoisted the heavily laden chest onto a sturdy low-framed cart. Two other chests destined for the new colony and previously scrutinized joined the cavalcade. They contained elaborate silks, jewels, expensive porcelain pieces, coin, and rare artifacts—all vested interests of Spain and England. Their combined value paled in comparison to France's receptacle bearing the queen's tiara.

A flippant remark made by someone in the midst of the parade pervaded the quiet atmosphere. "Has anyone considered the consequences of what a stormy sea might bring to bear on His Majesty's treasure?" Fuquay turned and poked a menacing glare in the direction of the inquisitive spokesman.

Continuing along its way, the entourage meandered through stately rooms passing from one corridor to the next. The pageant took on a bizarre appearance. Catherine, with the suggestion of her husband, walked with Fuquay, arm in arm. They loathed one another. The ministers and Captain De Villefort were next. Their gait was somber, as though they were in the midst of a funeral procession. The three chests moved very slowly, as the king's chamberlains had been instructed to be most careful of their every step and turn. The coffer containing Catherine's jewels was last in line. Wheels clicked in unison and echoed rhythmically in the vaulted gallery. Charles kept to the rear of the retinue, trying to conceal a mischievous grin.

———

Several carriages, flanked with heavily armed escorts, remained poised inside the palace courtyard. Destined for the docks of Versailles, the caskets were to be transferred to three ships waiting in the harbor to receive their precious cargo. In brief intervals, the *Calcutta*, *King Richard*, and *Vera Cruz* would depart under the protective escort of a heavily armed flotilla. They'd zigzag along the Seine to Le Havre where a fleet of fifty brigantines milled about in the English Channel awaiting their arrival. From there it was clear sailing to new and fascinating places that promised an abundance of wondrous adventures and untold riches.

Catherine broke away from Fuquay and turned to hide her tears. Perhaps if they were plentiful enough, she could drown in them. What the queen didn't know was that her husband devised a clandestine plan of his own. Catherine's most prized possession, her illustrious diadem, had been under the scrutiny of the king more than she could have ever imagined.

II

An Uninvited Passenger

The continuous plundering of cargo ships in the Caribbean had European merchants in an uproar. Their earnings had dwindled to alarming proportions. In response to the economic havoc plaguing the continent, a guarantee of "safe passage" to all trading vessels was proclaimed in an edict collectively endorsed by the sovereign powers of England, France, and Spain. All cargo ships destined for the West Indies would be escorted by a contingent of naval vessels sailing under the banners of each of the three countries. Portugal and other imperialist nations declined to recognize the terms of the proclamation and elected to conduct their colonial operations independently.

France, it had been agreed, was the first of the allied states to initiate the "safe passage" strategy. Upon learning that a flotilla of supply ships representing the three nations was soon to leave the port of Versailles bound for the New World, bankers and financiers flocked to the scene to invest their financial support. When King Charles publicly announced his intentions to dispatch France's crown jewels abroad to promote goodwill in the West Indies, enterprising capitalists applauded the news as a guarantee for their own valuable merchandise.

The edict also pledged swift action against all tyrannizers and marauders. One by one they would be hunted down and extracted from the Caribbean seaways, including the captain of the *Dantes's Revenge*, Jacques Lafitte, and his notorious band of sea rovers. For the capture of the rogue pirate, dead or alive, King Charles promised a handsome reward of five thousand gold florins. The euphoric news spread like wildfire. Tons of manufactured goods soon began to cram cargo hatches, and countless valuable items were recorded in each of the ship's manifests. The three vessels carrying supplies to the New World were fully loaded in record time. A stevedore, who had carefully reviewed his checklist, alerted the boatswain standing on the foredeck of the *Vera Cruz* that the cargo had been loaded and the ship's departure was now at the discretion of the captain.

As the harbor loomed into view, a woman tapped the roof of her horse-drawn carriage with a parasol. Casting it aside, she reached for the door and said hastily, "Bevier, are we in time? Which one is the *Vera Cruz?*"

"Yes, Your Majesty. That's the *Calcutta* leaving its berth. She bears the Spanish coat of arms. The *King Richard* is next. Notice the English emblem on the top sail. We're approaching the *Vera Cruz* just now. You can see the fleur-de-lis pennant being hoisted at the bow." The inconspicuous coach came to a sudden halt. Hurriedly the queen alighted from the conveyance without assistance. She wore a black cape and matching hood that caressed the sides of her face. In her hand, she carried a lofty traveling bag.

"Please, Your Majesty, I beg you," pleaded Bevier, her attendant. "This adventure is far too dangerous. I implore you. Come back with me before the king realizes you left the palace."

"Hush, Bevier. I am compelled to do what I must." Scrambling from the carriage, she added, "Remember, not a word until His Majesty has had his breakfast. Quickly, make haste, coachman. Adieu!"

Upon giving the horses a crack of the whip, Bevier exclaimed, "God save the queen!" The black stallions clicked their heels and darted quickly past the pier and out of sight.

Catherine scrutinized her surroundings with apprehension. She suddenly felt overwhelmed with fear and trepidation. Perhaps Bevier was right. The thought of voyaging across the sea may not have been such a good idea, after all. Who could predict what dangers lay ahead?

A multitude of soldiers bearing muskets were stationed along the promenade leading to the docks. They wore blue blazers garnished with epaulets and gold-tinted buttons that glistened in the sunlight. The queen was pleased her tiara and the rest of the crown jewels were being well protected. The *Calcutta* had already passed from sight, and the *King Richard* was just now leaving its slip. Smaller boats had been ordered to stay clear of the three treasure ships until they had all safely departed from the quay.

Impoverished peasants were swarming the wharfs. Their hope was next to none in gaining passage on any of the ships destined for the New World. Catherine pitied them and often wondered why the state wasn't taking veritable notice of their deprived conditions. Charles simply told her not to worry her pretty little head about such trivialities. The lower class had obviously squandered whatever wealth they possessed, and that was indeed the greater pity. Her Majesty mustn't overly concern herself on their behalf he insisted, but if it would make her feel any better, he'd talk to his economic advisers to make certain that no one in France wanted for food. She accepted this as his final word, put the matter aside, and never mentioned the subject again.

As Catherine approached the gangplank, a soldier dressed in blue confronted the hooded passenger. "Halt! In the name of His Majesty," he commanded. Withdrawing a letter from her cloak, Catherine presented it to the guard. It unmistakably bore the king's seal.

"For Monsieur Fuquay," she muttered in a muffled voice, "by order of the king." The monarch's stamp was sacrosanct, and Catherine knew it would never be questioned. She was motioned ahead without further inquiry.

As the queen crossed onto the deck, she encountered a bald, heavyset individual who wore a garment similar to attire befitting a monk. His hands and forearms were entwined within the droopy sleeves of the full-length brown habit that caressed his sandals. A thick leather strap encompassed his portly stomach where several combative weapons clung to his waist. Catherine once again flashed the dispatch and gruffly said, "Fuquay."

The ominous-looking man motioned the newly arrived passenger to follow him. Ascending a few wooden steps, the queen stood on a raised deck facing a cabin door. "Wait here," he said in a subdued voice.

Catherine looked around and momentarily wondered. What were the chances she'd ever locate Lafitte? If their paths did cross, would he be happy to see her? Had his feelings for Catherine diminished? She still believed Jacques loved her, not that her royal credentials were being compromised, so Lafitte could implement a personal vendetta against those he considered responsible for his father's death.

The queen's reflections were interrupted by the sound of a familiar voice that resonated from within the cabin by which she was told to wait. "What could His Majesty possibly want at this late hour? Inform Captain De Villefort we're passed due to leave port. Show the messenger in, Agular."

Catherine's heart jumped. Perhaps it would come to her later why the utterance of the burly friar's name gave her a chill feeling.

Giving Agular a nod as he left, Catherine entered the cabin and gently closed the door behind her. She lifted the hood to her one-piece cloak. It casually fell to the small of her back. Without looking up from the papers strewn upon his desk Fuquay snatched the dispatch from the queen's extended hand. Peeling away the seal, he unraveled the scroll and stared at it in disbelief. "What's the meaning of this?" he barked incredulously. "This parchment bears no message."

"It's only I, Pierre." Fuquay, completely taken aback, spontaneously jumped to his feet. With his mouth opened wide, he remained speechless. "Lost for words, Fuquay? It isn't like you. Aren't you pleased to see me, my lord?"

Coming to his senses, Fuquay stuttered, "Your Highness, wha-wha—"

"What am I doing here? Is that what you're trying to say?"

"Why I-I, please sit down, Your Highness. To what occasion do I owe this honor? Your Majesty, we're momentarily about to leave port!"

"Enough gibberish, Fuquay, where is it?"

"Where's what, Your Majesty?"

"The chest, Pierre, you know, the one to which my tiara has been vanquished."

"Certainly, madame, your crown is quite safe. It's in the compartment just behind you." Fuquay went over to a small door and unlocked it. Lighting a candle, he ducked his head and entered the chamber ahead of Catherine. Warningly he said, "Be careful, Your Majesty. Rodents! They seem to be everywhere." If his words were intended to frighten her, they failed to elicit a reaction. Crimson drapery covered the chest. A shard of light beamed through the gloom of a curtained porthole revealing speckles of dust that lingered in the stale smell of mold.

"The key, Fuquay," Catherine spoke in an authoritative voice. "Give it to me."

"Why, I don't have it, Your Highness," he blurted.

"What do you mean you don't have it? Of course, you must," retaliated the queen.

"Your Ma-Majesty," he stammered while removing an envelope from his silk jacket, "this will explain everything."

"Don't mince words with me, Pierre. For the last time, Fuquay, where's the key?" The queen's voice was emphatic. A sudden rap on the door quelled her voice.

"If you please, Catherine," Fuquay rarely addressed the queen without invoking Her Majesty's title. "Before you arrived, I ordered refreshment. Won't you come this way where you'll be more comfortable?" Upon leaving the closet area, Fuquay bolted and locked it shut. Glancing at his gold pocket watch, he continued to say, "There's a distinct chill in the air. Perhaps a cup of tea will warm you."

"Your timepiece, Fuquay, it's very curious. Haven't I seen it somewhere before?"

"Surely not this one, madame, I just received it recently as a gift from some friends wishing me safe journey." Turning toward the door, Fuquay said in a stout voice, "Come in, Francois."

Pierre's servant entered the room with a tray bearing a familiar aroma. "The libation you ordered, my lord." Recognizing the queen, he bowed respectfully. Turning to Fuquay, he said, "Is there anything else, Monsieur Fuquay?"

"Thank you, no, Francois. That will be all." The servant nodded and lowered his head to the queen before he left. "He is a gentleman of discretion, Your Majesty. Francois will say nothing to anyone that he noticed you incognito."

"Trusted servants are at a premium, Fuquay. I doubt there's a single one in my entire litter." Then she thought of Bevier and several of her other handpicked servants who she knew would never betray a confidence. Catherine's eyes focused on the fine mist of steam emanating from the freshly brewed pot of tea. "Obviously, Pierre, you did not intend to dine alone. Why, may I inquire, are there two drinking vessels on the porcelain tray? You couldn't possibly have anticipated my unexpected arrival." Noticing his loss for words, she went on to say, "Wherever did you find such an enchanting valet, Pierre? He's so young and handsome too. I don't recall seeing him in attendance at any of Charles's extravaganzas." Not waiting for a reply, she added, "Francois has a distinct English accent. Pierre, I thought you were French through and through." Sensing Fuquay was not captivated by her jocular mood, Catherine changed the subject.

"I believe we were discussing the whereabouts of a key, Pierre." Sipping her tea, the queen's composure seemed less curt.

"Yes, of course, the key." Removing a letter from the envelope he still cradled in his hand, Fuquay continued. "As you can see from this dispatch, your husband has ordered that the key to which you are referring be worn around the neck of Captain De Villefort until we have safely reached our destination. Should anyone approach Philippe with the intent of removing it, I-I dare not say the rest, Your Highness."

"Am I to think you are feeling a bit squeamish, Fuquay?"

"The details, my lady, are quite graphic. Would you care to read them yourself?"

At his last words, the queen burst into a sudden fit of laughter. Fuquay gave Catherine a quizzical look. "You mean to say," she continued in a lingering giggle, "he doesn't trust you either?"

Fuquay, surprised by Her Majesty's rhetoric, broke into a reciprocal laughter. For a moment the two of them seemed best of friends sharing intimate secrets. The ship's bell tolled three times. Gathering his composure, Fuquay said in earnest, "Surely, madame, you must exit the *Vera Cruz* at once. We'll be leaving port in minutes."

"Not on your life," she retorted.

"But, Your Majesty, the king will never understand. Think what he'll do. You must disembark before it's too late."

"Don't underestimate me, Fuquay. Think what I'll do, if I'm not on board when the *Vera Cruz* does leave port."

"But surely you can't stay in this compartment. My quarters will become a busy thoroughfare even before we reach the channel. There's very little room elsewhere on the entire ship. Where will you stay?"

With an amusing look, she glanced around and said, "I'll stay in there." Pausing, she added, "With the rats. That is, if they don't mind Her Majesty's intrusion." Then Catherine said quite seriously, "Fuquay, I will not be in the way. I promise. Go about your usual business, as though I weren't here. Right now, I'm tired, very tired. Undo the latch, Pierre. I insist. And don't concern yourself. I shan't make a sound."

Realizing it was futile to protest, Fuquay undid the lock and handed Catherine a lighted candle. She poked her head inside and turned to say, "For now this will do fine. You understand, Fuquay, tomorrow I must commandeer your quarters. I need plenty of air and space so I can think. Then we'll talk just you and me. Perhaps we can clear the air of a few misgivings I've been meaning to talk to you about.

"I'm confident the king's Treasury minister will not find it difficult in finding suitable lodgings elsewhere. Say nothing of my presence to Captain De Villefort until we've reached open sea. I know! We'll tell him I'm to be France's royal representative for Martinique's colonization ceremony at Charles's last-minute suggestion. I'm sure he'll understand. After all, I am the queen. If all goes well, perhaps I can don my tiara earlier than I anticipated. Monsieur Fuquay, it would look much better on me for all to see than displayed as some sort of prop in a museum, don't you think?" Very sincerely, Catherine added, "However strange this may sound, Pierre, I am in your debt and will not forget what you have done here. You will be duly rewarded."

"But, Your Majesty—"

"Not now, Pierre. The *Vera Cruz* has weighed anchor. We're moving. And, Fuquay, I'll take the key you have in your hand. It would be a pity if the door was locked and somehow it escaped one's memory that I was secured within."

Fuquay lifted his right hand to his throat and gasped, "Surely, Your Majesty, you are in one of your jesting moods."

"Three months is a long time without food or drink."

Ignoring her flippant remark, Fuquay replied quite graciously, "If all goes as planned, and there are no interruptions at sea, we'll reach our destination in less than six weeks, Your Majesty."

"Bonsoir, Pierre. Merci beaucoup."

"Think what you're doing, Catherine. There's still time to alter your decision. The journey will not be an easy one." Fuquay seemed quite sincere in his efforts to dissuade Catherine from her insistence upon making the voyage to Martinique.

"You ought to know me better than that, Pierre. Bon voyage."

"Sleep well, Your Majesty. A warm breakfast will greet you at seven bells."

As the queen pulled the door closed, Pierre Fuquay brushed aside a few beads of perspiration from his forehead. Wetness clung to his skin, but not in response to fear or trepidation. Pierre had been inwardly enveloped with a sudden burst of excitement. Charles, he knew, would never have approved the queen's voyage to Martinique, even if he were present to accompany her. It was too perilous a journey. For him to entertain the notion of placing Her Majesty in harm's way was out of the question. How to reconcile the present situation was Fuquay's immediate concern.

His secret plan was relatively a simple one. An earlier dispatch had been sent to Governor Belain d'Esnambuc at Martinique informing him that Monsieur Fuquay was to preside over the forthcoming inaugural ceremonies. The contents of the dispatch were to be made known publicly so that the former statesman, Jacques Lafitte, would be enlivened upon hearing the news. How could he resist the opportunity of cashing in on his revenge, as he vowed so many times to do? Naturally, if he dared to come anywhere near Martinique, it would be a fatal mistake. He could never escape the entrapment that awaited him. Lafitte had been a kink in Pierre's side long enough. It was he that should have been done away with first, not his father.

The queen's presence on the isle of Martinique could actually work in Fuquay's favor. When Catherine stepped onto the *Vera Cruz* and insisted upon taking the journey, she unwittingly sealed Lafitte's fate. Eyewitness accounts of her arrival at Saint-Pierre, the newly ordained capital of Martinique, would undoubtedly encourage her romantic adventurer to make a daring, chivalrous rendezvous with the woman he so much depended upon in the past. Ironically, the queen's persistence, not Fuquay's, would bring the lust-filled pirate to his demise.

However, for his plan to succeed, Pierre needed to resolve yet another problem, Captain Philippe De Villefort. Upon learning of the queen's presence aboard his ship, he had no other choice but to verify a handwritten letter from the monarch giving his approval. It had been necessary for Charles to protect his naval fleet from responding to counterfeit dispatches. The King of France had ordered all his commanders to be aware of a secret written code, a mark that he would use on whatever correspondence they should receive from him, once they had been given their initial orders. This procedure was employed to protect captains of French frigates from the possibility of being lured into ambush. If an enemy saboteur attempted to exhibit a forged dispatch for the purpose of entrapment, it would be detected immediately. Undoubtedly, Fuquay surmised, the queen had not been privy to this particular security measure. Whether it even pertained to her was an entirely different matter.

Pierre pleaded with Catherine at the outset to leave the ship before it set sail. Her decision to accompany the crown jewels to Martinique was irrevocable. He could hardly be responsible for the queen's persistence in having her own way. Fuquay had to find a way to persuade Captain De Villefort not to return to Versailles. Pierre had to think of something. His future depended upon what he must do next. If need be, he would have to rely on Agular to somehow dispose of Philippe. Perhaps the Treasury minister's devoted monk could assist the captain in falling overboard while attempting to retrieve one of his white gloves; Pierre mused with a self satisfied grin.

As the *Vera Cruz* slipped away from Versailles, Catherine peered through the porthole in her small congested room. The queen was appalled at what she saw. Peasants in great numbers were milling about the wharfs of the Seine.

With hands extended, they pleaded to passersby for food. Stately gentlemen and ladies in fine attire brushed briskly past beggars who attempted to gain their attention.

A recurring thought sharply returned to Catherine's mind. Hadn't Charles promised her that he'd see to everyone's basic needs, that not a single Frenchman, woman, or child would ever want for food, so long as he was king? How could she have been so naive? Why had she permitted the daily trivial distractions that preoccupied most of her queenly existence to distance herself from the throngs of French loyalists who more than graciously accepted Catherine as their beloved empress? Why had she allowed herself to become a prisoner of luxury? Had the mystique of royal grandeur completely deadened her senses?

Catherine remembered how Jacques on one particular occasion, like his father before him, had implored her husband's magistrates to address the impoverished conditions that permeated France's city streets. "The people are the salt of the earth," she recalled him saying. "Feed the poor and shelter the homeless. Give each man his just deserts. It is the humane and proper thing to do, for it is in the process of giving that we shall experience a revitalized France. It is our inherent duty to provide each man the opportunity to better himself before God and his country. Otherwise, I fear he will lose hope in his crusade for a better life, and we will have lost him to a fate worse than death. In the end, I fear too that France will be lost as well."

Sneers of dissent had followed those remarks. Evidently the king's council, chaired by Pierre Fuquay, believed the young minister of the Treasury was attempting to mend the broken pieces of a crusade his father, Dantes Lafitte, had begun before he retired.

Catherine suddenly felt numb. She saw enough. Her eyes started to close. She knew the ship would not reach the English Channel for several hours. Using the coverlet draped around the treasure chest, she made a bedding to make herself comfortable. There was no room in her head for a single thought more. Whatever tomorrow will bring, it would have to be dealt with then. So tired she was, not even romantic thoughts of Jacques Lafitte could keep her awake. Catherine was only an ocean away from her lover's embrace. What more can a queen ask for? Closing her fading blue eyes, she fell fast asleep.

III

The King's Ire

A servant parted the tall twin doors that opened from the center. He wore the usual buttoned tunic, white stockings that disappeared beneath his knickers, and buckled shoes that chimed an echo as he shifted his steps on the marble floor. Before he was able to announce her entrance, Beatrice, the queen's personal attendant, barged past him in a flash. Approaching the king who was about to eat a poached egg, Catherine's valet spoke as though she were unraveled. "Your Highness, the queen is nowhere to be found. She's gone!"

"Calm yourself, Beatrice. What do you mean she's gone?" the king shot back annoyingly.

"One of the gendarmes last saw her yesterday afternoon leaving the grounds in a carriage. Earlier Her Highness told me she didn't want to be disturbed, that she had a terrible headache. Her traveling bag and personal effects are not where they should be. Something is amiss, Your Majesty."

Clicking his fingers, Charles raised his voice toward his servant. "Bring Bevier to me, immediately!" he bellowed authoritatively.

Anticipating the king's summons, Bevier hastily entered the room unannounced and nervously approached His Highness. Fidgeting with a chapeau bras he held in both hands, the elderly steward stammered before

Charles even addressed him, "Her-Her Majesty ordered me not to speak a word until you had your breakfast, Your Grace."

"Very well, Bevier. Tell me now. Where is she?"

"You must believe me, Your Majesty. I tried in earnest to stop her."

Rising to his feet, Charles said disconcertedly, "That's not what I asked you. For the last time, Bevier, where is the queen?"

"Why, Your Majesty, I believe she's gone on a journey."

"A journey? What journey? Speak up, Bevier. My patience is wearing thin."

Bevier's words were slow and deliberate. "The Queen of France is with the crown jewels, Your Majesty. She boarded the *Vera Cruz* yesterday afternoon."

"The *Vera Cruz*?" Charles blurted in disbelief. "What in the name—" the king interrupted his sentence abruptly and scornfully added, "Bevier, do you recall my explicit instructions regarding your duties as carriage master to the queen?"

"Yes, Your Majesty, I do recall your explicit instructions very clearly."

"And what were they?"

"I was to be most gentle with the horses, Your Majesty, and never conduct Her Highness through the palace gates without your verbal permission."

"And did you receive such permission?"

"No, Your Majesty, I indeed did not receive such permission."

"And were you mindful of the consequences that I'd bestow upon you for not following my instructions to the letter?"

"Yes, Your Majesty."

"So why then did you ignore my orders, Bevier, knowing full well that you would be hanged for your disobedience?"

"But I pleaded with Her Majesty to reconsider what she was commanding me to do, that if I escorted her from the premises without your verbal permission, you would have me hanged."

"And?"

"She laughed and said she was the queen and that if I didn't immediately do as she so ordered, I would face a fate worse than anything the king could contemplate. Either way, Your Majesty, whomever I listened to, or didn't listen to, I'd be placing myself in a precarious position. Knowing you are a most noble and merciful king, I took my chances and obeyed the queen." Exasperated, Charles threw up his hands and winced at what he just heard.

Claude Truffaut, the king's valet de chambre, spoke candidly, "Your Grace, Governor Dupree is aboard the *Vera Cruz*. Surely he would delay the ship's departure until the matter of Her Majesty's presence was first confirmed with you. He'd never risk the queen's safety on such an arduous journey. They're probably moments away from the palace gates, as we speak."

"Monsieur Truffaut," Charles spoke solemnly while looking down at his undisturbed breakfast, "Governor Dupree, at the insistence of King Ferdinand of Spain, is aboard the *Calcutta*. His Majesty said he'd sleep more comfortably knowing that his consignment of jewels was accompanied by my most trusted minister of foreign affairs."

"Perhaps Monsieur Fuquay—"

The king interrupted Truffaut before he finished what he was about to say, "Fuquay is easily intimidated by Catherine. Haven't you noticed? She leads him about, as one would a goat on a leash."

"Captain De Villefort undoubtedly . . ."

"No, Truffaut, if Philippe had the slightest inkling Catherine was aboard his ship, he would have delivered her to the palace by now."

Lifting his head, Charles said in a voice that was more angry than authoritative, "Claude, find out how many brigantines are still in the harbor. Have them fully equipped and ready to set sail at once!"

The king's ire quelled everyone into a chilling silence. Short of steam emanating from his squinting eyes and wreathed mouth, Charles's disheveled hair, hunched shoulders, and spread-eagled fingers that clutched the table's fine linen gave him the appearance of a crazed beast about to pounce at the first utter of a sound.

Without further ado, the room cleared. The king limped awkwardly to a window from where he could observe the Seine meandering toward Versailles. He momentarily pondered what course of action Edward of England might take when the news of his daughter's departure from the continent reached his ears. Charles grimaced and purred angrily under his breath, "I've been such a blind fool, an empty, pigheaded fool. I ought to have known better. I should have told her."

IV

Ile de la Tortue

Like an octopus stretching its tentacles across the ocean, France's colonization of the West Indies encompassed a vast archipelago of virginal islands. Among these sparkling jewels of the sea, as Lord Governor Jean Dupree had heralded them to be, were Grenada, St. Lucia, Martinique, St. Vincent and the Grenadines, Dominica, and countless others.

Perhaps the most beguiling of these acquisitions was an island whose inlets were scented with jacaranda trees and lush hibiscus shrubs. The cay was inhibited with dense foliage surrounded by steep cliffs that provided suitable shelter from fierce hurricane winds. Ile de la Tortue abounded in wildlife and fruit-bearing trees. Though not yet inhabited by founding fathers, the island ranked high among France's finest newly acclaimed Caribbean treasures. Ironically, it was this paradise of abundant food and fresh aquifers that Captain Lafitte had chosen for his base of operations. For him and his followers, it seemed the perfect retreat.

Ile de la Tortue, the island of turtles, as it was called, had been the selected arena where Captain Jacques Lafitte sought refuge, prosperity, and revenge for himself and his brotherhood of French prisoners who had fallen from grace and deemed traitors by the sovereign Crown of France. Accusations made against them had ranged anywhere from grand theft and murder to conspiracy and high treason.

Jacques, as fate ordained him to be called, had explored the region in his early youth with Monsieur Dantes Lafitte, then French foreign minister to the king's court. During these tender years of maturity, the strapping, inquisitive garcon developed an obsession for sailing vessels. From stem to stern he cultivated an appreciative knowledge of ships by observing the intricacies of how they were rigged to survive tumultuous stormy seas. His formative years played a major role in a life that would hail him one of the most daring pirates ever to sail the Caribbean.

The Brotherhood of *Dantes's Revenge*, like so many other celebrities in history that have never been chronicled for their salient epic deeds, sought to accomplish a single specific goal: to achieve justice for the punitive crimes exacted upon them by the sovereign powers that governed them. Unlike some of the unsavory personalities that secured a footnote in the pages of the past, including the unscrupulous Henry Morgan and treacherous Edward Teach, written accounts of Captain Jacques Lafitte and his trivial band of marauders is nowhere to be found. Apparently, the glamorous, more infamous corsairs seemed to have captivated the historian's spotlight of attention in lieu of all that was transpiring at the time. Their dastardly deeds of piracy, murder, and terror evidently claimed center stage that appears to have immortalized them forevermore.

Pirates germinated from every circumstance repulsive to mankind. Some had been mutineers or escaped prisoners. Others evolved from the desperate, impoverished conditions they were forced to endure. Destined to intermingle with common riffraff, these homeless individuals had been abandoned by the state and shamefully ignored by aristocratic society. Indeed they appeared to have fallen from grace and deemed "the forgotten ones" by austere citizens of wealth and stature who happened to occasionally glance in their direction. Many too were falsely accused by opportunists who would profit from their demise. Lengthy terms of imprisonment blended into sentences of doom for those fortunate enough to survive the calumny of torture heaped upon them, or the executioner's noose.

Naturally, any prisoner would have submitted his loyalty to the emancipator who rescued him from a fate worse than death. Jacques Lafitte had been such a person. With the aid of the Queen of France, he stormed the Bastille and freed several condemned prisoners. Lafitte needed to even the score with those who betrayed him and his father, so he banded together a group of followers whose hatred for their oppressors burned deeply in their hearts, much as it did in his own. His twofold mission was to form a clique that would assist him in accomplishing the task of personal revenge against his enemies and to send a clear message to all sovereign powers that tyranny against the people will not be tolerated. The new order against oppression was appropriately called the Brotherhood of *Dantes's Revenge*, in deference to the memory of Jacques's father.

Lafitte's pirates appeared ordinary as any other. Their cloth jackets and loose-fitting shirts were tightly bound by a sash or belt that caressed a curved sword and other weapons secured tightly to their sides. Doeskin breeches, soft moccasins, high boots, peaked hats, and unshaven whiskers were the usual attire. The only distinguishable differences among the brood was the external mark of torture branded upon them by inhumane jailers whose contemptuous behavior in doling punishment had been outlandish. Scars, mangled fingers, a patch where an eye used to be, a severed ear, and gross imprints of branding irons were just some of the brutal traces of barbaric treatment bestowed upon the prisoners incarcerated in France's royal symbol of tyranny, the Bastille.

According to the pirate code of ethics, the captain of a ship is permitted a full share and a half of all contraband confiscated from any captured vessel. The first mate, quartermaster, boatswain, carpenter, and gunner shall receive one full share and a quarter of the total value of the cargo on board. Lafitte knew that avarice and greed were elements that one day might create disharmony and chaos among his crew. "We are not individuals," he often reminded his shipmates. "We are the Brotherhood of *Dantes's Revenge*. In everything we do, we do as one, and we do it in his name. If we must kill, we kill in self-defense, and we kill without hesitation those who have openly proclaimed to be our enemy. Though I am your captain, I am privileged to be your servant as well. We are equal partakers in our brotherhood, and I pledge upon my oath that it will be equal shares for all."

In the beginning there was not a single soldier among them that would hesitate to place himself in harm's way of a cutlass or pistol shot intended for Lafitte. So revered was he, each man's loyalty to his beloved captain superceded whatever regard the pirate may have had for his own personal safety. However, like any other, Lafitte's society was less than perfect. Occasionally, a disagreement among the men, or a vehement challenge to Captain Lafitte's authority, threatened the survival of the clan.

While the French founded new colonies on the sugar-growing islands of what is known today as the Lesser Antilles, miles to the northwest the isle of

Tortuga with its natural fortified buttresses and surrounding inlets became a suitable refuge to rogue pirate ships being hunted down by privateers who had been commissioned into a navy. These bounty hunters were bequeathed a letter of marque sanctioned by the European crowns of state giving them full authority to capture enemy ships that looted supply frigates carrying valuable cargo to or from the New World. The privateers were paid a substantial share of whatever goods were recaptured, the rest going to the sovereign power from which the booty was stolen. In essence the privateers maintained fleets to protect the colonies from unscrupulous renegade buccaneers because the various European governments that possessed them were unable to do so independently.

Regardless of the havoc played by pirates in the Caribbean, homeland protection had been the number one priority considered by all nations. Without a suitably fortified border patrol, any one of the European sovereign states would leave itself vulnerable to an enemy invasion. So it was. Privateers were given free reign in the lucrative business of hunting down renegade pirates without reprisals being sanctioned against them.

Tortuga nestled north of Hispaniola and other nearby landmasses that encompass that particular region in the Caribbean. Rocky mountains and dense foliage shroud countless craggy harbors and deep lagoons. Food was plentiful. For those who sought refuge from the bounty hunters, Ile de la Tortue served as a unique, protective hideaway that could withstand a siege of intruders. Dolphin Cove, by way of its proximity to the open sea, had the perfect camouflage of a barrier reef that was laden with foliage impenetrable to the spyglass. It is precisely because of its impregnable features that Captain Jacques Lafitte selected this safe haven as headquarters for the brotherhood. All captured treasures were safely stored here until the time came to divvy up the booty and disband to whichever paradise each man so desired.

Lafitte's followers had vowed to uphold him until he received full recompense in his father's death. Many clan members had personal reasons of their own to seek revenge for the ignominy they had been forced to endure by the state. Too numerous were the scores of retaliation to be reconciled. It was discussed and agreed by all that once their captain received full satisfaction—namely, the restoration of Dantes Lafitte's honor—it would be deemed a communal exoneration, whereby every member of the brotherhood would be collectively vindicated as well. For this to become a reality, Jacques needed first to improvise a timely plan of action. Seven months had elapsed since he fled France. An immediate confrontation with the villains at large was necessary.

Captain Lafitte began to pace to and fro, back and forth on the *Dantes's Revenge*'s lower deck. Several of his shipmates stopped what they were doing and looked at him curiously. His manly chest began to swell, as though he were taking in more than usual gasps of air. The veins in Jacques's exposed neck pulsated. Till now his spirit was in variance to what his father had constantly tried to instill in his adopted son's conscious spirit. "Before all else, let it be justice that governs your heart and soul," he remembered him saying. "Never betray, never betray," the dying words of his mother had suddenly enveloped his imagination.

Lafitte, in response to the urging of his meditative spirit, removed his cutlass from his waist and pitched it into the lagoon. "To hell with the past, and to hell with the future, all that is given to us is the present!" he shouted. The incessant ticking bomb of doubt and confusion he harbored within had left him, like a fever would suddenly vanish from one's burning forehead. Getting even with those who maligned and cast their evil spell upon him was never an option. This he now clearly understood. Love is greater than hate, and it is with love that he must conquer, not hate.

Lafitte had no other recourse but to return to France. He would negotiate before the high court a full pardon for those of his men who would willingly surrender his share of whatever booty had been confiscated from commonwealth merchant ships in exchange for amnesty. Just before Bevier left him at the docks of Versailles, he had given Lafitte a letter and said, "Catherine declared you must promise not to read this until you have left French waters. Give me your word so she may rest easy knowing you have honored your pledge."

"I give you my word." Lafitte distinctly remembered crossing his heart when saying it. Upon reading the letter nearly a week after the occasion, Jacques was prompted to return to Catherine immediately. However, should the king's ship have retreated to France prematurely, Lafitte and the newly released prisoners of the Bastille would undoubtedly never have made it back to Paris alive. Fuquay's assassins were sure to have seen to it.

Looking toward the east, Jacques stared into the calm sea before him. The time of reckoning had come. He spoke with determination. "We're not barbarians," he spoke coherently to a handful of men milling about the bridge of the ship. "Mateys, in our hearts each of us must surely agree the life we have chosen can never fully satisfy. Freedom to be, freedom to choose, freedom to love, and most precious of all, freedom to bask in the soil upon which we were born—nothing else can fill the restless void that tugs at the soul."

Muslim Green, Jacques Lafitte's quartermaster, was confounded when he heard his captain's shrill voice. "Viva la France, my brothers. Make ready to sail." It was the first part of what he said that boggled his mind.

The Queen Reminisces

The queen didn't know where she was when her eyelids suddenly parted in a subdued stare. A shroud of darkness gave Catherine the eerie feeling she was having a frightful dream. "Where am I?" she wondered audibly. As the ship sailed through a crest of waves that pelted the hull, Catherine was awakened to her senses. "The *Vera Cruz*," she uttered softly. "Now I remember."

Catherine could hardly breathe in the stifling small room. She had to fill her lungs with fresh air. Stumbling to the door of her cell, she unlocked it and lifted the latch. The portal creaked open. Peering into the outer chamber, the queen noticed a fully clothed figure fast asleep in a berth that seemed to have been fastened to the wall. Though she could not see his face, the slumbering body had to be Pierre Fuquay. Following the trail of moonlight that spilled into the cabin from a porthole, the queen unlatched the wooden door and found herself standing on the deck of a ship that was sailing briskly under a star-studded sky.

How beautiful! The heavenly night sparkled with splendor. A shooting star briefly illuminated the firmament with a stream of light that quickly faded into darkness. Catherine inhaled several deep breaths of air heavily scented with a salty, pungent odor. The chill of an offshore breeze felt refreshing. Once again the queen's thoughts focused on Jacques Lafitte. If news reached his ears that she'd be attending Martinique's inaugural fanfare, would he risk seeking a rendezvous? Did he still love her? Had he ever loved her? A sixth sense insisted upon the answers to all three questions being unequivocally *yes*.

Other queries raced through Catherine's mind as well. What must Charles be thinking? Would her indiscretion in going abroad, as she did, affect the alliance her marriage was meant to have endorsed? Catherine took another deep breath. Her thoughts strayed to when Charles and she were taking an early morning stroll prior to one of the preliminary meetings scheduled to determine Captain Jacques Lafitte's fate. It had been a powerful shock that day when her husband told Catherine of the devastating news.

*   *   *

Charles had placed his hand in hers while they chatted on the promenade adjacent to the palace gardens that overlooked the Seine. Spring flowers permeated the air. Pink and yellow roses exuded a delicious myrrhlike perfume. Poplar trees stood like statues along both sides of the walkway, as the sun played hide-and-seek with partially clouded skies.

Catherine knew the king was being pressured by self-indulgent magistrates. Charles would have given anything not to inform her of the council's decision that the queen's tiara was to be a crucial aspect of the elaborate royal display on the isle of Martinique. She surmised he had no other choice but to yield to the tribunal's final resolution. It was a preposterous proposal, she insisted. A most ridiculous idea! Out of the question! They must think of a more suitable strategy. Though she conveyed this to her husband in less than a stately manner, it had little effect in altering the course of his actions.

Because she was the daughter of a monarch, Catherine clearly understood that a king, in such times as these, had to acquiesce to those in power whose opinions dominated royal privilege. Charles had no alternative but to relent. His sovereign authority under the current circumstances had to bow to pressures exerted upon him by the third estate, namely, the bourgeoisie. These ambitious entrepreneurs were mainly comprised of wealthy silk merchants, learned doctors, skilled artisans, and bankers who controlled the economic structure upon which society revolved. To rebuke them in this matter would be a costly mistake. Conformance to solidarity with the powers "that be" was tantamount. Creating a rift between the king and majority of cabinet officials whose sentiments leaned toward those of mainstream society might possibly cost Charles his throne, or worse. Reluctantly, the King of France had to play the cards that had been dealt to him.

*　　*　　*

Catherine's thoughts fast-forwarded to the fateful, inevitable moment she knew would soon come. The queen was in her boudoir admiring herself in the full-length Victorian mirror. To the naked eye, she looked beautiful in her velvety crimson dress that caressed the marble floor. Her Majesty's lady in waiting, Beatrice, had removed the jewel-studded tiara from its encasement and carefully placed it on Catherine's head. She remembered giving her handmaiden a quizzical look, believing it would be the very last time she'd ever be wearing her most prized possession. The exorbitant diadem with its faceted multicolored diamonds and luxurious turquoise settings had been a gift to her by Charles on the occasion of their royal wedding. No other known jeweled ornament exceeded the beauty and grandeur that radiated from Catherine's elegant crown. But now, she had been told, it was to be used to entice the man she secretly loved into a defenseless game of entrapment.

Her melancholic trance, she recalled, had been interrupted by Beatrice who sensed the queen's dismay. Endeavoring to be optimistic, she said, "It will only be for a short time, Your Majesty. You'll again be wearing your coronet before the sun sets in ninety days. Is there anything else, Your Highness?" Before she could reply, Charles had entered Catherine's private quarters unannounced. Instinctively, the queen's attendant lowered her head and withdrew.

"I dare say, my sweet, the day is far too beautiful for you to look so forlorn." Placing his arms around her slender shoulders while facing the queen in the mirror, he said, "The charm you're wearing, cheri, I certainly can't recall giving it to you. Wherever, if you don't mind my asking, did you obtain it? Shush, let me guess. Ah, yes—it's a token from your father. No, on second thought, the charm doesn't quite resemble even a hint of English ancestry. Perhaps the pendant is a gift of a very dear friend? Am I getting warmer?"

Trying to disguise her startled reaction to his inquisitive questions, the queen flippantly replied, "My jealous husband, if you really must know, this key was given to me by a secret admirer."

"Anyone I may happen to know, my precious?"

"That, My Lord, you must find out for yourself." Attempting to change the subject, she quickly added, "Must I part with it, cheri" Adjusting her tiara, Catherine continued. "The crown is deservedly mine. Why must it be used to snag a lusty pirate?"

"Because, bon a mi, it will help rid your husband of this nagging thorn that seems to be tightly embedded in his side. And let us not forget, my pretty little

princess, it has been duly ratified by the assembly of idiotic buffoons, my own court mind you, that your crown's presence in Martinique, wherever the exact location of that godforsaken place might be, will gainfully represent France's colonial expeditionary leadership in the Caribbean."

Catherine remembered breaking into a fit of extemporaneous laughter. She rarely observed her husband behaving so comically ridiculous. Noting the queen's lighthearted reaction to his antics, he added, "Why couldn't have France's acquisitions of discovery been settled before I inherited the throne?" Regaining his composure, Charles sounded more like his usual self. "Don't fret, Catherine, my sweet. You'll be doting on your coronet much sooner than ninety days." Apparently he had been listening at the door and heard Beatrice's words before he entered the room. "Your elaborate symbol of authority definitely complements everything that you are," he spoke in an almost-whispering voice.

Appreciating her husband's compassion, Catherine chided hopefully, "A thought, Charles. Mind you, just a thought. Suppose I go to Martinique, as a gesture of goodwill, of course. In the event Captain Lafitte should take it upon himself to capture the crown jewels, do you suppose he would consider me a fair exchange for them?"

"Most certainly, my queen, and in the process he will ransom you for all I've got, the wretched scoundrel."

"His adventurous spirit seems to excite most of the debutants—in a barbaric sort of way. Beatrice tells me several ladies of the court bear an insatiable lust for him. Perhaps it's his absence from Paris that incites the female imagination."

"On the contrary, cheri, it's the absence of your touch that tantalizes me," he retorted with a slight wrinkle in his frown.

"Really, my handsome prince, at times you can be so flattering, so enchanting."

"No, my pet, there's no use trying to lure me into a compromise. I'm afraid the jewels will have to go." Then, as an afterthought, he said, "You couldn't possibly have the slightest notion of being romantically drawn to Lafitte? Why, he's nothing more than a common pig."

Suddenly realizing he had forgotten the time, Charles said quite soberly, "Enough bantering. The dignitaries have been waiting for nearly an hour. We mustn't keep them."

Catherine looked at her husband coquettishly. "A common pig, is that what you called Lafitte? I dare say, my husband, would you say that to his face?" Sensing her remark offended Charles, she quickly added, "I beg your pardon, Your Majesty. Of course he's a pig, but I think maybe in an attractive sort of way. You see, when I was a little girl my father raised pigs, lots of them. Naturally, I grew quite fond of pigs, especially the ones that liked to wallow in the mud." In saying this, the queen proceeded to unbutton her tunic. "Do help me with the clasp, Charles."

The king drew near and began to gently caress her slender throat. "You may be held accountable for seducing His Royal Highness," he said softly. The last words Catherine remembered her husband saying were "To hell with the dignitaries. They can wait a little longer."

Deafening her ears, Catherine clutched the king close to her bosom. Her thoughts turned to visions of fantasy, as they usually did when she was feeling ill at ease and despondent. On this occasion, the queen envisioned herself in the arms of a dreaded rogue. Captain Jacques Lafitte would heighten her passion to whatever lengths her imagination dare transcend.

Right now, however, her husband managed to wrestle her to the bed and was enjoying his own particular adventure, many fathoms from where her own thoughts flowed. She was far, far away. Catherine saw herself on a magnificent brigantine. A lofty regal throne was anchored to the crow's nest. Captain Jacques Lafitte held her with the grip of an octopus. The touch of his soft, evenly trimmed beard made every fiber of her body tingle. The decks were paved with gold, and sails garnished with gemstones glistened in the setting sun. Blue-finned dolphins circled the ship in unison, playfully leaping high above lush, pristine waters, while exotic birds flew above the pirate ship harmoniously flapping their colorful wings under an array of heavenly rainbows. Scintillating music filled the air. Dancing and laughter inebriated her spirit.

Catherine envisioned herself quite differently than she had ever before imagined. She bore no resemblance of a queen. There was no burden to carry. Protocol and duty had vanished. Her hair flowed freely past her neck, straight down to the small of her back. Wearing only a thin white veil wrapped about her shapely form, she surrendered herself to Captain Lafitte's embrace. For the first time, since she could remember, Catherine Stuart, daughter of King Edward of England, inhaled the brief experience of being a complete woman.

*   *   *

The queen's thoughts were interrupted by a familiar voice. "You really shouldn't be out in this chill air, Your Majesty." Placing a cloak around her bare shoulders, Fuquay added, "You'll need all your strength for the voyage, Catherine."

"Where exactly are we, Pierre? How far have we traveled?"

"According to my estimates, we've just passed through the port of Le Havre and are headed toward the Cape of Cherbourg. Once we have negotiated the channel, it will be clear sailing to Martinique, unless, Your Majesty, you'd rather we change course and sail due north. Undoubtedly your father would be most pleased to see you."

Ignoring his last remark, she said, "What do you think Captain De Villefort's reaction will be when he finds out that I'm aboard his ship?"

"He won't like it, Your Highness. You see, it is very unlike Charles not to inform him personally that you were to be, shall I say, a last-minute addition to the manifest."

"I think I have thought of a way to get around that." Catherine's voice seemed a bit excitable. "We can inscribe a directive on the blank dispatch I gave you earlier that Charles decided at the last moment to have me personally escort the crown jewels to Martinique. Neither you nor I wanted to disturb the captain's departure, so we waited to tell him after we set sail."

"It's nearly dawn, Your Majesty. Right now, try to rest for a few hours. I've already asked Francois to have my," he corrected himself, "your cabin made ready with fresh linens. He'll be serving you breakfast at seven bells, Catherine, unless you'd rather have something to sustain yourself before then."

"Seven bells will be fine, Pierre."

"Might I remind Your Highness that food on a schooner is quite different to what you are usually accustomed?"

"A cup of tea and a biscuit, I think, will be sufficient."

"We'll have a tête-à-tête with Captain De Villefort after you've acquainted yourself with the facilities on board."

"Thank you, Pierre. After we have settled things with the captain, you and I will have plenty to talk about, don't you think?"

"Certainly, madame, there will be more than enough time for us to"—he paused—"shall we say, clear the air of any misgivings either of us may have? Bonsoir, Your Majesty."

"Bonsoir, Pierre." As Catherine disappeared into the cabin, she thought of two things: Captain De Villefort's reaction to her being aboard and the word *plenty* she had made reference to before saying bonsoir to Pierre Fuquay. There was one particular question she needed to ask him, but it had to be phrased tactfully—lest he felt somehow threatened and deemed it necessary to have Her Majesty cast into the sea.

Tidings from the Sea Witch

Since the convoy left Versailles bearing the richest cargo ever to have left the European continent, it was business as usual in the Caribbean. Unable to achieve success in locating Lafitte's hideaway, bounty hunters concentrated their efforts on tracking down buccaneers who, in the process of evading their adversaries, threw caution to the wind. Prudence and personal safety often yielded to avarice and an impetuous affinity for gold.

Unlike Lafitte's brotherhood that prided itself in dodging predators, the lone wolf pirate ships were disorganized and unable to prevail in battle. Undisciplined and lacking astute leadership, they became prey to the wit and cunning of privateers who incessantly stalked them, as whaling vessels would similarly converge on a killer sperm. Soon notorious sea robbers gradually dwindled in number, and reigning monarchs once again prevailed in gaining control of the shipping lanes to and from the New World.

When Jacques Lafitte gave the order to make ready to set sail, four of his fleet of five ships swiftly swung into action. Storerooms and ammunition supplies were checked. Sailors scrambled to weigh anchor. Navigational charts were brought to the foredeck, while bluejackets climbed up and down rope ladders unfurling sails. Like clockwork the buccaneers tended to their prescribed duties. Amid the commotion, however, all activity came to an eerie halt when a sentry, perched on a high ridge overlooking Dolphin Cove, gave the shrill signal with his horn that a three-mast vessel was rounding the point.

"Friend or foe?" Lafitte's voice reverberated from the *Revenge*'s forecastle.

"Don't know, Cap'n," hollered a throaty voice from atop the crow's nest. Pointing his spyglass toward the approaching vessel, the sailor bellowed, "She hails three flags bearing skull bones atop its center mast."

"Ahoy, matey, what is the configuration of the three flags?" Lafitte retorted.

"Triangular, Cap'n," replied the sailor.

"It's the *Sea Witch*," Lafitte yelled back. "Let her through!" The sailor removed two green flags from a quiver tied to the crow's nest and held them straight up. Crisscrossing the banners twice he signaled the sentry that the vessel be allowed to pass.

Several concealed cannons protruded from either side of the craggy buttresses that lined the narrow entranceway to Dolphin Cove. Had it been an enemy ship attempting to enter the lagoon, or a bounty hunter's vessel seeking Lafitte's capture, the schooner would have been blown out of the water moments after its prow crossed the mouth of the estuary. The *Sea Witch* sailed into the cove and dropped anchor less than two boat lengths from the *Dantes's Revenge*. A dinghy was lowered into the water; and the captain of the newly arrived vessel, an Irish rogue, had two of his crew row him briskly to where Lafitte awaited their arrival on the bridge. Yates, Jacques's boatswain, called out. "Ahoy! Captain Brough." He threw a rope ladder over the portside of the *Revenge* and helped the visitors aboard.

Noticing Lafitte with his hair tied at the back, Brough greeted him excitedly. The two captains gripped each other by the forearms and acknowledged their mutual friendship with a hearty embrace.

"I seez yer gettin' ready to set sail, Cap'n. 'Tis a good thing, 'cause I comes to warn ya, matey. 'Tis time to move on, I tellz ya. 'Tisn't safe, not fer any of us."

"Warn me? What is it, John Brough? You sound as though the fleur-de-lis is bearing down upon your stern."

"Less than a week hence, ten days the most, I fears. A hundred ships is a comin', maybe more." Lafitte gestured to Captain Brough to be seated on one of the galley chairs bolted to the foredeck.

"Continue, my friend, your news intrigues me."

"Then I takes it ya haven't heered."

"Captain, for these past two weeks we've been hearing the same rumors." By now most of Lafitte's crew, including Captain Benitez Chavez of the *Seascape* and his first mate, gathered around and listened with great interest to what was being said.

"Rumors! So that's what ya thinks goin' on."

"It stands to reason that merchants are willing to pay more to protect their investments."

"Lend me ya ear, Cap'n. 'Tis a strange tale, I must tellz ya. I smells danger, Cap'n."

"We all here are fearless men. Only God can shake us to our knees. Speak your tidings, John. Tell us the news you bring." Looking at Yates, he said, "Rum for the captain. Rum for everyone!" A volley of cheers pervaded the galley.

Captain Brough waited for silence and then said, "Accordin' to one of me trusted kin, he's been lookin' out fer things on Martinique, taint a rumor, mind ya. Git this, the crown jewels of France be makin' a visit to Saint-Pierre, by order of King Charles hisself."

"So I've heard, John. The imperialist has acquired yet another colony to his litany of possessions. Does it surprise you he wants to herald an extravaganza at every opportunity that arises? Evidently, the fool's vanity has gone straight to his crown." Making eye contact with his men, Lafitte continued to say, "As I see it, His Highness apparently wishes to claim immortality by being the first sovereign ruler ever to publicly display his royal jewels in both worlds, the old and the new." Spontaneous laughter echoed among the gathered men. Lafitte's humorous remark had struck an amusing chord. The pirates lifted their mugs in unison. They appreciated their captain's barrage of words aimed at Charles who had banished most of these men to the pestilence and inglorious abominations of the Bastille.

"There's more, Jacques." Taking the cup of draught from Yates, Captain Brough engulfed a deep swallow of its contents. "'Tis fine rum, Cap'n." Setting the tankard aside, he spoke soberly, "Me thinks 'tis a trap. Three ships, I hears, the biggest cache to leave the continent. They's on its way. To Martinique, I's been told."

Brough paused and looked around. Satisfied his audience was giving him its undivided attention, the captain took a second gulp of rum before continuing. "No disrespect, Jacques, everyone knows ya took his ship." Pausing a few moments to peruse the remarkable architectural skill that went into the craftsmanship of the *Dantes's Revenge*, he added, "A mighty fine ship I's ever did see. Ya must knows Charles been hell bent ever since. He's wantin' to settle the score. 'Tis a trap I tells ya."

"What makes you so sure, John? Does he think I'd jeopardize my men for his crown jewels?"

"No, Cap'n, 'tisn't the booty that's the worm on the hook I fears. 'Tis what's the message in the dispatch that worries me."

"What dispatch? What message?" Lafitte revealed a trace of anxiety in his voice.

"I have a scout in Saint-Pierre sez 'tis true. He's privy to all ins and outs goin' messagees. He's seen it hisself. The dispatch. 'Tis Catherine, Jacques."

"What about Catherine?" Lafitte fired back.

"The dispatch sez she's on the *Vera Cruz*. Da Queen of France wil be in Martinique less then ten days, I tellz ya."

Jacques Lafitte was stunned. He asked no more questions. The captain of the *Dantes's Revenge* stood up and walked over to the center mast. Climbing the rope ladder, he pulled himself skyward passing sail upon sail until he emerged atop the crow's nest. The lookout, sensing Lafitte was in one of his quizzical moods, scurried down the ropes without acknowledging his captain. Removing the spyglass from its pouch Jacques peered into the distance searching for nothing in particular. His thoughts were numerous. He didn't know which to ponder first.

The mention of Catherine's name had jogged his senses. Through the spyglass he imagined he could see her. She was the most beautiful woman he'd ever encountered. He remembered comparing Catherine, as he reminisced, to a fragile vessel, afraid to touch her lest she break. Jacques's father, during one of the king's festive occasions, was introducing him to the queen who had been married to Charles for only a short time.

*   *   *

"Your Majesty, I don't believe I've had the pleasure of introducing you to my son, Monsieur Jacques Lafitte. Jacques, it is my esteemed honor to present to you Her Royal Highness, Queen Catherine of France." From the moment their eyes gazed upon one another, a sudden rush of euphoria swept over them. What seemed an interminably long time to Monsieur Dantes, they simply remained oblivious to their surroundings. Transfixed in a trance, neither of them could verbally acknowledge the other's presence.

Noticing Charles conversing with a few dignitaries, Jacques's father became inwardly alarmed. If the king happened to turn his head in the direction of his wife, he'd be blind not to detect the obvious blush that was transpiring between Catherine and young Lafitte. The elderly retired magistrate spontaneously stepped between the two. Tenderly taking each by the elbow, he casually whisked them to an unoccupied balcony adjoining the ballroom.

Relieved they were sheltered from Charles's immediate surveillance, Dantes attempted to end the lingering drought of silence. An impulsive ecstatic rapture had apparently captivated the young queen and his son. Endeavoring to break the spell, Dantes spoke in a stentorian voice, "The evening is truly beautiful, Your Highness. It suitably complements your loveliness."

Though imbued by Jacques's comeliness, Catherine was the first to emerge from her stupor. "Why I-I-what was it you were saying, Monsieur Dantes?"

The stately gentleman smiled and said, "I was just commenting on how fortunate it is for the people of France to have inherited such an enchanting queen."

"Convenir, Father, you have read my thoughts." Jacques had finally woken from his revelry.

Removing the fob from his vest, Dantes peered at his pocket watch. "You must forgive us, Your Majesty, but Jacques and I regrettably must bid you adieu. It's getting late, and you must be very tired."

Not yet ready to relinquish the moment, however, Catherine said, "Monsieur Dantes, your timepiece, may I ask where you obtained it?" Before he could answer, the queen added, "Perhaps Charles would fancy one just like it. He never seems to arrive, wherever it is he's supposed to be, at the duly appointed hour. A king should be punctual, at least occasionally, don't you think?"

Amused at her remark, Dantes replied, "Naturally, Your Majesty. Charles, I should imagine, is constantly inundated with numerous distractions, you included, I might add. Keeping to a precise schedule may not be so convenient for a king, as indeed it may be for a queen." Catherine smiled in appreciation of his kind sentiments. "As for my timepiece, Your Majesty, Jacques gave it to me on the occasion of my recent retirement. And I am proud to convey, he has been chosen by the Board of Governors to be my successor, the newly appointed secretary minister to the Treasury."

"So I've heard. Congratulations, Jacques. May I call you Jacques?"

"Certainly, Your Majesty, it would indeed be an honor." Turning to Dantes, Jacques continued to say, "Father, why don't you go ahead? It's nearly ten o'clock. Poor fellow, with the long hours you have assisted me today, you must be fatigued. Besides, I have my own carriage."

Dantes took his son's hint without so much as raising an eyebrow. "I bid you adieu, Your Majesty. As usual, my son is right. I'm not as gay as I used to be in my earlier days of reckless adventure. Au revoir, my princess."

"*Bonsoir, Monsieur Lafitte. I am privileged to have shared these few moments with you. Happy dreams,*" *Catherine said, as a daughter would to a father.*

Bowing his head to the queen, Dantes turned toward Jacques. "*Don't tarry, my son. We have detained Her Majesty long enough.*" *As he was leaving, Dantes said emphatically,* "*Bonsoir, Jacques. I think we nearly have him.*"

Catherine waited for Dantes to disappear into the night before asking, "*What did he mean, Jacques? 'We nearly have him.' To whom was he referring? Was it my husband he was alluding to?*"

"*Of course not, Your Majesty.*"

"*You would tell me, if it were so?*" *inquired Catherine.*

"*He's got a lot on his mind, that's all. Please, Your Highness. You needn't be concerned. On my sacred oath, it was someone else, not your husband.*"

The queen, somewhat relieved, noticed Lafitte tugging at the nape of his neck. "*What is it, Jacques?*"

"*It's nothing, Your Majesty.*"

"*Must you call me 'Your Majesty'? Here, let me have a look.*" *Catherine without hesitation undid the handsome magistrate's tie and unbuttoned the top clasp of Lafitte's blouse. A sterling silver chain had apparently been the cause of his discomfort. Loosening his collar, Catherine felt for the tangle of twisted links.* "*Am I making you nervous, Monsieur Lafitte?*"

"*Not at all, madame, your delicate touch seems to be soothing the problem.*"

"*So now it's madame.*" *Catherine was beginning to show her frustration.* "*In the future, Monsieur Lafitte, try to remember I am not just an ordinary woman.*"

"*You're not?*"

"*Contrary to what others may think, my husband insists that I am first a queen, then*"—*she paused*—"*a woman.*"

"*Is there a difference?*"

"*Monsieur, I'm not in the habit of revealing royal secrets.*" *Catherine changed the subject by asking,* "*May I satisfy my insatiable curiosity by examining the charm that clings to this lusty chain; that is, if you don't mind my inquisitiveness?*"

"*Be my guest, Your Majesty.*"

The queen slipped her fingers along the metal string. In the process Catherine's touch caressed Lafitte's manly physique, tantalizing him to near distraction. Upon locating the trinket, she clutched the amulet tightly and withdrew it from behind Jacques's blouse. Whatever curious other treasures that were tucked away beneath his stately garments needed to be thoroughly explored, she mused quietly to herself. Examining the pendant closely, she inquired, "*Why it's a key, quite unusual to be sure. Perhaps it's a gift from a-a—*"

Jacques, realizing what the queen was about to say, smiled and said, "Since you asked, Catherine"—At last he called me Catherine, *she thought to herself*—*"and who could deny such a lovely princess anything her heart may so much desire . . ."* At those words, the blood in Catherine's veins began to quicken. *"The key is a duplicate. There is only one other like it. You see, it fits into the back of my father's timepiece, the one you were admiring a few moments earlier. Precisely every ten days the chronometer must be wound with a key; otherwise, the clock loses its accuracy. Dantes asked me to keep the spare in the event he misplaced his. If I didn't wear it about my neck, I too shall be an unpardonable victim in the realm of forgetfulness."*

Through the glass doors of the balcony, Catherine caught sight of Charles meandering toward where the two were cavorting. Quickly turning to face Lafitte who was off to one side, Catherine said, *"Jacques, we need to talk again soon. Will you come, if I should send for you?"*

"That depends, Catherine."

"Depends? I don't understand."

"It depends upon which of you it is that summons me, of course—the queen or the woman?"

"Which do you prefer?" Before Lafitte could answer, a king's steward parted the balcony doors.

Charles, in a festive mood and barely keeping his chalice in an upright position, cheerfully entered the portico. *"Ah, there you are, cheri. It's unlike you to keep our guests from your usual tease."* Noticing Jacques positioned away from the light, he momentarily paused. *"I stand corrected, Catherine. Monsieur Lafitte, I didn't see you lurking in the shadows."*

"Lurking? Your Excellency," Jacques replied questioningly.

"It's the wine. The fools, they keep filling my goblet to the brim."

"And you keep emptying it," Catherine chided.

Looking into the near-empty vessel, Charles said, *"Apparently so, my observant princess."* In an awkward turn of his head, Charles said to Lafitte, *"I didn't see you is what I meant to say."*

"No matter, My Lord. Your charming hostess has been showing me the splendid view."

"It looks much better during the day, when one is not inhibited by a darkened sky. Don't you agree, Catherine, my dear?"

Ignoring her husband's apparent observation of a moonless firmament, the queen, anxious to avoid a barrage of inquisitive questions, clasped his arm and said, *"Are we nearly finished entertaining, Your Worship, or do you prefer that* we continue humoring our pompous noble guests until sunrise?" Glancing toward Jacques, she quickly added, "Excluding present company, of course."

"Need you ask?" Turning to Jacques, he said, "Monsieur Lafitte, it appears Her Highness is ready to retire. We'll converse another time. Would you excuse us?"

"Certainly, Your Eminence, I bid you and Her Highness bonne nuit."

Charles tilted his head in acknowledgment. Turning he whispered to Catherine, "Imagine that. I hardly know him, my own chief minister of the Treasury. Perhaps I should give him a lesson or two on proper décorum while in the presence of the King and Queen of France. Did you happen to notice his disheveled appearance? Even in the black of night he looked half indisposed."

As the royal couple exited the balcony, Catherine turned and stayed her eyes on Lafitte. "It's always an honor to share a few moments with one of His Majesty's loyal and dedicated subjects," she said. "Incidentally, Monsieur Lafitte, your collar is askew. Bonsoir."

Charles murmured to Catherine, "My precious, what do you really think of him?"

"Monsieur Lafitte? Well, for starters, he appears to be very astute, quite intelligent, and somewhat unkempt—"

The king interrupted her words of appraisal by adding a few of his own, "Obviously youthful, relatively attractive, coy—to be sure, reservedly sensuous, and let's not forget—positively seductive."

"You're not jealous that we were talking alone, Charles?"

Yawning uncontrollably and ignoring Catherine's last remark, Charles said, "I've had quite enough entertainment for one evening, and if I'm not too inebriated to have noticed, so have you, my princess. Shall we make our escape—together?" If it weren't for Catherine's tight hold, Charles would have unceremoniously collapsed amid his austere guests.

Lafitte's waning thoughts of the occasion, as he recalled, focused upon Pierre Fuquay assisting Catherine with her husband. He had been a moment too late in grasping the just-filled cup of crimson wine that casually slipped from the king's unsteady fingers. Falling to the marble floor, the spattered contents pelted several nearby guests, as blood from a freshly slain dragon would much have done the same.

* * *

Monsieur Edmund La Ruche lost his name a few weeks after being liberated from the Bastille by Jacques Lafitte. During its maiden voyage, the *Dantes's Revenge* had anchored off some unknown tropical island in the Caribbean to replenish its storehouse with fresh food. While seeking a secluded area behind a coppice of palms to relieve himself, he stepped onto a tract of sand in which a pool of spongy, still water had collected. La Ruche immediately began to sink in the soft mire that was unable to support his weight. By the time anyone responded to his screams for help he was already up to his shoulders in thick oozing muck. It took a dozen men to finally extract him from the bog. Though some of his mateys first started to call the buccaneer Quagmire, it wasn't long before he latched on to another name which the majority of the men thought more suitable.

"Captain!" It was Peter La Ruche, alias Quicksand, Lafitte's chosen first mate, who interrupted Jacques's interlude with the past. The corsair had climbed the mast ropes fearing his captain was engaged in one of his trances. The entire crew, from the very beginning, had been aware of Lafitte's intermittent abstractions of Catherine. He seemed at times completely transfixed, as though imprisoned by his own thoughts. Occasionally, Jacques could be heard invoking her name while in the twilight of one of his mystifying hallucinations. It was the one thing about their captain that created anxiety and apprehension among the crew.

"Captain! Captain!" retorted Quicksand, again and again.

"I heard you the first time. Is Captain Brough still on board?"

"Aye, he's fixing to leave, Captain. Says it's no use getting his ship all blown up."

"Where to, Quicksand?"

"'So far'z da win takes me.' His exact words, Captain." Pausing, he added, "There's more, Jacques."

"More?"

"It's Patrice."

"Go on."

"He's been drinking, heavy like. So have the others. They're talking crazy. They fear you're having another one of your—"

"Never mind."

Without a moment's hesitation, Jacques took hold of the rope line and slid past Quicksand straight down the main mast. Alighting on one of the cannons near to where the men were gathered, Lafitte raised both arms signaling the crew's attention. Before anyone could lay hold of Patrice, he swept forward and brandished his cutlass. It was then that several men, including Captain Brough, pounced upon the buccaneer and rendered him powerless.

"Let him be!" ordered Lafitte. Stunned, as most of them were, no one moved. Raising his voice even louder, Jacques's voice penetrated the lagoon's tranquility, "Let him be, I said!"

Released from his bondage and still clinging to his weapon, Patrice collected himself and stammered closer to Lafitte who promptly said, "Patrice, since when does the loyalty of a buccaneer yield to the bitter spirits confined to a keg of rum?" Not waiting for a reply, Jacques gestured with opposite arms while continuing to say, "Which is it you seek, my right hand or my left? Or would you rather extract an eye?" This time he made a gesture with a finger pointing to each of his eyes. "Is one ear enough, Patrice, or would you prefer both of them?" As he said this, Lafitte tugged at one lobe, and then the two of them simultaneously.

Removing a dagger from a sheath strapped to a nearby masthead where the crew had assembled, Jacques held it tightly in his grasp and pointed it directly at Patrice. All murmurings stopped, and an uncanny silence broke over the ship. Everyone's eyes were riveted on their captain in anticipation of what he intended to do next. Leaping from the cannon to the deck, Lafitte alighted close to where Patrice had been standing. "Step forward, and do what you must," Jacques's words resounded loudly.

Lurching toward Lafitte, Patrice plunged the cutlass at his intended victim. Jacques, alert and agile, stepped to one side and caught him by the arm. Pinning his attacker to the ship's deck, Lafitte held the blade of his dagger to the sea rover's throat. It was hardly a fight. Inebriated, Patrice could not withstand the brute strength of Captain Lafitte's hold. Engaged in a helpless stare, he just looked on as Jacques pressed the point of the dagger to his throat. Everyone choked, anticipating Patrice's final breath of life.

To the assemblage's amazement, Lafitte removed the weapon from its position and turned it toward the side of his own neck. Piercing the skin, he drew a few drops of blood. Pointing to the bleeding wound, he screamed vehemently at Patrice who had been startled from his stupor, "Is it one drop of my blood you wish to draw from your captain, or do you want all of it? Tell me, Patrice, which of the two do you prefer?"

"'T's the regal mistress that has yer head spinnin'. Ain't it so, Cap'n?" Patrice spewed forth. "She has ye in a spell. We all knows it. Come out of it, Cap'n, afore 't's too late. Open ye eyes, Cap'n, afore ye send us all to hell."

Patrice's words penetrated Jacques's mind and jogged him to his senses. Helping his longtime friend to his feet, Lafitte turned and plunged the dagger he was holding into the polished wood of the ship's mainframe. Maneuvering himself atop a bulkhead, Captain Lafitte motioned for everyone to rest at ease. Surmising from his body language that he wanted to speak, they drew closer and relaxed themselves from the turmoil that had just taken place.

"Mateys, it's time I told you things, till now, I've kept from you. Captain Brough, I want you to hear this too, before the winds take you to distant shores."

"Aye, Cap'n, ya have me fools attencien." Several spontaneous snickers emerged from the gathered men. Brough's words could have been taken to mean something else, by the way he said them.

"Brothers, when I have finished here, I am determined to fulfill the oath I have made upon my father's death—to uphold his revenge. Whatever each of you chooses to do, I hereby give you that right and freedom to uphold that decision. Whichever of you steps forward to claim his full share of the treasures we have amassed, I say take it and go in peace.

"Maybe it is true. Perhaps I am bewitched, as Patrice so eloquently rebuked. But not before you have heard my tale shall a single malignancy be cast upon your captain—least of all not by any of you. Reserve your judgment, my brethren, until first you have listened to that which I've told no one, not even the regal mistress. So help me God!"

VII

The Captain Heeds a Warning

Once the chest containing France's elaborate consignment of abundant riches of wealth and opulence was safely stored in the anteroom of Pierre Fuquay's quarters, Captain Philippe De Villefort, satisfied the king's wishes were fulfilled, prepared to set sail. Since there had been adequate security on board the *Vera Cruz*, the commander went about his usual duties very much the same as he would have done on any of his other previous voyages.

Prior to this particular journey, Philippe had traversed the Caribbean twice with Governor Dupree who successfully negotiated the acquisition of several island territories. Charles placed his complete trust in De Villefort. The captain's impeccable qualities of intelligence, astute adroitness, and navigational superiority loomed high on his list of competent military standardbearers.

Unlike most captains in the French Navy, Philippe was short in stature. His recessed eyes, pointy nose, and lengthy sideburns gave him an austere appearance that summoned respect. However, he possessed a queer fetish that his crew found quite amusing. Whenever one of his white gloves received a smudge or slight blemish, he'd casually remove it from his hand and discard the blotted object directly into the sea. Though he never heard anyone use the term, White Gauntlet, it was the nickname whispered round and about the ship during such times anyone happened to notice the action being revisited.

Four days into the journey, Captain De Villefort had not yet been informed of the queen's presence on his ship. Fearing he would interrupt the voyage and return her to France, Pierre Fuquay advised Catherine to remain cloistered until they were far enough out to sea, whereby Philippe had no other recourse but to acquiesce to Her Royal Highness's pensive desire to proceed as scheduled to the isle of Martinique. When the news had been finally broken to him by Fuquay, that Catherine was aboard ship, Philippe's squeaky voice could be heard by the watchman manning the crow's nest.

"Out of the question, Pierre! Why wasn't I informed earlier of this-this breach of command?"

"My good captain, might I remind you, we are nothing more than two pawns, you and I. Tell me, Philippe, on a chessboard the queen moves about for what particular purpose?"

"To protect the king, naturally."

"Quite so, Philippe, but she is motivated for even a far greater reason."

"She is?"

"What is the usefulness of a king unless his kingdom remains intact? Once he's checkmated, the game is lost. If Charles fails to gain control of the Caribbean, he will dispossess his stronghold at home and abroad. Whose wrath would you rather incur, the king's, who clumsily moves hither and yon seeking self-indulgence, or the queen's, who sweeps from one side of the ocean to the other for one purpose only, to protect her husband's rank among all nations?"

"What you say, Pierre, does denote a sense of logic, but I'm afraid we must turn back. Charles would never permit Catherine to take such a preposterous journey under any circumstance."

"Don't be a fool, De Villefort. Set aside your fears and think for a moment. We're expendable, you and I. There is no law that supercedes the authority of a king and, I might add, a queen's. Right or wrong, all royal subjects exist for their amusement. Ponder this. What if Catherine, because of your insistence upon returning her to France, informed Charles that she was displeased with the way you spoke to her, that your demeanor was inappropriate?"

"She wouldn't."

"Never underestimate our beloved queen, Philippe. Think for a moment. Do you really believe it matters to Charles to see you hanging from the gallows, especially if it suited his precious Catherine's whim?"

"But surely you're not serious, Pierre."

"I've never been more so in my life," Fuquay retorted emphatically. "Is she not on a mission to represent the king? Under the extenuating circumstances, though you are the captain of this ship, you must reconsider your position. If this journey is interrupted, all is for naught. Everything has been set in motion—to the minutest detail. My plan must not be compromised, De Villefort."

"Your plan! So that's it. I should have known. Well, whatever it is, Pierre, it won't work. Jacques Lafitte is far too clever to be waylaid by your"—he paused—"sporting little game of chess."

"Your confidence overwhelms me," Fuquay blurted sarcastically.

"My decision is irrevocable. I must signal the flagship, *Calcutta*, that we are returning to France."

Fuquay's voice softened noticeably. "Is this your final word on the matter?"

"It is!" Captain De Villefort exclaimed vehemently.

"You're aware, of course, how your decision will affect France's foothold in the New World. Do you really think Charles will very lightly dismiss your inexcusable disregard for the primary purpose of this pending mission? 'Why did it take you four days into the journey before the queen's safety suddenly became of great concern?' he may very well ask, among other things."

As Fuquay prepared to leave the captain's quarters, De Villefort retorted, "Send for Catherine. I wish to speak with her, immediately."

"Don't you think it wise, Philippe, to acquiesce on this one occasion? Her Highness will assuredly appreciate the fact that you, in our little game of rooks, bishops, and knights, used jurisprudence in making the correct move. After all, a queen's authority does outrank a captain's. Philippe, your king's bishop is on the wrong colored square. I think it a wise move that you pay tribute to the queen, not the other way around."

*　　*　　*

For the first time since boarding the *Vera Cruz*, Catherine inhaled the ocean breeze in the light of day. Feathery cirrus clouds pervaded the sky above the sea. Like gulls she remembered hovering over the Thames, sails of more than fifty ships billowed in gusty winds that coaxed the fleet speedily westward.

The queen's interview with Captain De Villefort went better than expected. Philippe, after careful consideration, relented to Catherine's insistence upon continuing forth with the journey to Martinique. The tête-à-tête she was anxiously anticipating to have with Pierre Fuquay was the next thing on her agenda. More than once he had mentioned at the last council meeting that Jacques Lafitte accused Pierre for having something to do with Dantes Lafitte's murder. It was about time, she mused, the Queen of France knew precisely what was going on in her kingdom, particularly in matters that concerned the man that made her heart throb at the very mention of his name.

VIII

Two Kings in a Pod

The *Monticello*'s navigator knocked on His Majesty's cabin door. Turning from the casement where he was gazing upon the sea with his spyglass, the King of France replied, "Yes, who is it?"

"It's Monsieur Gerard. I need to speak with you, Your Majesty."

"Is it urgent?"

"Extremely urgent, Your Majesty."

"Well then, come in." An impeccably well-dressed gentleman entered the room with several scrolled-up charts cradled in his arm. One of them fell from his grasp to the floor. "You seem quite beside yourself, Monsieur Gerard. What is the meaning of this intrusion?"

"Intrusion? Why, Your Majesty, you haven't given me the details of our destination. We're nearly halfway into the channel. It's imperative I plot our course."

"Tell me, Gerard. Exactly who am I?"

"Why, Your Majesty, you're the King of France, naturally."

"Naturally. You are rather an observant individual, Monsieur Gerard. Do you envision me a fool?"

Bewildered by the question, Gerard addled nervously, "Why, yes-I mean . . ."

"Quite extraordinary. Answer me this. Do you think your king is a pompous baboon?"

"Your Majesty, why, no, of course not!"

"So much for your honesty. Tell me, Monsieur Gerard, how do you suppose I became ruler of France?"

"Why, I don't rightfully know, Your Majesty."

"Monsieur Gerard, it's time you came to realize the fortunes of life. It was my destiny to be king, ordained by God to lead the people of France into a new millennium, one that promises wealth and prosperity never before imagined by any of my predecessors." Charles, noticing Gerard's dubious expression, continued to say, "Relax, my navigator. Affix your sextant due north. I believe that's the direction we are presently heading."

"But, Your Majesty, we're on a course that will take us to—"

"England! Very good, Gerard, I'm relieved to know your competence in plotting the intended direction of this ship is most reassuring. Kindly relieve yourself of those confounded scrolls and step this way." The nervous navigator released the charts he was holding and watched them gingerly fall to the cabin floor. "Now cast your eyes northward. Here, use this to assist you." Charles handed Gerard his spyglass and said, "Now tell me, my astute navigator, exactly what do you see?"

"I see a ship, no, three-five ships, Your Majesty!"

"Very good, Gerard, now fix your sextant according to the coordinates of those five frigates which, my learned navigator, is the precise destination of our rendezvous. Would you care to alleviate from your inquisitive mind any other inquiries that may at the moment be tugging at your curiosity?" Gerard remained speechless. "No?" continued Charles. "Then kindly inform Captain Fontaine I request his immediate presence. We mustn't keep King Edward waiting. It appears his escort reached the rendezvous coordinates before we did. Let it be a secret between us, Monsieur Gerard, that promptness has never been one of my strong points. And please be so kind as to remove those awkwardly strewn scrolls from the floor. I wouldn't want to give His Majesty, King Edward, the impression that aside from lacking punctuality, I was guilty of being untidy as well."

* * *

The King of England was robust in stature. His round face and double chin gave him a congenial expression of contentment. However, Edward's eyes looked very tired, as though the responsibilities of royal accountability gave him no rest. Instead of a crown, he wore a hood that covered his retreating hairline. Anxious to respond to the message he received from Charles's courier, it was he that made the transfer from his ship, the *Prince of Wales*, to the *Monticello* where the King of France greeted him with open arms. This unprecedented meeting between two kings in the middle of the English Channel had happened so spontaneously, any evidence that it actually ever occurred has been conspicuously omitted from the pages of history.

To ensure privacy, Charles made certain that the door to his cabin was barred for the duration of the encounter in which Edward and he had been engaged.

"This I must give you, Charles. You know me too well. It's almost frightening. How could you have been so sure that I would jeopardize my personal safety and England's as well by responding to a cryptic message that made no mention of a reply?"

"The gold fleur-de-lis that accompanied my dispatch, the one you so graciously gave to me on the occasion of Catherine's and my betrothal, it could not have come from anyone other than me. And your dedicative spirit to your daughter is most predictable. Though I must admit, I hadn't anticipated Your Majesty's prompt arrival, knowing full well there was always the chance you didn't receive my carrier's letter. Indeed, it would have been a pity for my small convoy to have participated in an exchange of cannon fire with a flotilla of your elite naval vessels, just by chance they may not have been informed in time by Your Liege of our unceremonious rendezvous."

"You needn't have been concerned about that. Charles, you are an ally now. Don't ever forget that. The French banner will always be a welcomed sight to the shores of England. Now, what's this disconcerting news about my daughter? Has she affronted you in any way, Charles? You must be straightforward in this."

"No, sire, Catherine has done nothing to dishonor me."

"But this expedition you mentioned in your letter, surely you didn't give your consent that Catherine be a part of it?"

"I was shocked to have learned that my beloved princess left the palace without so much as mentioning a word to me."

"And these rumors I hear, only rumors, mind you, that my daughter is involved in some sordid affair with one of your former statesmen, this-this Lafitte? Charles, there must be some plausible explanation for all this."

"Apparently gossip is more contagious than the plague. Your Highness, you know, as well as I do, every realm has its insidious despots. They'll stop at nothing to cause disharmony and chaos. Their purpose is to incite the people to rebel against the throne."

Before Charles could verbalize what he intended to say next, Edward was distracted by something he just heard and injected, "Ah, yes, I've been meaning to ask. Charles, have you recently been inundated with the people's unrest? My entire kingdom seems to be riled up by instigators yelling 'Treason!' whenever they encounter the royal coat of arms."

"Your Majesty, it amuses me to think that you should concern yourself with such trivial matters."

"Trivial?"

"It goes without saying, Edward, one can never sweeten the fermented pulp that clings to the inside of a barrel."

"Say, what?"

"I'll put it another way."

"Please do."

"It's a historical fact that each of the monarchs that preceded you was incumbent upon hearing such insurgent outcries as 'Death to Taxes' or 'Death to the King!' Your predecessors had to endure it, and so must you, and so too will your son, Henry, when he assumes your sovereignty."

"None too soon, I pray. Incidentally, Charles, I've been cogitating. At what point in time do you and Catherine propose to honor me with a grandson and bestow upon France an heir to the throne?"

Charles turned away to hide a disconcerted look on his grimacing face. Pretending a smile he said, "Edward, you predictive rascal, Catherine is already in the process of fulfilling your wishes. Hopefully she will have returned to France before coming to term. It was to be a surprise. Our son, Louie, is nearly a reality."

"Splendid, Charles, congratulations, Your Royal Majesty." Pausing, he added, "The lass, I see, didn't waste any time in fulfilling her husband's aspirations. Wonderful news, such wonderful news, I couldn't be happier!"

"I beg you, Edward, don't be too premature in your well wishes. After all, the young fetus prince is presently in the midst of a perilous journey."

"Fiddlesticks! Surely you don't anticipate cause for concern?"

"Right now, Your Liege, I'm befuddled. I don't quite know what to think."

"I shouldn't be overly alarmed, if I were you, Charles. You know Catherine's obstinacy. She'll not let the slightest harm come to her unborn child. A prince, you say. What makes you so certain the fates haven't decided for your successor to be a-a—"

"A charming little princess? I doubt very much, sire, that even the gods can circumvent Catherine's dogged determination."

"You did say, Louie? Why, in heaven's name, did you choose the name Louie to be the next King of France? I don't recall that particular nomenclature ever being associated with your lineage of descendants."

"Because, noble one, your daughter beseeched most imploringly that if our firstborn was, in fact, to be a son, would I terribly mind very much that we called him Louie. You're well acquainted with those lovely, bewitching blue eyes of hers. How can I deny her anything, least of all, the name of her firstborn son? Undoubtedly, the people of France will be certain to remind me of the proper bloodlines in my ancestry that I've carelessly managed to overlook."

"Never mind them. So I'm to be a grandfather. How splendid. For starters I think I'll gift the newborn prince with a collection of my swiftest colts. And if perchance Catherine obliges you with an enchanting princess, they'll be the finest gentle fillies that ever graced the palace stables."

"Your words of anticipation are most gratifying, Your Majesty. I only wish Catherine were here to embrace them."

Edward, anxious to resume a trend of thought he had been contemplating earlier, said, "Charles, not to change the subject, but I'd like to make a point about something we touched upon a few moments ago. We are in agreement the masses comprise the bulk of a nation's kingdom. This being a fact, don't you think it a wise decision to minimize tariffs in their behalf? I've been thinking. It behooves the nobility to make concessions. If the bourgeoisie and lower classes are not compromised, we're inviting the damned revolutionists to further their tyrannical interests."

"Edward, you're beginning to sound like Catherine. Might I remind you that taxes are not the true enemy of the people? Sloth and indifference are what makes them weak and pitiful. Though the majority of the populace is not in agreement with its monarch's decisions on matters of revenue, as I see it, they have two alternatives—either pay the levees or suffer the consequences."

"Which are?"

"In France, it's the Bastille. Therein abide many devices of persuasion which sooner or later convinces debtors to regularly pay their tithes to the crown."

"You mean, pay to you."

"No, to the government of France is what I think is more what I meant to say."

"But you represent the government of France."

"Not quite. You see, Edward, I 'am' the government of France. And if you think about it rationally, you likewise are the government of England."

"Charles, I've always deemed the majority of the people my pillar of support, but of late they seem to want everything handed to them on a royal platter, even after the concessions I've made."

"Perhaps, Your Liege, you should consider offering them your royal boot instead."

"I've given it much thought, Charles. It's time I acknowledged the people's needs. I intend to lower their burden of tithing. We, aristocratic society, that is, drink nectar of the gods, so to speak. Recently I've seen with my own eyes, mind you, people begging in the streets for mere morsels of food. They appeared destitute beyond words. I could hardly believe it. It was ghastly, I tell you. Naturally, it's not in my place to tell the King of France how to manage his affairs, but, Charles, consider what I'm saying. For the good of all France, rethink your position on this particular issue.

"Join with me in changing the tides of history. There has been too much unrest in Europe for a number of reasons. Religious bigotry, feuding families, political factions are just a few that have kept me awake at night; but the recurrence of my worst nightmare, I'm convinced, is due to the damn financial burden my advisors have prompted me to heap upon the common laborer. By God, Charles, levees and taxes are the true anarchists. They can squeeze the life out of a person."

Edward paused to elicit a response from Charles who had been casting his eyes through the casement of his ship during Edward's entire mollifying speech. Though he had succumbed to near pleading, the King of England received not the least sign of acknowledgment. Realizing his words were being cast upon deaf ears, Edward reverted back to the primary concern of his journey. "Now, about Catherine, tell me everything."

"Whatever news you've heard is undoubtedly nothing more than outrageous innuendoes and fabricated lies. Your daughter has always been faithful to me. As for Lafitte, my former Treasury minister, he apparently inveigled Catherine for the purpose of promoting his personal treasonous acts against France. His father who held the same post before him, much to everyone's surprise, betrayed France as well. It has been reported that Catherine and the young master of deceit had been seen together in the palace gardens on a few occasions and, well, you know how wagging tongues embellish the imagination. The dukes and duchesses of my court seem to have little else to do but create scurrilous, insinuating chatter whenever it suits them. Anyway, all this happened several months ago. Lafitte absconded with my ship, a relic Catherine had France's finest craftsmen build in honor of my coronation's anniversary. Evidently piracy suited him more than nobility."

"Pray tell, what was she thinking?"

"I suppose, Your Lordship, Catherine was caught up in one of her whimsical moods. Anyway, it's all forgotten. Her latest fancy was to adventure off to the West Indies, of all godforsaken places. Evidently, she sustained the misguided notion that it would prove beneficial to France by personally representing me at the upcoming colonization ceremony that is soon to take place on the isle of Martinique."

"Surely you intend to do something about it."

"Your Majesty, at the moment, Catherine's safety is my primary concern. Though she is securely protected for the time being by not less than fifty armed vessels, I intend to reinforce her escort back to France with as much naval power that's available to me."

"Charles, you have my empathy and support. Catherine means everything to me. She has been my pride and joy from the very first moment she came into this world. When she lost her mother to the pestilence that plagued Birmingham's countryside, where she spent her earlier years gathering eggs from the palace barn, I had forgotten what it was like to be alive. Catherine and Henry were all I had left. However, it was she who rejuvenated what little pulse of life still lingered in my crestfallen spirit." Stretching out his hands, Edward took firm hold of Charles's forearms. "Bring her home. However many ships it takes, whatever the cost may be, bring her home, Charles, if it's the last thing you do. In three days' time a consignment of twenty ships will be dispatched to Cherbourg. Expect them in less than ten days. The fleet commander will abide by your instructions."

"Rest assured, Your Eminence, I'll do everything in my power to return the Queen of France to where she rightfully belongs. It will not be the last thing I do. It will be the very first thing I do, and I will do it personally. All will be in readiness when your brigantines arrive at Cherbourg, Your Highness."

A firm rap on the door interrupted the two kings. "Yes, what is it?" Charles blurted.

"Your Majesty." It was Captain Fontaine. "The clouds are thickening in the distance. A squall is fast approaching."

"Very well, make ready His Majesty Edward's transport. We're nearly finished here."

Fontaine's reply was affirmative. Edward and Charles embraced and bid one another farewell. Upon his departure, the King of England returned the gold fleur-de-lis Charles had sent him in the dispatch by pressing it firmly into his hand. "I believe this belongs to you," he said.

"My Liege," Charles delayed Edward a moment longer, "which of us would you wager will die first?"

The King of France was quite amused by his father-in-law's reply. "Your question is most curious, Charles, but I think the answer is logical enough. 'Which of us would you wager will die first,' you ask? It depends, I suppose, upon who it is that gasps his last breath first."

*   *   *

Charles keenly watched Edward, as his oarsmen quickly rowed the small craft to the larger ship waiting to take him back to England. It would be the last time they'd ever see one another. *My poor Edward,* the King of France thought amusingly to himself, *if the squall doesn't get you first, your ambitious prince Henry undoubtedly will.*

IX

Lafitte's First Revelation

Jacques Lafitte had climbed atop a bulkhead so he could be seen by his assembly of gathered listeners. Perhaps it was because of a previous notion to become a Jesuit minister that prompted him to launch into the solemn exhortation, as he did.

"My brethren, hear me now, and hear me well. When I am finished, the gauntlet will have been cast. Either I will stand alone in my purpose, or you will remain steadfast at my side until what you and I have resolved to do is no longer a matter of debate but a reality that has indeed manifested itself."

A clap of thunder sounded in the distance. No one turned his head or seemed to notice the gathering cumulus clouds in the darkening skies above.

"Mateys, I say to you, cast your woes to the wind. Believe in whom we are and what the brotherhood truly means to each and every one of us. Release whatever it is that's binding you up inside. Let the funnels of doubt and fear that linger in your hearts be stripped away by a renewed vigor of faith.

"In doing so, I promise, you will be cleansed of whatever uneasiness torments the soul. God alone has the power to free you from the shackles of grief and despair that bind each and every one of us to the four corners of the earth. Cast away the evil shadows of the past. If you dare to approach the enemy face-to-face, then arm yourselves with the power of strength that only God's trumpet of angels can bestow. They will not deny the just in their quest against evil. After our work is done here, peace and contentment will abide. What those who took from you in the past, let them have it, I say. Nothing of this earth is worth a single precious breath of freedom, which is every man's lot. Let not the hordes of treasure in our midst beguile you into thinking the trinkets they bear are more worthy than a single man's soul. Like the dust and sand beneath our feet, every tangible thing we deem precious will crumble before our eyes and return to the ashes from whence they came.

"Do not preoccupy your minds with idle concerns. Judge not your brothers. If others should calumniate you, let them receive the satisfaction of believing they received the upper hand. Be still in your impatience to defend your sullied honor. The moment will pass, and you will have won the victory. The prize will not be a laurel conquest over one's opponent but a triumphant mastery over one's own forged shackles of sin."

The blood in many of Lafitte's lusty pirates began to hasten through their veins. What they were hearing could not be coming from a mere mortal, so engrossed were they in what their captain was saying.

"Do not pretend for a moment that 'time' heals all wounds. Time is merely periods of intermittence. It caters to no one, nor does it proclaim allegiance to any particular passing epoch. Within a few tics, a generation briefly germinates, and then completely expires—taking only its accountability to the next level of judgment. Heed me, brothers; we are presently impaled in just one of those tics of the universal chronometer that will be stilled for no one. Whatever fleeting time remains, it behooves each and every one here to use it for the greater honor and glory of Him who graciously saw fit to bestow it upon us. Though try as you may, mateys, the Creator's inclination in granting you and me the prosperity of life, for whatever His reason, is incomprehensible to imagine and fathomless to ponder.

"Is there wisdom in accumulating that which will eventually vaporize into oblivion, or is it wiser to cast one's hopes beyond that which we have already witnessed to be temporal in nature? It's the latter, I say. There's a far greater reward for the man who places his trust in Him and upholds that trust with an unyielding faith. Mateys, we have been granted hope as well. It is the fulcrum which keeps us on an even keel. It ultimately points to a distant paradise where, like the woman who planted the mustard seed can attest, there will be an endless jubilation of wondrous, unforeseen expectations.

Safeguard these treasures, I tell you—faith, hope, and love. Let them take root and abound within. Inhale these gifts with your last earthly breath so that in dying inside you, they will blossom forth new life which can never be compromised. Remember too, in the end fire, water, air, and earth will pass away; but I solemnly tell you, His words will not pass away."

Captain Lafitte looked up and momentarily searched the heavens. Dark impending clouds billowed overhead. Seemingly to ignore them, he looked into the eyes of his men and spoke with a vibrantly renewed passion, "The prescribed time has come when you must hear from my own lips that which I have kept from you. My tale must be shared, if I am expected to solicit your support in swiftly resolving matters which I am bound in conscience to uphold. Needless to say, without your assistance it will be an impossible task for me to achieve that which I am compelled to do."

As Lafitte hesitated, Captain John Brough stood up and spoke admonitory words of caution, "Ennyone heres dinks udderwiz ter interup the cap'n." He reached for his cutlass. "Sure as litinin', Iz run ya thr—" Realizing what he was about to say, he returned the weapon to its position and said respectively, "Goze on, Cap'n. Weez lisinin'."

Captain Lafitte began first with a revelation that had little to do with the present time. "There's this story about a boy I'd like to share. I think it will help you understand your captain more than you do and, perhaps too, explain why he is motivated in his curious ways. The boy's name is Louie Grapier."

*   *   *

Louie Grapier had been brought up near a roadside bordello overlooking the English Channel in Cherbourg, a busy thoroughfare northwest of Paris, where unsavory sailors came and went with the tide. He and his mother lived in a dingy apartment by the sea. Leticia eked out a living by tending a roadside tavern where mariners caroused and spun yarns of their latest adventures until the wee hours of the morning. Louie's father, whom he had never seen, was killed when his fishing vessel capsized in the wake of a vicious sea storm.

Consequently his mother, who never remarried, took it upon herself to raise the child. She did her utmost to instill in her son, above all things, he must never lose sight of God—that in His wisdom He has cultivated a plan for all of his human creatures. There were the good and the bad. They all fit under the umbrella of his creative design. He left it to each of us, she told Louie, to decide upon which side of eternity we preferred to bask.

At such times when he was able to break away from his menial chores, young Grapier climbed a nearby hill and watched with great excitement the sailing ships that gracefully moved along the sheltered seaport. He imagined himself, as Columbus once did, venturing on a wondrous voyage to exotic places that promised an abundance of happiness and fulfillment.

The boy's fortune of fate soon took an abrupt twist. One night when the moon was full, he had been awakened by screams of terror. Instinctively, the youth snatched up the cutlass he always kept by his bedside and rushed to his mother's boudoir from where the disturbance reverberated. Without hesitation, Louie thrust the weapon into the side of a drunken sailor who had followed Leticia home and persisted, with a dagger to her throat, that she bed down with him.

Half turning before he expired, the sea dog precariously attempted to fire his pistol. Leticia, fearing for the safety of her son, spontaneously jerked the sailor's arm toward herself. A puff of smoke and the sound of a seaman's weapon filled the room. Leticia slumped back on her bed, revealing a pellet wound to her heart. Grasping for her beloved son who took hold of his mother, she managed to choke out the words "Never betray, never betray." Moments later Leticia's body stiffened and relaxed peacefully in Louie's arms. Realizing she was dead and fearing reprisals for what he had done, young Grapier bolted to the docks. With chapeau bras on his head and a cutlass secured to his belt, it was all the boy had in facing whatever the grim future would bring.

The port of Cherbourg had been particularly active that evening. Several ships were being loaded with last-minute cargo supplies. As the tide was at its fullness and the time for departure neared, merchants began shouting orders to hurry up the loading. To Louie everything seemed surreal. The inlet looked like a busy ant colony with people barking and scurrying in every direction.

"Git yer back into it!" a rustic overseer yelled to a jaundiced-looking mariner. Without hesitation Louie retrieved the heavy load from the sickly, burdened sailor. Attempting to mask his identity, he lifted the clearly marked sack of hardtack onto his shoulder, the one nearest to where the boatswain was taking inventory of everything being carried on ship. Standing in a line of crewmen hauling dried meat and countless other supplies, Louie slipped on board without being noticed. Little did the young stowaway realize, he had smuggled himself onto one of the king's merchant vessels bound for the Caribbean. Fear and trepidation ran through his veins. Filled with apprehension that he would be discovered, Louie groped about seeking a place to conceal himself.

Several hours into the journey, however, Grapier was found out by a deckhand who heard muffled sobs emanating from the coverings of a small dinghy.

"Lookee now! What do we have here? Ah, I found meself a blanket. Matey, you'll do me jus' fine. What da ya say? Jus' you and me, we'll keep each udder warm tanight. Dat'll be fair, ain't it? Cum ouder therr, boy. We don't want to ketch cold now, does we? Git yerself movin', afore I throws ya to der sharks!"

"I-I have a cutlass," Louie stammered. "I already killed one man today."

"Have ya now, youngin? A real feisty one, eh? Well, we'll see about that." Reaching for a bullwhip tied to a cinch at his waist, the scoundrel was about to remove it when a hand protruded from the shadows.

"Leave it be," an authoritative voice commanded.

"Sir, I caught this here youngin—"

"You've done your duty," interrupted the harsh voice. "Off with you!"

Recognizing the gentleman intruder, the sailor pulled himself together. "Yes, sir. Why, yes, sir. Right away, sir."

As the rogue scurried from the deck, the boy spoke first, "Are you going to throw me overboard?"

"Now why should I want to do that?" said the tall man whose voice considerably softened.

"Because of what I said."

"You mean about killing a man?"

"Yes, sir."

"Why don't you come out of there, and we'll talk about it over some hot porridge. I'm starved."

"Can I bring my cutlass along, just in case?"

"Only if you promise not to run me through," said the gentleman with a slight chuckle in his voice.

"I won't," Louie had whispered to himself, "so long as you don't plan on using me for a blanket."

*   *   *

"Yer Louie Grapier, ain't yer, Cap'n?" It was John Brough who spoke out. He had been transfixed by everything he heard.

"Yes, John, I am he."

Quicksand, Jacques's first mate, was perplexed. "But your father, Dantes Lafitte, you're his son. How could it be otherwise?"

"There's got to be an explanation, Quicksand. Let him finish," rebuked Yates, the *Revenge*'s boatswain. "Go on, Captain. Tell us more. We're listening."

"Yes, Yates, there's more, much more."

* * *

While the giant bearded man and Louie Grapier, that is to say, I, satisfied our hunger, it's somewhat curious as to what transpired next. He wore a long buttoned-down coat that reached to the top of his boots, and his chapeau bras was askew on his forehead. He didn't look much like a pirate, but his prolonged stare into my face gave me a frightful chill. The fears I harbored quelled a bit when the big fellow spoke in an almost fatherly tone of voice.

"Tell me, garcon," he said, "what brings you to hiding away on the Orgueil de France?" I just stared back at him, speechless. "Come now, my boy, I'm not going to harm you. Tell me, what is your name, and what brings you here?"

I managed to eke out, "Are you the captain, sir?"

"Oh, no, I'm not the captain; but the ship is in my command. He'll do what I tell him. Right now, that's not important. What I need to know is your name. Surely your parents must be concerned in not knowing what's become of you."

Still feeling ill at ease, I tried to circumvent the tall man's inquiry of whom I was. "I can climb those ropes, right to the top," I said.

"That's part of the rigging, and the crow's nest is right above it."

"I know that. I know a lot about ships."

"Sure you do. I was just making sure you could maybe help us look for, for Henry Morgan."

"Henry Morgan!"

"If I'm not mistaken, I believe he's not too far away from where we're going."

"He is?" I spurted excitedly.

"Not so loud, my young buck. You never know who might be listening." The seaman reflected for a moment, then continued. "Of course, my boy, I can't recruit you into His Majesty's service unless I know your name and a little something about you."

"If I say anything, you'll throw me overboard, sir," I remembered saying fearfully.

"Whatever gave you that idea? I promise, from one gentleman to another, you have nothing to fear. Now come, tell me your name."

Just by the way he said, "You have nothing to fear," I felt a sudden sense of trust in the stranger; but I was not yet ready to place my entire confidence in him. "My name is Louie Grapier, sir, and that's all I know."

"I wasn't eavesdropping, mind you, but I overheard you telling the sea dog with a whip that you killed a man today. Tell me, Louie, is that what's bothering you?" The tall man invited me to sit down on one of the steps leading to the

quarterdeck. He assumed a similar position two steps below, so I wouldn't have to look up at him.

"I can't talk about it," I said. "I promised myself not to tell anyone about what happened. It's a secret."

"You and I must trust one another, Louie. You see, I too have a secret that I promised myself never to tell anyone. If you share your secret with me, then I'll share mine with you. Don't you think that's a reasonable proposition?"

"I guess so, but if I tell you my secret, you might throw me to the sharks."

"Heavens no, my boy. I surely can never do that. When two men share secrets with one another, it's a sign of friendship. You do want to be my friend, don't you, garcon?" Though I felt a sense of awe for the elderly gentleman, there remained a doubt of skepticism as to what he might do if he learned about what happened in Cherbourg, so I remained silent.

"Now listen carefully, Louie Grapier." His voice was still kindly, but his patience was obviously less than mellow. "You have two choices. Either we can share our secrets right now, or I'll have to take you back to France immediately. Since you haven't told me where you live, the lawful authorities will have to tend to the matter in their own way. Mind you, it's a serious offense to stow away on one of the king's royal ships. They're liable to do anything."

"You mean use thumbscrews?" I was suddenly afraid again.

"Maybe, if that's what they think would be necessary to get the truth out of you." It wasn't till later that I realized the tall man blinked his eye at me when he said those frightening words and that we wouldn't have returned to France because of my being on board one of His Majesty's ships.

"But I didn't know this was the king's ship, honnete."

"It doesn't matter," insisted the kindly gentleman whose name he told me was the marquis Dantes Lafitte. He had been on a special voyage with Governor Jean Dupree to acquire islands in the Caribbean for the Commonwealth of France.

"Don't take me back," I remember whimpering like a homeless she dog. "He'll kill me."

"Who'll kill you?" retorted Monsieur Lafitte quite concernedly. "Tell me," he said, "who is it that has instilled in you so much fear that you think he's going to kill you?"

"The king, for what I've done," I recall blurting out in a panic-stricken voice.

"Nonsense, the king has more important things on his agenda than to rid the population of his precious children. His Majesty, King Henri, would first have to know all the circumstances as to what prompted you to do such a thing. People are killed every day for a just cause. Perhaps you too had sufficient reason for doing *what you did. Think for a moment, Louie, if that sea rover insisted on using you for a blanket, and you killed him, do you think the king would punish you?"*

Monsieur Lafitte had a point to what he said. His words did make sense. He convinced me with his sympathetic tone of voice, "It'll be easier for you to tell me what happened than for you to needlessly stand before King Henri's deputies of justice."

I explained the circumstances of my scuffle with the drunken sailor and how my mother lost her life during the incident. I also mentioned that my father died at sea in a fishing accident when I was too young to remember much of anything. No longer able to control my emotions, I cried, "Mum, I want you back."

It was then that Monsieur Lafitte put his arm around my shoulder and said, "Now it's my turn to tell you my secret. Whatever you told me, I will share with no one. Whatever I share with you, I expect for you to do the same. Tell absolutely no one."

"You have my word, sir. I won't say anything, I promise." And I never did, until now.

"Good, I believe you. I'll get right to the point," he said. "You see, my wife, her name was Elizabeth, died before she and I were able to have any children. We've always talked about having a boy for our first child. And then it really didn't matter what came afterward, so long as the children were healthy. Anyway, it was a very cold winter when she passed away quite suddenly. Many people died that year. The physician said Elizabeth expired because of a terrible disease that was going around. It didn't have a name. He just called it the plague.

"You can imagine how sad I was, just as you must have felt to see your mother, what was her name?"

"Leticia."

"Ah, yes, a beautiful name, Leticia. She must have been a splendid woman to have raised such a fine garcon as you. It had to be extraordinarily difficult to have witnessed such an ordeal, as you so described. In any event I, I mean we, Elizabeth and I never did have that son we so very much wanted. Since I knew in my heart that I could never remarry, I prayed to God that if He ever saw fit for me to someday inherit a son, I would see to it that the boy would be taken care of, as if he were my very own. Somehow, I'm prone to believe God has answered my prayers this very night. That's what I'm thinking right now."

Standing up and looking into the moonlit sky, Dantes Lafitte said to me, "It's getting late, my boy. I decided we're not returning to France after all, not just yet anyway. If we did, France would undoubtedly lose the opportunity of obtaining a colony or two. Louie, what I want you to think about in the meantime, before our voyage is completed, is the prospect of becoming my son, the boy Elizabeth and I always dreamed upon having. My promise in return is to love and protect you, so long as I live. Even if you say no, there are some friends of mine who will look after you until you've had enough time to decide what particular vocation it is that you'll find comfort in pursuing. The man you killed, Louie, deserved to die. If need be, I'll defend you before the king myself."

With my eyes filled with innocence, the little rascal in me replied, "Will you protect me from Henry Morgan too, Father?" He then gave me the grandest hug I ever did receive.

I remember Dantes cautioning me, "Be careful when you speak, my son, especially on board ship. You never know who may be listening to the very things you don't want others to hear." How right he was. The rogue sailor, you see, the one who accosted me on the Orgueil de France *that day, apparently heard every last word that transpired between Dantes and me. After we returned to France, nearly two years later, not only did he receive a handsome reward for his malicious betrayal of the secrets Dantes and I shared, but in doing so, the traitor had to pay a premium price as well. He apparently signed a sworn statement in front of witnesses as to all that had transpired in the conversation on board that evening. The eavesdropper, according to Dantes, was found dead hanging from a tree not too far from Pierre Fuquay's country estate.*

*　　*　　*

Lafitte was gratified that his men listened intently to what he said. The truth never hurt anyone, he always believed. It pleased him that some of his comrades were intimately sharing in the heartfelt thoughts he was endeavoring to communicate. Rugged as they were, he occasionally noticed one of his crew attempting to conceal his efforts in wiping away a tear or two, even as he spoke.

"So now you know, mateys, how the magistrate who always wanted a son had lifted me from the bowels of despair and officially adopted me into the tenderness of his mercy and affection. We spent nearly two years in the Caribbean. I learned much about the West Indies and how to configure navigational charts. It was euphoric to be among the mapmakers who tirelessly chartered newly discovered land masses according to their position beneath the stars. The sea was my love, and a ship was my passport to riding its waves.

"At the time the *Orgueil de France* returned to Paris, Father introduced me to his inner circle of esteemed associates as his son who had been living in Toulouse with cousins until Dantes completed his administrative duties abroad. Schooled in the disciplines of law, philosophy, economics, and science, the newly acclaimed Society of Jesus to which my father insisted I be scholastically nurtured, instilled in me a fervent knowledge of truth and wisdom. Theology had been a favorite pursuit, and for a time, I seriously contemplated a life dedicated to Him whom I loved all the days of my life.

"However, my aspiration to fulfill this notion, though in accordance with my father's utmost approval, was abruptly set aside. He had aged noticeably, and my filial devotion prompted me to, whenever possible, remain by his side. It was during the *automne* of his life Dantes tutored me in all I needed to fathom in the realm of fiscal, financial discipline.

"When I reached the age of twenty-seven, it was a proud day for both of us. I was duly accepted to the king's court and appointed chief minister of the Treasury, a position the marquis Dantes Lafitte previously held with impeccable honor before he retired. At this moment in my life, I had reached the height of mortal bliss, so I thought.

"My colleagues addressed me by the name I had chosen to be called fifteen years before, on the deck of the *Orgueil de France*. I distinctly recall Dantes asking me why I particularly wanted to assume the name Jacques. It was my mother who once told me that when I was born, she wanted me to be christened Jacques; but because my birth father's name was Louie, she abided by his wishes. Not until I was old enough to understand that I learned from Leticia the translation of both names. Jacques means 'romantic; ingenious' and Louie 'powerful ruler.' I preferred Jacques to be my newly chosen name. You see, after killing a man, I didn't feel much like a ruler of anything, or powerful. Louie Grapier was a name of the past. After what I had done, I no longer held it in esteem.

"Mateys, I'm aware that there are other matters I have kept from you." Looking skyward, Captain Lafitte said, "Before the impending storm forces us to take cover, does anyone have anything to say, for now is the time to speak?"

Captain Brough spoke up before anyone else had a chance to say his piece, "Cap'n, jus how'd ya manige to steels dis manficent ship? An' rites frm unda 'Is Majestees noz."

A bolt of lightning shattered the eastern sky. Heavy raindrops pelted the lagoon. "Take shelter, mateys. After the tempestuous cloudburst passes over, all there is to know about the *Dantes's Revenge* will be laid bare. This I promise."

———

Heads or Tales

The interruption of a tapping sound on Catherine's cabin door caused her to replace the quill in its holder. What she was writing to Charles, for the moment, had to wait. Carefully disposing the unfinished letter in a drawer of the escritoire at which she was sitting, the queen said, "Entrer."

"Bonjour, madame." It was Pierre Fuquay. "Your Highness, I thought you might like to know, according to Monsieur Beauford, the *Vera Cruz's* navigator, we have crossed the midpoint of our voyage. We should reach our destination in less than three weeks."

"I was just about to send for you. Can you make arrangements for a ship to carry a dispatch to Charles, the moment we arrive at Martinique?" Catherine's abruptness and lack of enthusiasm in Fuquay's greeting, or what he had to say, was quite obvious.

"Most certainly, madame, as you wish." Turning to leave, he was stopped by Catherine's words which softened considerably.

"Pierre, I was just about to have some tea. Would you find it convenient to join me? Perhaps we can have our talk, the one we discussed in Versailles."

"My option to be anywhere in particular is quite limited, Your Majesty. While I pour the tea, ask your first question. I'm fairly certain there will be more than one."

"No, Fuquay, you're very much mistaken. I clearly have no reason to turn this tête-à-tête into an inquisition. We've witnessed enough of those to last a lifetime, don't you think?"

"Madame, I couldn't agree more heartily." Fuquay poured the tea and made himself comfortable on a cushioned chair opposite the queen.

"Pierre, I am adamant about this. Do not misunderstand the point of this interview. There are things I've heard that I cannot intelligibly piece together without knowing the facts pertaining to the discourse we're about to share. I trust you will be candid and avoid mincing words."

"I have no reason to do otherwise, Your Highness."

"Merci, Pierre. There is one thing that has been troubling me. Related questions may follow, but in the main, I've been in a quandary over a scenario of events that simply mystifies me. Contradictory remarks I've heard need to be put into proper prospective."

"What exactly is it that's puzzling you, Catherine?"

"At least twice I heard you mention that Monsieur Jacques Lafitte reportedly accused you of being responsible for the death of his father. Right now, I want you to tell me whatever it is that makes him so certain of this, to accuse you, as he has."

"A large sum of money was reportedly missing from le Banque de Paris. Since I am the duly appointed king's administrator, I naturally had access to it. Dantes confronted me with the false accusation that it was I who pilfered the vault of a substantial sum of assets. Naturally I rebuked Monsieur Lafitte for his blatantly false accusatory innuendos.

"The last thing I recalled him saying was that he had certain documents in his possession that would render proof of my guilt in a proper court of law. When I challenged him to produce the alleged documents, he said that he would do so in due time."

"So then, where are they? Surely Dantes would have presented his findings to the tribunal of justice if he possessed such incriminating evidence against you."

"Madame, there were no such documents. It is I who possess a letter signed by Monsieur Percival Huxley, president of le Banque de Paris, stating that Dantes, with the help of his bastard son, pilfered the treasury with the intention of making me the scapegoat."

"Monsieur Fuquay, how dare you bring dishonor to such a beloved statesman, in what you just said, and to his son, one of France's most trusted—" Catherine did not finish what she was about to say, knowing

Dantes and Jacques had both been publicly accused of grand theft. "In all honesty, Pierre, there must be a plausible explanation for all this. I find it incomprehensible that either of the Lafittes is capable of being unpatriotic. Do you have Monsieur Huxley's letter with you?"

"No, Your Majesty, the letter is in Paris where I'm sure it's quite safe. You see, right now it's in the possession of your husband. And I might add, he has a second document as well. At the proper time, I will produce both letters of correspondence to the tribunal. Catherine momentarily found herself in a compromising position. Charles never mentioned any of this to her, and Fuquay, scrutinizing everything being said, must have realized this by now. She decided to move on with what seemed to be an obvious question."

"A second document, Pierre?" Catherine asked.

"You prompted me to recount what I know. Apparently, you were not expecting to hear that Jacques Lafitte is not the legitimate offspring of Monsieur Dantes Lafitte. The elder made a mockery of France when he publicly proclaimed the return of his absentee son from Toulouse, where his wife, Elizabeth, supposedly gave birth to a male child before she passed away. The truth of the matter is, prior to his adoption young Lafitte had been a stowaway by the name of Louie Grapier who, incidentally, had earlier killed a French sailor. I do possess a sworn statement from one of His Majesty's naval recruits, a Monsieur Garret, attesting to this fact. He was aboard the *Orgueil de France* when he overheard everything I just said. Monsieur Dantes was in the process of sailing to the Caribbean with Governor Jean Dupree when all this transpired. He'll attest to Garret's presence on board ship, if you'd care to discuss the matter with him when we reach Martinique. Naturally, Your Majesty, you could never have been privy to any of this, since it happened nearly sixteen years ago."

Catherine was speechless. She found it impossible to believe that Jacques was not Dantes's sired child. It was as though she had been bludgeoned with a barn stool.

"This Monsieur Garret, where would he be today?"

"Unfortunately the gentleman had disappeared soon after the *Orgueil de France* retuned to Versailles. However, his story had been confirmed by several yeomen. I strongly believe Dantes may have had something to do with the seafarer's disappearance, but it's only a matter of conjecture on my part. So I'll leave it to your discretion as to what or what not to believe."

"Go on, Pierre, I shall not interrupt you again," Catherine managed to eke out.

"Before anything could be proven, one way or another, the next thing I knew, Dantes Lafitte was killed in the streets of Paris. The scurrilous deed was undoubtedly committed by the same riffraff he was crusading to deliver from, to use his own words, *the iron hand of tyranny,* your husband's own regime, so he implied.

"Of course Dantes had been discussing his false accusations against me with his"—Fuquay momentarily paused, and then continued to say—"his son, Jacques. When he heard of the subsequent foray, Jacques Lafitte naturally believed I had something to do with it. From what I was able to ascertain, he rushed to Dantes's side before lawful authorities were able to secure the Bourbon Street Bridge where the attack occurred. An on-the-scene witness apparently saw the elderly statesman whisper something in Jacques's ear. Undoubtedly, it was a repetition of slanderous accusations against me to ensure that his reputation remained unsullied.

"According to a documented ledger, certain items were taken from the deceased: jewelry, some francs, you know, the usual things. Officially, Your Highness, Dantes Lafitte was killed, not murdered, in the throes of a common robbery that takes place more than a hundred times a day in Paris alone.

"Concisely, it's simply a matter of tossing a coin. Heads you believe me, tails you don't." As he said this, the queen noticed Pierre unhinging a timepiece from his waistcoat. Reaching into his vest pocket, he removed a small key. Inserting it into the back of the chronometer, he proceeded to twist it in a winding motion. Catherine nearly swooned.

"What appears to be ailing you, Your Majesty? Have my words made you feel ill at ease?"

"No, no, Pierre, quite the contrary. You have enlightened me considerably. The ship's incessant bobbing makes me nauseous at times."

Gathering her composure, the queen sighed nonchalantly. It would be the last thing she ever did, if Catherine made the slightest mention to Monsieur Pierre Fuquay what she was thinking. "Heads or tails," she mimicked. "It all depends, I suppose."

"Upon what, Your Highness?"

"Upon which side the truth lays, Pierre, the head or the *tale.*"

"Touché, Your Majesty, Charles can learn a thing or two from your adroit diplomacy. Is there anything else?"

"No, Pierre, I've heard quite enough for one day." As an afterthought, Catherine said as Fuquay was about to leave, "There is one thing you can do for me, Monsieur Fuquay. I'd like an audience with Captain De Villefort at his earliest convenience, of course. There are numerous formalities I've been meaning to discuss with him upon our arrival at Martinique. And, Pierre, I trust that what passed between us in conversation will remain that way, just between the two of us, at least for now."

"Certainly, madame, there are much less foreboding subjects with which either of us might find more comforting in prioritizing one's time."

Fuquay gave Catherine a contorted smile, replaced the timepiece back into his pocket, and turned to say as he was leaving, "Bonsoir, Your Majesty."

Before she could respond, the door to Catherine's cabin had already closed behind him. Reaching into the drawer of her secretary, the queen withdrew the letter she was writing to Charles. Tearing it up into pieces, she tossed the remains through an opened porthole. What she had to say to him needed to be said to his face.

XI

Lafitte's Second Revelation

The storm passed almost as quickly as it had come. A scent of misty salt air permeated Dolphin Cove. Turbulent clouds gathered along the eastern horizon toward the northern shores of Hispaniola. Captain Lafitte asked Quicksand to assemble the crew. Before Jacques revealed his intentions as to what he planned on doing next, Captain Brough's inquisitive inquiry concerning the *Dantes's Revenge* had first needed to be addressed.

Those assigned to maintaining the ship's unceasing tidy appearance swabbed away whatever dampness the cloudburst showered upon the foredeck. "The *Dantes's Revenge*, have any of you cast eyes on a nobler prize?" Lafitte began to address his men. "The brigantine you have all come to cherish and share with one another, I say, rightfully belongs to His Lordship, King Charles of France."

At his words, murmurs of protest reverberated among the crew. "However, mateys, for the moment this magnificent ship belongs to the brotherhood." The grumbling quickly transcended into cheers of spontaneous applause.

"If Sir Charles thinks he ought to have it back, he must first ask each one here to kindly relinquish his inherited share."

A cadence of aye ayes resounded amid the listeners. One buccaneer shouted, "I'le relinkwish me boot up 'is royal highniss' mulish ass, I wil." The remark brought forth a flurry of cackles from the assemblage.

Holding up his arms, Lafitte said, "Mateys save your guffaw till you've heard the truth of it all."

Taking a few moments to peruse the decks, and then the masts that extended overhead, Captain Lafitte retorted, "Look around you, men. She's a beauty. It was Catherine who insisted this schooner be a vessel worthy of only a king to possess.

"The construction of the *Dantes's Revenge*, formerly the *King Charles*, initially required the sagacious planning of a great craftsman who outclassed his formidable peers. The architectural dexterity and ingenious imagination required in manufacturing such a brigantine had to surpass all previously conceived designs. Renee Dubois was such a man, and at Queen Catherine's behest, he presided over the task of revolutionizing French naval history by developing an illustrious schooner fit for a king. Its expense transcended mathematical conjecture. There were barely enough financial resources available to build a single prototype.

"The renowned bell, if you've neglected to notice, has been tailored to highlight the forecastle instead of the stern, as is the usual location of the belfry in most brigantines. Its exquisite ornate features of gilded fleur-de-lis and French royal coat of arms indeed accent the ship's dignity. Three-tier adaptable cannon stations embellish the gun ports from every vantage point. From the decorative molding and unique chain pumps that discharge the periodic deluge of storm and seawater we occasionally encounter, to the sturdy mastheads and formidable living quarters garnished with beveled overhanging bay windows, it was she, I say, Catherine, not I, who is responsible for this creative masterpiece we call our own.

"Have you ever wondered why the *Dantes's Revenge* has never been fired upon by a single cannon shot? Do you think it is because we are mightier than our enemy? No, mateys, it is because His Eminence, King Charles, would rather lose a fortune in gold than see the gift of his beloved queen, though he has never actually seen it, receive a single blight or slightest indignity— regardless who controls the rudder. He will persist with all his regal power and cunning to seize this ship one day, if it takes all France to assist him in doing so. And by God, in the end he shall have it!"

An absolute hush stymied the atmosphere. The buccaneers were confounded by what their captain just said.

"Allow me, comrades, to go back to the very beginning from whence it all started. The narrative you are about to hear is tantamount to what the future may bestow upon all of us as to how we elect ourselves to proceed.

"Mateys, I am neither greater nor lesser than any of you. Our basic needs are relatively the same. Who among you has never loved a woman? When I first laid eyes on Catherine, I was enamored by her. Some of you may abide by the term *bewitched*. Needless to say, at the very outset of our first encounter, the moment our eyes interlocked, we became ethereally imprisoned.

"Difficult as it may be to explain, the Queen of France and I were caught up in the shackles of blissful imprisonment. At such times when we were alone together, the world seemed motionless. All else was inconsequential. Everything simply stopped. And there we intermingled, the two of us, enraptured in an uncanny, scintillating captivity.

"Unaware that a plot existed to assassinate the man I considered to be my true father, Dantes Lafitte, I focused my every whim and fancy on being as near to Catherine as I often dared without inviting curious eyebrows to be raised in what may have been construed as interludes of impropriety.

"Catherine wished to amuse Charles with a most noble and extraordinary gift. Since the presentation was to be made on the anniversary of his coronation, it had to surpass anything commonplace. She wanted it to be awe inspiring, majestic in nature. Try as we may, neither of us could think of a suitably unique gift, something that hadn't already been presented to a sovereign monarch in the past; not until the day, that is, one of my steeds caught a stone in its shoe. Quite by chance the incident occurred near an emporium that Dantes often frequented. While my coachman pulled up to see what he could do to remedy the situation, I happened to glance toward the display in the grand window before me. My imaginative spirit was totally consumed by what I saw."

*　　*　　*

The facsimile of a five-mast barkentine displayed in Gilbert's Curio Shop is what sparked my attention. The wheels spun round and round in my head. It was as if I were beguiled by countless flashes of light popping off all at once. Everything came to me in a sudden rush. The complete scenario of how I could please Catherine unfolded before my very eyes. Did such a vessel really exist? I had to take a closer look.

Upon entering the shop, a bell above the door tinkled sharply. A clerk wearing spectacles had just returned a feather duster to its cradle. "Good afternoon, monsieur, my name is Gilbert Montclair. Welcome to my humble gallery of objets d'art. How may I be of service?" He appeared to be in his midfifties and approached me as though I may have reminded him of someone. Perhaps it was my aristocratic demeanor that gave the shopkeeper reason to pause. Though I was not overly concerned by his curious look, I began to suspect he may have recognized me but could not recollect the precise occasion.

"I'm in search of a gift for a lady, not an ordinary woman, mind you. She's, one might describe her to be, a cut above the patricians of ancient Rome."

"I so happen to have something that's just come in that positively exceeds the sheerest elegance. You'll be most pleased; rather, if you forgive me, the lady of whom you speak will be eternally mindful of your intuitive foresight. Right this way, monsieur."

"If I may delay the proceedings for a moment, Monsieur Gilbert, might you shed some light on the remarkable display in the window? I couldn't help but notice the fascinating features of the model. Perhaps you can enlighten me on the artist's conceptive designs."

"Why, certainly, what would you like to know about it?"

"Everything, I'm thinking of procuring it for a very dear friend."

In a distinguished tone of voice, the curator inquired, "Might the person for which the gift is intended, could it possibly be someone employed in His Majesty's service?"

"Astounding, you are most clairvoyant, Monsieur Gilbert. However did you know?" I replied.

With a satisfied expression, he said, "Won't you step this way? I will be happy to tell you all I am able." Turning toward me, he surprisingly said, "Your father, Monsieur Dantes Lafitte, is a long-standing friend of mine. You must be very proud of him, as I'm sure he is of you, Monsieur Secretary Treasurer. Jacques, there's nothing I won't do for your father. You see, we go back a long way. He speaks of you very highly, you know. Do you recall the many gifts Monsieur Dantes bestowed upon you after your return from the Caribbean? You were just a lad then. A good deal of them came from this very shop."

I immediately recalled to mind the grand rocking horse I had received from Dantes and the numerous books, pirate memorabilia, and several other superfluous gifts I really didn't need. For a moment or two I was reliving those precious memories, as though they happened recently. Gilbert jostled me from my revelry when he began his brief dissertation on the remarkable galleon in the window.

"As you can see, Monsieur Lafitte, this particular model differs from existing ships in that it bears an unprecedented five masts. Its elongated tapered hull is

designed to give the vessel stability in a turbulent sea. It also reduces wind resistance which provides swifter movement and maneuverability. With a square stern and elegantly shaped snout projecting forward from the bow, this beautifully crafted frigate is engineered to cross the sea in half the measure of time indicative of any other seafaring vessel afloat.

"There are one hundred sixty elevated cannons, as you can see," he continued to say. "I counted them. Because of their long-range firing capacity, they can annihilate a small fleet. Each cannon is equipped to eject five rounds in less than three minutes. Of course, it takes a feisty crew with brawny arms and cool heads to maintain the necessary discipline in keeping step with the ship's nautical capabilities. Simply speaking, since every last detail is synchronized to fulfill a specific function, it would hardly be a chore for the gun crew to take aim and sink a predator within a distance of one hundred yards. Each cannon can be angled to whatever desired degree is mandated by cranking the innovative turnbuckle attached to its carriage.

"The galleon's keel, according to the indicated specifications, would be constructed of specially treated oak, and its mast spars from only the most durable pines. Various hardwoods trim the decks, and—"

Interrupting him, I said, "To manufacture such a wonder, how much would it cost?"

"Remember, Monsieur Lafitte," he answered, "at the present time this is only a prototype, a forerunner, if you will. We're talking about the most heavily armed, swiftest futuristic warship ever conceived in man's imagination. The approximate cost, you ask? Why, there's the designers, tradesmen, engineers, materials, and, of course, the financiers. To build a vessel such as this, for it to become a reality, it would take the wealth of a nation. Surely you don't, monsieur, you're not contemplating on, it's only a facsimile."

"One can dream and wonder, I suppose. You've been very kind, Monsieur Gilbert. Please have the model delivered to my father's house this very afternoon, 15 le Boulevard de Chateau."

"I know the address. And about your previous inquiry of a gift, would you like to see to it now? You know, the matter concerning the lady who is not so very ordinary?"

"I believe you have already helped me find what I was searching for."

"And what is that, Monsieur Lafitte?"

"The ship, Monsieur Montclair, the ship." As quickly as I had entered, with a gait in my stride and leaving the curator speechless, I exited Gilbert's Curio Shop.

*   *   *

"I was ecstatic. So was Catherine when I showed her the model ship and explained what Monsieur Montclair had told me. She thought the idea was absolutely ingenious and that it was possible for a prototype of its kind to be built in time for Charles's anniversary ceremony. But we had to act swiftly. Somehow, I believe the queen would have agreed to anything I suggested. For me, at least, it was an added excuse to rendezvous with Her Majesty without bringing undue attention to ourselves. Catherine and I would meet almost on a daily basis to consider the feasibility of making the model brigantine's transformation a reality."

"Dat ya did, Cap'n. Sheez a butee."

Ignoring Captain Brough's comment, Lafitte continued. "Catherine's intended gift for Charles had to be secretly entrusted to a number of people including her most loyal servants. This way I could enter and leave the palace gardens, as a gendarme would ordinarily do during the changing of the guard. Since much work had to be done in less than a year, Catherine and I tried to set aside the vibrant feelings that constantly tugged at our hearts. Though our interludes were frequent, we did manage to concentrate on the task at hand. It would have devastated Catherine if her husband's ship was not completed on schedule."

"Tellz us abowt da ring ya warein arownd ya nek." Captain Brough shifted his weight to the peg leg side of his body where a knee, calf, and foot normally would have been, if a shark hadn't feasted upon him at the time he fell overboard in a drunken fight. Right now, John intended to satisfy whatever mysterious facets remained in his head concerning Captain Lafitte's shrouded past.

"Shush, John. Don't interrupt," admonished Quicksand.

"In the garden of the perennials, near the great fountain, is where Catherine and I usually carried on our clandestine relationship," Jacques continued his story.

*   *   *

While the queen sat at her easel in the garden, I would arrive unannounced and exit the same way through the Fontaine Bleu Portail, as prearranged. Catherine saw to it that her cloistered moments were not disturbed during the queen's leisurely hours of meditation and preoccupations with nature's intimacies.

To: Roland Sineneng

Best wishes,

John Nuzzolese

It was so peaceful for the two of us. We'd cajole at the most trivial things. During such times we were alone, Catherine was no longer the Queen of France, and I was void of being Monsieur Jacques Lafitte, Treasury minister of France.

We were two ordinary people totally inveigled in a mutual infatuation. Our hearts seemed to convey to one another that which words, under any circumstances, could not possibly achieve. Though Europe was in turmoil, and the people of France were in an uproar over an oppressive regime, none of it seemed to get in the way of our amorous obsession with one another.

On one particular occasion, when Catherine and I were engulfed in child's play, she asked me to give her something I possessed that had a special significance assigned to it. The object didn't have to be of monetary grandeur; just something I treasured that delineated personal value. When I asked why, she said the memento would help quicken the lonely hours she had to endure during my absence.

Without hesitation I removed the chain that I wore from around my neck and gave it to her. Unhinging the clasp, Catherine slipped the attached token into her hand. "Ah, yes," I remembered her saying. "This is the spare key to your father's timepiece. It would not be right for me to have it. How will he ever be able to wind it should he misplace his?"

"I'll simply have to request a special audience with the Queen of France. It will give me yet another reason to seek your presence," I remember saying quite sincerely.

"Are you sure you want to part with it?"

"I can't think of a safer place for it to be than with you, cheri. At times I too am guilty of misplacing things, particularly my heart," I said.

Removing a ring from her finger, Catherine smiled. "This once belonged to my mother. Take it, and let it be a constant reminder of me, lest you forget I ever existed." Securing it to the chain she previously removed, Catherine added, "Remember me, Jacques, forever and always."

Catherine's words were worth a thousand pictures.

Prior to my father's assassination, Pierre Fuquay succeeded in discrediting Dantes and me by presenting King Charles falsified documents incriminating us of collusion in pilfering substantial amounts of gold and silver from le Banque de Paris. Ironically, about the same time, Dantes received a letter from a reliable source indicating that it was Fuquay who committed the very crimes he had accused my father and me of exhibiting. Indubitably, the mysterious letter proving our innocence, if it still exists, will undoubtedly become a relic of antiquity, as it was never recovered.

When word reached me of my father's demise, I rushed to the scene in a complete frenzy. Clambering down the wet cobblestone surface, my carriage arched forward into the night. I can still see the streams of light stemming from curbside lanterns that cast shadows of my fleeting horses galloping briskly beneath the darkened Parisian skies. After a few tenuous turns, my carriage came to an abrupt halt near a divide by the river's edge.

In a matter of moments, I found myself kneeling beside a pool of blood that belonged to my father. The driver of his coach had been killed, and Dantes's disheveled body was found next to his carriage on the Bourbon Street Bridge. He had been bludgeoned about the head. Lifting him partially into my arms, I eked out in a quivering voice, "Father, who did this to you?"

Before he expired, Dantes managed to weakly whisper, "Be careful, my son, Fuquay, Agular, they're looking for the let-ter."

"Father, what letter?" I cried. It was too late. He was gone. Finding myself in a precarious position and being confident that one of Dantes's loyal comrades would tend to his lifeless remains, I lifted him into his carriage and sped away in my own to the palace.

I'd been informed earlier that Agular had once been a Franciscan monk. Though he was a thief and a murderer, seeing a usefulness for him, Fuquay managed to sway the tides of justice by proclaiming his innocence before members of the court who happened to be indebted to Pierre for certain indiscretions of their own.

Just recently, when the Dantes's Revenge intercepted a cargo ship from a frigate that lifted anchor at Versailles, I ascertained that suspicion of Dantes's murder had fallen upon disenfranchised patriots who dubbed themselves the Enemies of France. According to official records, as I was told, the unfortunate incident had been reported a robbery, since personal items were missing from my father's person. His wallet had been emptied of its contents, and the gold watch given to him by me on the occasion of his recent retirement had been removed from Dantes's jacket.

In attempting to piece things together, my thoughts began to wander. Since I had been elevated to the station of Treasury minister, the position vacated by my father some months ago, Fuquay had become furious. He'd been next in line to assume the same prestigious office. However, the commission chose me to the elite position for two apparent reasons. My credentials were impeccable, and it was thought to be an appropriate gesture by the French parliament to honor Dantes by making me his successor. Fuquay, being twice my senior, must have been consumed in a jealous rage. He wasted little time in fabricating evidence to imply that my father and I were confidants in misappropriating treasury funds for reasons of self-indulgence.

Fuquay already dispatched his cutthroats to intercept me, thinking I would return to the chateau where my father and I lived. I later ascertained from Bevier, the queen's personal coachman who'd been looking for me there, that our house had been ransacked. Whatever letter Fuquay was searching for evidently did not surface. Dantes told me only a few hours before, the evidence he'd been trying to procure to convict Fuquay for his heinous crimes against the state finally fell into his hands. My father, in obtaining it from an undisclosed source, withheld his identity to safeguard the individual until lawful authorities were placed in a position to protect him. Fuquay, believing I had the letter, sent his assassins all over Paris to hunt me down.

Having no clue as to where Dantes had concealed the letter, I rushed to the palace to inform Catherine about the horrible turn of events. If you recall, Her Majesty held my father in high esteem for being a loyal servant to France, particularly because of his unrelenting crusade in assisting the poor and destitute.

However, before I arrived at my usual entranceway, a carriage cut directly across from mine. We nearly collided. Thinking it was Fuquay with his accomplices, I reached for my scabbard. You can imagine how happy I was to see Catherine alighting from her coach. She hurried into mine, and we embraced. All anger and fear suddenly subsided in me, and I began to breathe easily. Her Majesty clutched several letters in her hand. Before I could say anything, Catherine held me tightly. I could tell she was frightened by the way she kept looking back over her shoulder to see if any of Fuquay's spies followed her to the gate.

"Jacques, the palace is being watched. News of what happened to your father has not yet been received by the king." She was obviously distraught. "When I heard what happened," she continued to say, "I told the courier that Charles was asleep and insisted he could not be disturbed." With rivulets of tears streaming down her face, Catherine lamented, "Jacques, how awful. I'm so terribly sorry."

Wiping the moisture from her face, she emboldened herself and said, "Cheri, listen most carefully. There isn't a moment to lose. Fuquay has all the main roads watched in hopes of locating your whereabouts. You must leave France at once." I remembered her saying this with echoes of fear and trepidation emanating from her voice.

Several more carriages pulled alongside of mine. "Don't worry, Jacques, they're here to assist you. Now listen very carefully." She was very explicit. "Take these. The first letter is a written decree granting you permission to take His Majesty's ship, the King Charles, *for a turn in the Versailles harbor. This one is an order for the warden of the Bastille, Stephan Vega, to release into your custody fifteen prisoners whose names are inscribed in the contents. I got them from Bevier whose associates* have been monitoring the prison. Monsieur Vega has been led to believe that it is the king's wishes to show a gesture of good faith to the people of France by releasing the prisoners on the occasion of his forthcoming fifteenth coronation anniversary. If the men are still able to, they will serve as the crew for your voyage."

"My voyage, Catherine, to where?" I inquired.

"To wherever you think it'll be safe. When Charles is alerted by Fuquay's twisted tales to what happened this evening, his first priority will be to bring you before the tribunal of justice so you can be hanged legally. Your father's sympathizers are already gathering at the palace gates demanding justice. I'm hoping they'll divert Charles's attention, at least for a while, when he is awakened. Hurry, Jacques, I'm frightened."

"What about you, Catherine? You've already placed yourself in harm's way. Charles will be furious when he learns you helped me to escape."

"At first, perhaps, but I'll convince him I requested you to take his ship for a turn around the harbor to ensure its sea worthiness, that I was clueless to all that has happened these past few hours. Jacques, I have to get back before I'm missed. Bevier will take you to Versailles after your visit to the Bastille. Go now. Godspeed. Come back to me. Au revoir, amoureux."

Before I could ask her to come with me, Catherine grasped the key she wore that I had given her. It was then I held tightly the ring she had imparted to me. We briefly embraced, and in a flash she exited the carriage and hastened back to the palace.

It all happened so quickly. Bevier's words were uttered with alarming overtones. "Fuquay has spies lurking everywhere. We must leave at once."

I turned to wave good-bye to Catherine. Kicking up a plume of dust, her carriage had already passed through the Fontaine Bleu Portail.

Stretching my neck through the casement, I then yelled to Bevier, "To the Bastille!"

"You heard the master," he beckoned to the horses, "to the Bastille!"

As the pacers pranced away, the other coaches followed briskly behind. I hoped to God in my heart that I would see Catherine again, but deep down inside I knew it could not be anytime soon.

*　　*　　*

Luckily the King Charles had just been completed. It took nearly a year for the extravagant warship to be constructed. The idea to endow Charles with such an opulent brigantine overwhelmed Catherine. Without reservation, she gave *me full dominion over the project and to use whatever financial resources were available at my discretion.*

Renee Dubois, one of France's most renowned architects, was issued a warrant to fulfill the dubious task of making what was merely a facsimile into a reality. The assignment was to be one of absolute secrecy and, fortunately for me, administered in the shipyards of Versailles. With Her Majesty's seal of approval, the birth of a new era in naval history commenced under the auspices of a woman.

Naturally, I had to acquire a substantial amount of money quickly. I had to do it in a way that would not implicate Catherine, since she did not have Charles's approval to authorize the business expenses involved. Dantes and I spent long hours pondering how it was possible to circumvent large sums of cash in and out of the treasury without anyone becoming suspicious. He suggested it was highly irregular and that if I did it without the king's knowledge, I would be placing myself in harm's way, even if the queen defended my integrity.

His fatherly advice to me was to drop the entire episode, but if Catherine and I insisted upon going through with the adventure, it would be best to speak with Monsieur Percival Huxley, president of le Banque de Paris. Being it was an expense incurred by the crown, there may be several options in negotiating the financial issues involved.

After discussing the matter with Monsieur Huxley, it was agreed that the project could go forward but that a substantial sum of interest would never be recovered from His Majesty's investments. Since I was the Treasury minister, he had no recourse but to follow my instructions in the matter. He'd have to have a written statement from me that Percival was acting in accordance with my authority, exonerating him of any personal financial implication associated with the enterprise. Knowing I was placing myself in a precarious position, I decided to go forth with the project.

There were many details to be worked out regarding the King Charles *operation, particularly regarding its precise specifications. I served as liaison between the queen and Dubois. It did give me the perfect opportunity to seeing Catherine frequently. As time progressed, we both marveled how such a gallant ship could take form and shape, how it could evolve from mere planks of wood into an unprecedented five-mast schooner equipped with one hundred sixty magnum-powered cannons.*

As it turned out, it was partially because of the King Charles *enterprise that Catherine's and my relationship became hopelessly entwined. Being in her presence seemed to be a constant flow of nectar, just enough to sustain me until our next rendezvous. Needless to say, Catherine felt the same way. The singular moment soon arrived when we became one in spirit and one in body. Love between a man and woman is a thing of beauty ordained by God, not something one can contrive through manipulation or deceit; at least, that's what Catherine and I infallibly believed.*

The two of us were actually happy for Charles. Once he was presented with such a magnificent prize, the king would be intoxicated with joy. Catherine planned to tell him that his newly built ship was a gift from the people of France. Perhaps then, he may look more kindly upon them in the future. I too was ecstatic, but for a different reason. Just being with the one I loved took away my craving for all else that existed.

It was precisely the time auditors were looking for answers when accusations had been summoned against my father and me. Evidently, Monsieur Huxley had been somehow coerced into divulging my improprieties to Pierre Fuquay who went out of his way to make sure his suppositions were coated with false allegations. I had no way of defending myself, unless I implicated Catherine. You see, the president of le Banque de Paris was found dead in his office. His throat had been cut. The letter I had given him was nowhere to be found. An eyewitness in the bank remembered seeing a heavyset, hairless man enter Percival's office before he was murdered. The person in question was wearing a brown frock. It could only have been Fuquay's defunct monk, Agular.

*   *   *

"I believe you know the rest, why my father was butchered in the streets of Paris, and how Catherine intercepted me at the Fontaine Bleu Portail. Mateys, if you have any further inquires, ask them now or forever hold your tongues."

Captain John Brough's hand went up, as though it belonged to a shy schoolboy who already asked too many trivial questions.

XII

Martinique

Scattered across the Caribbean Sea are the Windward Islands, so called in that their prevailing trade winds blow east to west. These routine air currents coupled with the transatlantic flow of water in the same direction gave the brigade of fifty-three ships destined for Saint-Pierre, Martinique, favorable speed across the vast ocean.

Numerous islands form the larger part of the West Indies. The Antilles, the term given to these islands, as opposed to the East Indies, is divided into two major theaters, the Greater Antilles which skirt the northwestern sector of the Caribbean and the Lesser Antilles which are comprised of smaller islands that bask more to the southeast.

The larger islands which include Hispaniola, Jamaica, Cuba, and Puerto Rico, geologically speaking, are comprised of continental rock. The smaller islands which include the Grenadines, Saint Vincent, Dominica, Grenada, Saint Lucia, and Martinique were formed mostly by volcanic activity and sometimes referred to by early explorers as the coral jewels of the Caribbean.

Governor Jean Dupree and Dantes Lafitte were among the forerunners who chartered their precise location under the dome of brightly lit northern hemispheric stars. The marquis Lafitte, while exploring the islands with his newly adopted son, often made reference to Martinique as "the Pearl of the Antilles." Its lush green rain forests and tropical plants exuded a spectacular beauty difficult to describe in words. The various varieties of flowering plants and orchids impressed Jacques even as a young garcon. He especially enjoyed watching the colorful species of birds flapping about the pristine waters. Young Lafitte had often imagined himself riding bareback on a blue dolphin that would take him to one of the surrounding mysterious islands laden with Henry Morgan's hidden treasures.

French brigantines imported slaves from Africa to work the richly endowed soil. Later, natives from South America moved into the region. These Caribs, as they were called, drove out the Arawak Indians who migrated to Martinique before them.

During the time the island of Martinique became a "department" of France, sugar plantations were being cultivated. Permanent settlements were already taking root in Saint-Pierre, Fort-de-France, Saint-Marie, and smaller villages along the coast. The governor of Saint-Pierre, Belain d'Esnambuc, received Fuquay's dispatch that the Queen of France was to attend the forthcoming coronation ceremony. This information was not to be kept a military secret, that the news should be transmitted to neighboring islands, so the event will grace the queen with proper homage and respect. Invitations to prominent dignitaries within reasonable sailing distance were meticulously drafted by d'Esnambuc's secretarial staff at his behest. The gala occasion was to be the first of its kind in the new part of the world.

And so, with Charles's approval, the letter indicating Catherine was to attend the French acquisitional ceremony on Martinique was dispatched to Governor d'Esnambuc. Its contents were intended to have reached Captain Lafitte well before the actual event was to take place. According to Pierre Fuquay, the cleverly designed plan was certain to entrap the ex-patriot in a snare impossible to escape. However, when the queen actually did show up at the pier in Versailles, the contents in the letter received by the governor of Martinique validated what was to be "truth" rather than "fiction."

At this time Martinique was not officially a "department" of France. However, Saint-Pierre, its "capital" city, had already reflected French architectural edifices. A grand fort protected the harbor's entrance with cannon turrets that could easily stave off a siege. Lafitte was certain to find his way into the harbor in a disguised merchant vessel or ordinary fishing bark, but once he passed the security ships, it would be next to impossible for him to retreat. The governor's mansion eked of newly acquired furnishings worthy of garnishing a king's stately parlor. It was the perfect setting for the hoopla about to be unleashed.

Included in the invitations sent to the dignitaries invited to the noteworthy event was a grand banner that bore a purple, white, and red stripe. They were the colors of Martinique's newly proclaimed flag. Only those brigantines flying Martinique's pennant would be permitted to enter the Port of Saint-Pierre. If Jacques Lafitte did decide to attend the festive proceedings, he would have to enter the harbor without the support of His Majesty's conspicuous five mast ship, as it was impossible to mask its identity.

Catherine had noticed Fuquay talking to someone while she happened to be on the forecastle of the *Vera Cruz* one evening. She was standing in the shadow of one of the sails that shielded her from the moonlight. Not thinking it important at the time, the gentleman she saw conversing with him strangely looked like Fuquay's identical twin. Had Pierre Fuquay procured a look-alike for this particular occasion, as a matter of insurance, just in case Jacques Lafitte decided to show up after all? she wondered.

She had to confide in Captain De Villefort before the fleet reached Saint-Pierre. He was the only one Catherine could trust with what she had recently discovered to be the unequivocal truth. Several murderers were on board ship, and the queen had to risk breaking her silence, that whatever they intended upon doing next, it would not come to fruition, so far as she could help it.

XIII

Agular

A gentle *tap, tap* alerted Catherine's attention. As she was expecting Captain De Villefort, the queen said, "Come in, Philippe." To her surprise, it was Agular who entered. Attempting to hide the startled look in her eyes, Catherine turned her head to one side and uttered, "Agular, I was expecting the captain. Do you have a message from Monsieur Fuquay?"

"Yes, Your Highness, it slipped his attention to remind you that I am to be your personal escort when we disembark at Saint-Pierre."

Having little sufficient time to synthesize what the hooded monk had implied, Catherine's voice was casual. "Thank Monsieur Fuquay for his thoughtful proposal, but I don't think it will be necessary for me to have a chaperone, Agular. I feel quite safe with the security arrangements Captain De Villefort has previously discussed with me. Adieu, Agular."

Instead of leaving at the queen's suggestion, Agular went on to say, "Forgive me, Your Majesty, but Monsieur Fuquay insists that you are not to be left unattended during your visit to the island of the Caribs. It has been rumored that some of them have an abhorrence for imperialists."

"Won't you sit down for a moment, Agular?" Catherine thought it best to keep her fears in check by not indicating to Fuquay's peculiar reverend friend that he gave her the shivers, and she completely distrusted him. Changing the subject, the queen asked, "Agular is your first name, not your surname?"

"Agular is my only name, Your Majesty. Circumstances were such that I never learned the identity of those responsible for my existence."

"I'm intrigued as to why you decided to become a man of the cloth. You see, when I was much younger, I too had an ambition to enter God's service."

"Why didn't you, if I may be so impertinent to ask, Your Majesty?"

"It's a fair question, and I shall answer it, but first you must satisfy my curiosity as to why you became a monk."

"Certainly, Your Majesty. You see, I'd been an orphan ever since I could remember. I have no idea who my parents were or what may have become of them. It wasn't until I reached the age of reason that I realized I'd been a ward of the state living in an asylum for unwanted *d'enfants*. If you could only imagine what it must have been like. The sanitarium was overrun by pestilence and disease. It was less than human to live in such ignominy. Naturally, I developed loathful resentment for the institution to which I was banished, including its austere administrators.

"I won't weary you with the particulars, Your Majesty, but when I was sixteen, during which time I was being thrashed with a whip, in the process of defending myself, I killed an orderly. After my trial was concluded, the court solicitor to the case, Monsieur Pierre Fuquay, took pity on me. He gave me three alternatives from which I was to decide my own fate."

"And what were they, Agular?" Catherine's attitude toward him seemed to soften considerably.

"He said I could either choose to hang for the crime I had committed or rot in the Bastille's dungeon." Agular paused for a moment. Though Catherine could have guessed, she asked anyway, "And the remaining alternative, Agular, what was it?"

"Monsieur Fuquay offered me the opportunity of spending the rest of my life doing penance in a cloistered monastery. Since hanging seemed quite final, I briefly contemplated the two remaining options. Both suggested a form of melancholic imprisonment, but the latter appeared less intimidating."

"Weren't you happy being in God's service?"

"I was completely happy, Your Majesty, in a bittersweet sort of way."

"What prompted you to leave the monastic life, Agular?"

"It was the plague, Your Majesty, the one that revisited the continent when you were too young to remember."

"Revisited?"

"Do you recall in the Book of Exodus how the infidels were smitten by the various scourges of pestilence cast upon them by Yahweh?"

"Yes, I do recall."

"Likewise, the entire order of friars to which I belonged had been stricken by the plague of Europe. Every last one of them died within weeks; that is, excepting for me."

"Oh, how awful!"

Agular, somewhat in a trance, ignored Catherine's intervening cry of compassion. He continued to say, "For days I wandered about in a stupor until I came upon a roadside *auberge*. Extremely hungry, I begged for food which was nothing new to me. Several patrons, who had had their fill of spirits, suddenly lashed out at me for the pathetic fool I must have seemed to them. 'So's yer hungry,' they cajoled. Their taunting escalated. Grasping hold of their *entrejambes*, they cried out in unison, 'Then eat this.' Losing control of my senses, I retaliated. There was anger in my fists. While striking one of them on the temple, the buffoon fell backward and collapsed. He died instantly. If there weren't so many, I would have killed them all.

"Monsieur Fuquay, it so happened, held the office of magisterial solicitor to the king's court. At my trial, he recognized who I was from the last time he interceded for me. Because my benefactor despises drunken disorderliness, he rescued me for the second time in my life. From that day forward, I have dedicated my complete allegiance to him, Your Majesty. If necessary, I would die for him." Catherine reflected. She wondered how many times Fuquay would have sentenced Charles to the Bastille for his inebrious behavior, if he had the opportunity.

The queen thought it best not to probe Agular any further. What he said frightened her beyond words. Jacques, she wondered, may not be able to defend himself from this robust goliath of a man whose personal weaponry constituted an arsenal in itself. She had noticed him shining his thick plate of armor and helmeted shield that glistened in the moonlight when walking on the deck shortly after leaving Versailles. Somehow she needed to gain Captain De Villefort's assistance in keeping Agular at a safe distance once they reached Martinique. Jacques, she knew, would stop at nothing in seeking a way to rendezvous with her; so did Pierre Fuquay. Agular had every intention, Catherine was certain of it, to stay within proximity of the queen and wait patiently for her lover to appear.

Hearing enough, Catherine thought it best not to probe the defunct monk any further. She already concluded in her mind that he was a black angel who had been summoned from the depths of hell to obey and defend Satan, or rather, Pierre Fuquay. The two appeared to be vicariously one and the same, evil and barbaric in nature.

Although Agular's revelation seemed sincere, Catherine wasn't about to accept the distorted facts she had just heard. Fuquay was an out-and-out murderer, liar, and cheat. This she already confirmed to be true. The lout seated before her, however, had obviously been spiritually wounded for all that transpired in his wretched past. He unconditionally embraced Pierre whose self-interests lured the misguided monastic servant into a web of deceit and corruption.

"I decided not to enter the cloister, Agular," she began to say, "because—" A knock on the door caused Catherine to pause. Completing her sentence, she said, "Because ever since I was a little girl, I also wanted to be a queen." Raising her voice toward the door, Catherine breathed a sigh of relief and said, "Entre."

Upon entering the cabin, Captain De Villefort said, "You wanted to see me, Your Majesty?"

"Why, yes, we need to discuss the forthcoming itinerary of events. Monsieur Agular was just leaving."

Rising, Agular first bowed his head to Catherine and then turned to face Philippe. He gave him a villainous stare and abruptly left.

"Before we return to France," De Villefort whispered softly to Catherine, "I'd like to leave that creature chained to a ship's anchor on Cannibal Island, if there is such a place."

Catherine smiled at his words and said, "Won't you have a seat, Captain De Villefort?" As though she wanted her words to transcend the cabin walls, the queen elevated her voice, "Monsieur Fuquay has had the foresight of seeing to my protection once we arrive at Saint-Pierre. Unfortunately I cannot in conscience convey to Charles, when we return to France, that you had the same intuitive regard for my personal safety."

Astonished, De Villefort said, "But, Your Majesty—"

"Enough, Philippe!" Catherine's voice pierced the atmosphere. "In the future kindly remember the proper respect you should have for your queen." Slipping a hurriedly scrawled message across the table to the mystified captain, he picked it up. Before De Villefort could say anything, Catherine held a finger to her pursed lips. "Read it, but don't say anything," she whispered softly. The communication sounded somewhat cryptic to Philippe.

Urgent. The walls have ears. Meet me by the mizzenmast in one hour. Speak to no one.

Retrieving the note, Catherine said vehemently, "Leave me, Philippe. I have another of my splitting headaches. We'll have to discuss the details of Governor d'Esnambuc's agenda when I'm feeling less incapacitated. Adieu!"

Captain De Villefort nodded to Catherine. He arose and made some apologetic remarks before he left.

*   *   *

Neither Pierre Fuquay nor Agular appeared to be anywhere in sight during Catherine and De Villefort's brief rendezvous under the mast nearest the stern of the *Vera Cruz*. The queen surveyed the galley to make absolutely certain no one was within listening distance. Only a few sailors were on deck toward the center of the ship. They were preoccupied with mending one of the lower main sails. It had been torn by a piece of the rigging that entangled in a crosswind.

Captain De Villefort spoke first. "What is it, Your Majesty? Your note sounded as though . . ." He paused. "Is something troubling you?"

"Shhh, Philippe, not so loud. I've got to warn you."

"Warn me? About what, Your Majesty?"

"I have reason to believe both our lives are in danger. Do you ever recall seeing a gentleman on board that looks to be Pierre Fuquay's identical twin?"

Before Philippe was able to reply, Catherine suddenly cringed and painfully clutched the lower part of her abdomen. "What is it, Catherine? Tell me, Your Majesty, what's ailing you?"

"Help me back to my cabin, Philippe. Quickly, before it's too late."

From out of the shadows, Pierre Fuquay suddenly emerged. Agular was with him. Noticing them, Captain De Villefort said, "Help me get Her Majesty back to the cabin, Pierre. She's in great pain." As Fuquay took hold of Catherine, Agular gently lifted the queen in both his powerful arms.

"What was Her Majesty doing on deck, Philippe? I thought she was in the midst of another of her splitting headaches."

Captain De Villefort immediately connected to what Catherine said earlier in her note.

The walls have ears.

"If you must know, Monsieur Fuquay, Her Majesty's splitting headache subsided much sooner than she had expected. We must hurry. For god's sake, be careful, Agular." Philippe was in such a panic, he never noticed the obvious smudge on one of his white gloves.

The burly monk's cumbersome stride caused Captain De Villefort's heart to palpitate. "Careful, now, careful," Philippe repeatedly sputtered. Agular loped gingerly across the foredeck until he reached the cabin door. Several onlookers, unable to decipher what was going on, watched in amazement. Once inside, Philippe said, "What do you suppose is the matter, Pierre? Is it her appendix?"

"Quite possibly, Philippe, her appendix or—" Interrupted by an agonizing scream Catherine could no longer suppress, Fuquay motioned to Agular. "Get me a wet towel and some blankets, quickly."

As Catherine let out another uncontrollable screech, Captain De Villefort looked at Fuquay. "What is it, Pierre? For god's sake what's happening? She appears to be convulsing."

"You're the captain. Don't you recognize the symptoms, Philippe? The Queen of France is in labor."

XIV

Lafitte's Third Revelation

Although Captain John Brough was not among the men who had been emancipated from the Bastille, he had befriended Captain Lafitte when they crossed paths off the southern coast of Hispaniola. John and his small band of sea rovers were being harried by three bounty ships seeking their capture.

The sequence of events that followed gave the *Dantes's Revenge* its first taste of action on the high seas and a reputation that spread quickly to every island port in the Caribbean. As bounty hunters bore down upon the *Sea Witch*, a notorious pirate ship that combed the Caribbean searching for plunder, Lafitte's five-mast brigantine intercepted the scavengers before they could close in on Brough's schooner.

It was hardly a fight. Lafitte's gunners turned their starboard cannons on the frigate closest to the *Sea Witch*. A thunderous roar of artillery fire ripped into its bow and sunk the vessel immediately. The second assailant turned and blasted a volley of cannon shot at the *Revenge*. None of the rounds found its mark. Twelve of Lafitte's cannons blasted away within five-second intervals. The first two errant missiles fell short; but the ensuing volleys struck the main mast, bulkhead, and bowsprit in succession. The ship caught fire and, like a wounded whale unable to stay afloat, began to founder.

Realizing it would be futile to engage the ominous five-mast brigantine in a head-to-head confrontation, the third alien ship attempted to elude the powerful vessel. It was no use. Before it could distance itself from the *Revenge*, several rounds of gunfire slammed into the mastheads, splintering them to pieces. Others pummeled the hull below the waterline. The frigate began to list and slowly retreated to its watery grave. Since both ships were being sought by Europe's sovereign powers, the *Dantes's Revenge* and *Sea Witch* agreed to form an alliance that remained in good standing until the bitter end.

Though Captain Brough and his crew weren't bona fide members of the brotherhood from the start, they had been accepted into the coterie after the two factions joined forces at the conclusion of the brief skirmish with the bounty hunters. A common enemy had made the fatal mistake of attacking a lone pirate ship whose "big brother," so to speak, happened to be sailing by.

Being that Lafitte never disclosed the details to Captain Brough as to what happened at the Bastille that fateful day, he thought it was fitting to explain what had transpired when he heard the inquisitive captain say, "Cap'n, tellz us hows ya manigged to foolz the gards in da Bastiell. Me an me mateys wants to noze."

It was a fair request. Captain Lafitte promised to explain to the men everything they wished to have clarified. How could the alliance trust him if he held back anything they needed to clear up within the blurred vision of their skeptical minds? Once again the men gathered on the foredeck to hear what Jacques thought to be the conclusion of his tale. Looking toward the horizon, he spoke with renewed vigor.

$$* \quad * \quad *$$

The king's ship had just been completed. Catherine foresaw in her clairvoyance that I needed a crew to sail it. Who better to choose than men who desperately had to flee France, the same as I did? It didn't take very long before my coach reached the heavily fortified prison. Though I was being hunted down, there didn't appear to be any sign of unusual activity in the vicinity of the great house of detention. The Bastille would hardly be the place a fugitive from the law would seek refuge. Not finding me at home, Fuquay's watchdogs presumably rushed to the palace gardens. Fortunately I had already rendezvoused with Catherine and was well on my way before they reached the Fontaine Bleu Portail.

From the river to the Bastille runs the Arsenal Basin which provides water to a moat that surrounds the giant fortress. The tributary runs underground for nearly a mile and then emerges to form the Saint-Martin Canal. This is the escape route I chose for how many of the prisoners I could manage to help free. The Swiss Guard patrolled all of the exits, and to walk through the main gate over the bridge with a parade of prisoners was not an option. Though Catherine was the catalyst, Bevier and I devised a plan of our own.

Aside from my carriage, there were four others Catherine had sent along to escort the released prisoners to Versailles. We stopped short of the Bastille, the ominous eight-towered state prison linked by walls of equal height that loomed over one hundred feet tall. Bevier knew what to do. Signaling to a coachman who was familiar with the escape route, the fellow jumped into one of the small wooden boats that was moored to the canal. These conveyances were used to transport supplies through the underbelly of the Bastille. The crafts also removed dead inmates from the premises to avoid contamination and disease.

"You know what to do, Victor," I remember Bevier telling him. "One of the others will lift the inner grating from the inside. Go quickly." We then watched the small boat disappear into the narrow aperture of the Bastille.

It was just then two prison sentries approached the small cluster of coaches. They confronted me with a "Halt! Who goes there?" Before a reply was given, the guards were waylaid by two of the coachmen who jumped from their carriages. Knocking the junior officers senseless, they removed their uniforms before tying them up. The fourth coachman feigned to be a madman and acted in a feisty manner. As the carriage approached the Bastille, visions of the worst imaginable horrors flashed through my mind.

I often frequented the mammoth prison for the purpose of giving hope to several detainees incarcerated for false charges of miscellaneous offenses. Dantes had told me that many of the most trusted and reliable Frenchmen he knew, for reasons of fraudulent convenience, were regularly condemned to the foul dungeon. The governor of the Bastille, Monsieur De Launay, had little reason not to grant me admittance whenever I happened to show up at the cast-iron gates. Ranking government officials were always granted the high level of respect associated with their office.

Bevier pulled the coach to a halt at the prison gate. I then alighted. The two men who confiscated the sentry's uniforms stepped down from their exterior perch and pulled what appeared to be a disheveled-looking character from inside the coach. It was difficult for me to read the hands of the great clock that hung above the vast doors of the main entranceway. I did not procrastinate in making my next move. It was a simple gesture. I waved the dispatch that Catherine had concocted to the sentry at the first gate. The drawbridge immediately descended and the heavy doors parted. This brought me and my small entourage to the next set of portals.

"Bonsoir, a lettre de cachet from His Majesty," my words echoed in an authoritative voice. The letter was a direct order of internship from the king which gave the prisoner in question absolutely no recourse. It could be years before a proclamation of release was so ordered.

"Ouvir!" the senior guard exclaimed.

The clanking of metal bars being lifted could be heard, and lighted braziers hanging from the stone walls within gave me a clear view of the turnkey's quarters.

Among the 189 prisoners detained in the Bastille were high-ranking naval officers, parliamentary deputies, businessmen, and common felonious offenders, all of whose future state of existence was tenuous. Three to five prisoners, mostly convicted murderers, were either hanged or executed by a firing squad every ten days. Persons of influence and wealth who escaped the death sentence usually paid a handsome stipend to jailers in exchange for palatable food and sanitary accommodations. Prisoners deemed insane or incorrigible were placed in dungeons where rats and pestilence germinated.

An attendant whom I had never seen before approached me. "Governor De Launay has left for the day. How may I be of service?" he said.

"I'm to carry out His Lordship, King Charles's two written requests." Holding the dispatches at a distance, I continued to say, "The first is a lettre de cachet ordering this lunatic a lengthy stay in the lowermost dungeon. It's a miracle that he hasn't already been hanged."

The prison master reached for the sealed letter, but I pulled it back and continued to say, "May I see your ledger of registered prisoners. I believe that's what His Majesty ordered me to ask you next."

"I beg your pardon, Monsieur—"

"My name is unimportant," I interrupted. "His Majesty's order conveyed in this second letter, however, is important. It must be carried out immediately."

"May I please see it?"

"If you insist, but I'm in a hurry. I've received an invitation from Her Majesty to attend one of King Charles's festive occasions, and I don't wish to be unnecessarily delayed. Can you understand that?"

I then handed the second letter to the well-groomed jailer. After opening it and surveying its contents, he said, "This is rather an unusual request. I'm afraid you'll have to wait until the warden gives his approval."

"Might I remind you, Monsieur—?"

"Monsieur Malcolm de Salle, I am the keeper of the keys at the moment."

"What you have in your hand, Monsieur de Salle, is not a request. It's a direct decree of the king. His Majesty, as you can clearly see, wants the fifty-five prisoners whose names are inscribed released forthwith."

"But, monsieur—"

"However irregular it may seem, there's no time for banter. Would you rather His Highness, Sir Charles, personally attend to the contents of his own edict? I assure you, Monsieur de Salle, if you delay a moment longer, you're apt to find yourself sharing a cell with this poor excuse for a human being." Extending my hand, I said poignantly, "The ledger, if you please."

"How will you transport them, monsieur?"

"They can walk. Surely they still have legs; that is, if you haven't already chopped them off for your personal amusement." The jailer was speechless.

I had inscribed a 5 over the 1 in the number 15. I'd needed more than fifteen men to sail the king's ship out of the Versailles harbor. Catherine could not possibly have known this. Perusing the ledger, I recognized the names of French patriots who had been arrested for various punitive acts against the crown. Cassis Yates, Peter La Ruche, Muslim Green, and a host of naval seamen were on the list.

"You shall be duly rewarded in fulfilling the king's wishes in a timely manner, Monsieur de Salle. The keys, if you please. While this rascal of a fellow is taken below by my escort, you and I will see to the rest."

"Fifty-five prisoners, oh my, are you certain His Majesty wants fifty-five prisoners released?"

"That's what the letter says, in honor of his fifty-fifth birthday anniversary. Perhaps His Majesty consumed too much wine and had intended to inscribe only one 5." My facetious remark failed to elicit a response from the befuddled Monsieur de Salle.

The rest was routine. Once the gate beneath the Bastille was lifted, so Victor's boat could get through, the prisoners exited by way of the underground canal. Several other small crafts were employed in the evacuation procedure. Though it took several trips to complete the task, we managed to free seventy prisoners that evening.

Needless to say, tears spilled from my eyes for what I'd seen at the lowermost level of the Bastille. I never before had recourse to venture to that particular facility. It was horrific. To describe the conditions therein would only sicken you for what transpired in a world beyond imagination. My only regret was that many of the inmates were in no condition to be moved. The exodus would have killed them. Sadly to say, we were also unable to evacuate anyone who was chained to his cell wall. The keys to their manacles must have been in the absentee superintendent's possession. I believed Monsieur de Salle when he assured me that was the case, as he too was sickened by what he saw.

After finally realizing that an unprecedented escape was taking place right beneath his very nose, Monsieur Malcolm de Salle rallied to his senses. Knowing full well that he had been duped, and not having any family with which to be concerned, he thought the prospect of adventuring with the prisoners was better than having to answer to Charles for what he had done, or failed to do. At any rate, overwhelmed with compassion for the caged inmates whose dignity had been ripped from the depths of their souls, Malcolm de Salle acquiesced to what any God-fearing man would do. It was he, dressed in his finery, who hailed several passing carriages so that the entire troop of seventy emancipated prisoners could journey to Versailles expeditiously.

*   *   *

The entire gallery of listeners turned toward Malcolm de Salle who was perched on one of the lower mastheads. Brandishing their cutlasses to the sky, they resounded with repetitive hoots of "Aye, aye! Aye, aye!" Jacques too acknowledged the gentlemanly pirate with a nod of approval.

"It had taken nearly a year for the extravagant war ship to be constructed. The thought never occurred to me that the king's galleon had not been fully certified to embark on its maiden voyage. Our survival ultimately depended upon a power far greater than any ordinary man or king.

"When we reached the port of Versailles, the prisoners needed suitable attire for the long journey ahead. It was heartwarming to witness common folk eager to support those of us they recognized to be victimized inmates of the Bastille. Whatever necessary supplies were needed for the imminent voyage, various shopkeepers rallied to our assistance. None of what transpired in Paris had reached the attention of government officials in Versailles, so the queen's letter permitting me to take the king's ship for a spin was not challenged by the harbor master.

"It was just before we left the quay that Bevier removed Catherine's letter from inside his jacket. He made me promise before giving it to me that the ship would be well beyond the borders of France before I contemplated reading it. My oath, he said, would give Catherine peace of mind and the assurance that no harm had come to me.

"While most of you here were scurrying about amid the confusion, I drafted a letter to Charles. Bevier, who I had come to trust, respect, and admire, said that he'd have it circumvented to His Majesty in the usual manner.

"Bewildered and no longer seeking answers to questions that surged through my mind, I became a different person. 'To hell with France! Damn Fuquay!' In an instant I swore my revenge. The fuse had been ignited. What seemed to be an armory of ticking gunpowder swarming in my head, I had to diffuse it before it exploded prematurely. It was imperative for me to devise a plan to satisfy my vengeance. How else could I ingest the hope and belief of righting the wrongs that had been flagrantly heaped upon my father and me?

"With venom in my heart, His Majesty's newly constructed brigantine, equipped with all the trappings imaginable, sailed under a moonlit sky. In commandeering the *King Charles*, as the ship was to be named, it suddenly struck me that the magnificent brigantine had been my rightful inheritance. After what happened to my father, I thought it only fitting that I should christen it, *Dantes's Revenge*.

"Once we reached the English Channel, we set our course in a west-southwesterly direction. It would take us to the Caribbean where I had traversed as a youngster. I remembered it being a refreshing time of my life filled with exhilarating recollections, and I always dreamed one day of again returning to its pristine waters.

"It wasn't until we were clear of France that I opened Catherine's letter. After reading it, I became extremely troubled, and my mind has been in a quandary ever since. What she said in her letter was indeed overwhelming. I instantly wanted to turn the ship around and go back. However, prudence prevailed. Instead, I buried the contents of Catherine's letter in my heart where it's been lingering ever since.

"Many of you, not knowing what was ailing me, witnessed the effect it had upon my senses. You see, though my behavior has betrayed me, I'm truly not bewitched, or the mad dog many of you so seem to think I've become."

XV

A King Is Dead

"**W**hich of us would I wager will die first, you ask? It depends, I suppose, upon who it is that gasps his last breath first,*" Charles remembered vividly Edward's final parting words.

News that King Edward of England died in his sleep did not surprise Charles in the least. Without reservation he was certain that Prince Henry orchestrated his father's death so he could assume power over a country suffering under the tutelage of a weak monarch. He thought Edward's concern for the peasant class's welfare created a divided regime. It wouldn't take long for his successor, King Henry, to regain control of the chaos created by his deluded father. Like a deluge propagated by a spontaneous thundercloud, blood ran through the parish streets of England. Charles had inwardly predicted this would occur upon Edward's passing. The reign of terror lasted longer than the one Charles would experience before his own rule came to a disenchanted climax.

Naturally, the twenty ships Edward promised to send Charles, the naval vessels that were to reinforce Catherine's escort when she returned to France, had gone by the wayside. The newly ordained King Henry, learning of his father's intentions, wasted no time in countermanding Edward's orders on the eve of his death, only hours before the fleet was to leave the shores of

England. Although Henry's sister was married to the King of France, the alliance between the two countries deteriorated quickly. In the short weeks that passed, after Edward's untimely end, heavily fortified gun ports would stretch along the coastline on either side of the channel that separated the two countries.

Reassessing the situation, Charles decided to keep whatever ships he had at his disposal poised for a possible attack, in the event young Henry lost complete control of his senses. He would oversee what the ramifications of England's sudden exchange of kings entailed for France. Catherine, for the time being, at least, had to rely on Captain De Villefort and Jean Dupree in bringing her home safely, as Charles strongly felt they would do. She'd better have a plausible excuse for her impudent behavior in sailing off, the way she did. Attempting to apply the tourniquet of magical potions she kept on ice for Charles, it would be futile for Catherine to even try.

After the Queen of France once learned of her father's death, her sympathetic husband would do everything in his power to suave the tears that were sure to flow profusely from his wife's melancholic eyes. Perhaps Catherine should indeed be grateful that Edward did expire; otherwise, Charles may not have had sufficient reason to curb his temper or lashing tongue when next he beheld her in his arms—for the unforgivable thing she had done in leaving him to brood over her absence.

XVI

Moment of Truth

"Cap'n, weez wants to know what's in da letter dats bin givin yer da spelz yer bin havin'. If weez trespasin' on sakerit grownd, den leavz it be, jus leavz it be, weez undastan."

Jacques didn't care for Captain Brough's inquiry about the contents of Catherine's letter. He was trespassing on sacred ground. Under any other circumstance, he would have challenged Brough to retract what he said, that it was none of anyone's business.

"Mateys, I promised to lay bare all that you asked me in the hope that you will uphold me as to what I must do next. After the last word is done, when my tale is finished, either we will go forth together, or I will go forth alone." Jacques, in saying what he just did, invited yet another possible question pertaining to what exactly his intentions entailed.

Before Lafitte could respond to Captain Brough's request, another voice echoed loudly. It belonged to one of the buccaneers who was with John when they boarded the *Dante's Revenge*. The unforeseen outcry carried the equivalency of a piercing dagger to the heart. "Tell us, Cap'n, did you bed down with the queen? It's a fair question, ain't it?" The rum that flowed in the sailor's veins obviously inebriated his sense of propriety.

"Enough!" It was Quicksand who dropped down from a rope ladder and confronted the inquisitor face-to-face. "What's between a man and his woman is personal, I tell you. It doesn't have to be shared with anyone else, least of all, any of us. Let it pass, mateys. Enough, I tell you, no more!"

Captain Lafitte began to perspire, for he knew what he was about to say would not be easy. "No, Quicksand, I promised to tell all. The men have a right to know everything."

"Everything, Captain, even this?" Quicksand raised his voice in disbelief.

Retaliating, Jacques hollered back at Quicksand, "If I must be crucified for what I have done, then let it be so."

"In God's name, Captain, not by us!" Lafitte's first mate was irate. "We're not the enemy, Jacques."

"My transgressions are the enemy!" Lafitte's words stirred everyone. "Every morsel of truth must come out of me, Quicksand. Otherwise, I'd stand guilty of betraying myself more so than they."

The crew began to grow restless and ill at ease. It was the first time they witnessed their captain steeped in a compromising position. The stirring grew to a grumbling.

"Hear me out, my brethren," Lafitte raised his voice to quiet the din. "We're not through here, but when all the facts have been laid straight, we'll be stronger for what has transpired among us this day; and what must be accomplished, by God, it will be fulfilled."

Relaxing his tone of voice, Jacques continued to say, "What I'm about to disclose needs no retelling, nor shall I hear it whispered among you afterward—lest you suffer the consequences. This warning I command even to the sea, that she keeps her silence, no matter to what distant shores she traverses."

"We're with you, Captain. Bare your soul, but only if you must." Muslim Green, the *Revenge's* quartermaster, by his words, seemed to prevent the crowd of mystified buccaneers from unraveling.

Captain Lafitte peered toward the sky and saw a magnificent rainbow. The multicolored arc fanned the entire northern part of the Caribbean. It was as though the heavens were prompting him to disentangle that which had been pent up inside him. *Free yourself of the pain and anxiety that has shackled you to the gremlin fantasies that have gripped you so. Bare your soul. In this your brethren have a right to know. Release the burden you carry within. Only then will you arise victorious in your purpose.* Surely the voice from above was not a figment of Jacques's imagination.

Lafitte could feel the blood stirring in his veins. Every fiber in his body came alive and was rampantly exchanging meekness for strength. Even the muscles in his neck began to pulsate rhythmically. Whatever fears or weaknesses that had adhered to his wounded spirit were suddenly siphoned from his mind, body, and soul. It was a holy transformation. Jacques was certain of it. The Lord provided him with a vigor that transcended all doubts.

Jacques's loyalty to God and Country, his brotherhood, Leticia, Dantes, and himself seemed all one and the same. However, his loyalty to Catherine was first and foremost in his heart. *Never betray, never betray,* Louie Grapier's mother's last words pealed loudly in the belfry of his memory. Undoing the buttons of his sanguine shirt, Lafitte removed a letter that clung to his heart. Holding it high, he said, "Mateys, this is the letter I received from Catherine of France, the one her trusted servant, Bevier, gave to me on the day of our departure from Versailles. The words herein speak for themselves. I cannot find it in my heart to read them to you now, but I will place it here."

Turning around, he propped the folded piece of parchment behind a rope attached to the mast post by which he was standing. "It shall remain in place for anyone who wishes to read it. Upon three hours from now, if it has not been disturbed or summoned by Almighty God to fall one iota from its perch, I shall remain your captain. However, I say, if it has been violated by any of you, or released from its position by the wind or rattle of the sea, then what I must do, I will do alone. Three hours, I tell you, not a moment more nor a moment less. Only then, if it remains undisturbed, I will take it as an omen that your curiosity be satisfied in ascertaining its contents."

XVII

Fuquay's Discovery

The Queen of France lay on her cot fully clothed. It appeared she was resting comfortably, after her sudden painful attack had stricken her while talking to Captain De Villefort toward the stern of the *Vera Cruz*. Francois was appointed to the task of informing the captain of any change in her condition. Monsieur Beauford, the ship's navigator, and Pierre were in Captain De Villefort's office. Smaller islands in the vicinity of Martinique had already been sighted. Philippe was saying, "I only pray we will reach Saint-Pierre before Catherine," he paused.

"Before Catherine gives birth?" Fuquay had anticipated his point.

"How long will it be till we arrive at our destination, Lambert?"

Beauford, standing beside the seated De Villefort, hastily referred to a chart sprawled on the captain's desk. "Once we pass through St. Lucia Channel, here, the fleet will head northward to Saint-Pierre, three days at most."

"What's this configuration?" Philippe inquired, pointing to a small circle on the western coast of Martinique.

"That's Fort-de-France. It's a little closer to our ultimate destination. Do you wish to make port there, for the queen's sake?" It had been necessary for Captain De Villefort to take Beauford into his confidence regarding Catherine's condition. Fuquay had concurred with the notion as well.

"Only if her condition worsens, Lambert, I do not wish to alter any of Governor Dupree's originally scheduled plans unless it's absolutely necessary."

"That is a wise decision," Fuquay agreed. "Philippe, I've been meaning to ask, have you informed Monsieur Dupree of Catherine's presence on board your ship?"

"Certainly, my communication was specific. To be exact it said, 'Queen of France aboard *Vera Cruz*.'"

"And what was his response, if I may ask?"

"Two words: 'Dominus vobiscum.'" As Fuquay put a hand to his mouth in an attempt to suppress a chuckle, Francois burst into De Villefort's cabin.

"It's Her Majesty, she's heavily perspiring. I think Her Highness has a fever."

*　　*　　*

Upon giving Catherine a thorough examination, the *Vera Cruz* physician, Monsieur Bernard Trousseau, said to Captain De Villefort, "Which do you prefer, Philippe, patting Catherine's forehead with a cool cloth or delivering the baby?"

"Bernard, are you quite sure she's ready to give birth?"

"I should think very soon, Philippe, very soon. Next time, perhaps you'll heed my suggestion, Captain. A handful of women aboard ship would be most useful during times such as these, I dare say."

"To say the least, Monsieur Trousseau, my entire crew would agree with you, but I assure you a handful will not be enough."

Attempting to ignore De Villefort's quip, Dr. Bernard asked Pierre Fuquay who had been standing by to help Catherine feel more comfortable. Philippe nodded, giving him consent to do what Trousseau just suggested. Fuquay delicately undid a few buttons from the top part of Catherine's dress. The tight collar seemed to be interfering with her breathing. While doing so, he noticed a chain tightly wound about her neck that could have been causing the queen considerable discomfort.

Pierre proceeded to loosen the hold it had around her throat. Unclasping it, he carefully drew the attached keepsake that was lodged between the cleavages of her breasts from its precarious position. What he saw caused Treasury minister, Pierre Fuquay, to warrant a few beads of perspiration of his own.

The duplicate key to the one he possessed in his coat pocket, the one that displayed the same ornamental filigree design, the one Fuquay had lifted from the person of Dantes Lafitte after Agular had killed him, stared him stone-cold in the face. As he diligently removed the chain and placed what it held in his pocket, Fuquay softly whispered, "Now there, Your Majesty, rest quietly. You'll be yourself again in no time at all. Surely you won't need this. After all, what's mine is mine."

If she were alert enough to have heard him, Catherine undoubtedly would have gone into shock.

"Did you just say something, Pierre?"

"Yes, Captain, I was just quietly reassuring Her Majesty everything was going to be fine and that once we reach our destination, I will endeavor to see to all her needs—every last one of them."

XVIII

Catherine's Letter

After the three-hour moratorium had passed, Captain Lafitte emerged from his cabin. He was clean shaven and wore two broad leather straps that crossed his chest in the form of an *x*. Two pistol butts protruded from the crease of his belt, and a sword caressed his thigh. It appeared the captain of the *Dantes's Revenge* was prepared to do battle.

The crew, curious in its ways, had remained on deck by the mast where Catherine's letter had been posted. Jacques, realizing it had not been disturbed, removed his crimson turban and said, "Mateys, it's an omen that I remain your captain. God has answered my prayer, and our trust has not been violated. Neither you, nature's wind, nor the sea has jostled Catherine's letter one iota."

Taking up the folded parchment, Jacques opened it and began to read. Nary could a bird in the sky be heard, not a sail in the cove did stir. The letter was undated.

Jacques, ma cheri,
    My heart is with you, as I write this. Though it be torn and shrouded with fear, I believe my prayer, that no harm will come to you,

---

shall be upheld. If I had the slightest doubt it were not true, I would already be dead inside.

There is so much I want to say, but the sands of time have long since passed through the hourglass. Just knowing you are alive and well is sufficient to sustain the dreadful drought that awaits me.

The void created by your absence can only be endured with the knowledge that you have left France and are safely away from the reign of terror that has suddenly reared its ugly presence. The gendarmes will soon be alerting Charles of the people's hostile reaction to your father's death.

For the sake of my husband, I, as Queen, would sware an oath that the child I am carrying within is his; Catherine, the woman, Jacques, you know what I mean, attests before God that the babe I have conceived is yours. In all fairness, cheri, this I thought you had the right to know.

However long it takes, I will endure. May the saints be with you. Come back to me, Jacques. Needless to say, if you cannot, I will somehow seek a way in finding you.

+Catherine+

"Shez quite a woman, Cap'n," Captain Brough perked up with a satisfied grin on his face.

"Who," Yates shouted, "the queen or the woman?"

"Take ya pik, loggerhead."

The multitude of swashbucklers cajoled in unison. High spirits dominated the aft deck. A swirling wind filled the air, as sails began to billow. All was as it should be, vivacious and mettlesome. Whatever tension previously existed between Lafitte and his men had been cast into the sea, as an object no longer to be savored.

Jacques Lafitte addressed his men with a renewed spirit, "Mateys, from the depths of our hearts, each of us here pines for France. This I know because I am one of you. France is our home, the beloved country for which you and I incessantly yearn. Ask Patrice. Though he longs to be reunited with his family, the tyranny exacted upon him by the state has borne an irreconcilable hatred in his heart." Looking directly at him, Lafitte said compassionately, "And who among us can blame you, Patrice. The punishment bestowed upon you, my brother, should not have been applied to even a lesser animal than ye—what, for want of a loaf of bread?"

Turning toward his first mate, he said, "Who among you need to be reminded that Quicksand's inheritance was taken from him by dishonest solicitors. His abhorrence for France is not focused on the fatherland that suckled him from infancy. Rather, it's the venomous poison of his betrayers what's eating away at his heart." Two of the men standing on either side of Quicksand patted him vigorously on the shoulders, as everyone nodded his approval of what Lafitte just said.

"Yates, if it weren't for you, I wouldn't be standing here today. It was ye who held me back from returning to Catherine during the time my fit of temper in Versailles would not listen to reason. I can still feel the bump on my head, the only force of constraint that would have deterred me from my purpose." The men ratified their captain's boatswain with a hoot and a cheer. "I know now, Yates, that I would never have made it back to Catherine, as I had hoped to, not with Fuquay's band of cutthroats drooling for my blood, anxiously anticipating for it to mingle with my father's."

Summoning his strength, Captain Lafitte cast his voice toward the direction from which the wind was generating a mild vortex. He spoke briefly, but his words were as cutting as the sharp edge of a sword. "They say we are the degenerate ones, unholy criminals and thieves, murderers and beleaguered despots. We are none of these. We, my brothers, are the offspring of our forefathers. We are the inheritors of our birth rights, and we shall reclaim that which was taken from us. We are the Brotherhood of *Dantes's Revenge*, and we will go forth to confront our destiny. Who here is with me?"

Tumultuous bursts of "Aye, aye. Aye, aye" echoed throughout Dolphin Cove. The men were once again united in thought and purpose. Faith had been completely restored in their captain.

"This very day we will caucus to devise a plan that will settle the score with those who had the audacity to interfere with our lives. A vast treasure, as I speak, is crossing the sea, quite close to the waters we have proclaimed our own. Think lads, upon capturing it, we can procure for ourselves a bargaining chip. What do you say, mateys? Once we have it, is it not a fair exchange for our freedom? Whatever you decide to do, know full well, I am resolute in recapturing the woman I love. Who's with me?"

A unanimous cheer of endorsement filled the ship's gallery. Captain Benitez Chavez of the *Seascape* was not amused at what he was hearing. Whispering quietly to his mate standing next to him, the buccaneer said, "What does freedom have anything to do with the price of gold? To hell with France and to hell with Spain, to hell with the brotherhood and to hell with Lafitte—and he can take his regal mistress with him."

XIX

An Audience of One

"Your Majesty, a gentleman is here who wishes to have a word with you."

"A gentleman? What's his name, Truffaut?"

"He didn't give his name, Your Majesty."

"He didn't give his name? Send him away. A king can't be too careful these days. Perhaps whoever it is, he may want to kill me. Get rid of him."

"In lieu of his name, he says he has a letter for you, Your Majesty."

"A letter? What letter?"

"He says it's a letter addressed to you."

"Addressed to me? How would anyone ever obtain a letter addressed to the king, unless he was the individual who wrote it?"

"He says it's a letter addressed to you from the president of le Banque de Paris."

"You mean Monsieur Dumuree?"

"No, Your Majesty, the gentleman says it's a letter written in the hand of Monsieur Percival Huxley."

Charles thought for a moment and, in recalling the name he just heard, remarked, "Percival Huxley, why, he's been dead nearly eight months. I've never received a letter from a dead man before. How curious. I wonder, do you suppose he's risen from the grave? Truffaut, what did you say the gentleman's name is—the one who's waiting to see me?"

"The gentleman didn't give me his name, Your Majesty; however, from what I know of him, he's the proprietor of an exclusive antique shop located in la Saint Marie Esplanade. I don't know him personally, but I believe the curator's name is Monsieur Gilbert Montclair."

"Why in heaven's name didn't you say so in the first place? Never mind, show him in."

"Right away, Your Majesty."

*   *   *

"Let me get this straight, Monsieur Montclair. Monsieur Dantes Lafitte gave you this letter just before he was—"

"Assassinated, Your Majesty, I believe that's the correct term."

"Monsieur Montclair, you seem quite sure of yourself. Why?"

"His exact words to me were 'Gilbert, this letter contains sufficient evidence to hang Monsieur Fuquay. It's addressed to the King of France. If for any reason I am unable to deliver it myself, see that he gets it. My son's life depends upon it' is what he told me, Your Highness."

"Continue."

"Shortly after Dantes was killed, I was paid a visit by a Monsieur Fuquay."

"Monsieur Pierre Fuquay?"

"Yes, Your Majesty."

"Go on."

"Apparently he knew about Monsieur Huxley's letter."

"Yes, now I remember. Le banque president was found dead in his office. Quite an ugly affair, as I recall."

"From what I gather, he was killed only an hour or two before Monsieur Dantes Lafitte had met his fate on the Bourbon Street Bridge."

"Yes, yes, go on."

"When Monsieur Fuquay learned from the banque president that a letter existed incriminating him of certain indiscretions, he evidently paid him an unscheduled visit. Failing to beat it out of him, the whereabouts of the letter in question, Fuquay searched everywhere. Not finding it, he must have assumed Huxley gave it to Dantes."

"Why would Monsieur Fuquay believe Dantes Lafitte even possessed such a letter?"

"Your Majesty, from what Dantes told me when he brought it to my shop, I gather Monsieur Percival Huxley apparently made a grave mistake."

"Mistake, what mistake?"

"Monsieur Fuquay, even before he was appointed secretary treasurer, had been borrowing large sums of money from le Banque de Paris without sufficient collateral. This I know because Dantes had been monitoring his every move. You see, Your Majesty, my esteemed colleague had taken me into his confidence believing that he was being closely watched by Agular, who I'm prone to believe is Monsieur Fuquay's duly appointed assassin."

"The mistake, Gilbert, get to the point. What was Monsieur Huxley's mistake?"

"Le Banque de Paris was about to be audited. He told Pierre that unless the treasury notes to which he was accountable had been returned, Monsieur Huxley would have no other recourse but to inform the banque solicitors of Monsieur Fuquay's delinquency. The mistake you ask? Percival believed the incriminating letter would dissuade Fuquay from doing him physical harm. It should have been sent directly to you, but I assume he was still in the process of trying to salvage a situation that was beyond repair. He wanted Fuquay to learn of its existence, but the letter would only come to Your Majesty's attention in the event anything happened to him. Percival believed Pierre Fuquay would resolve his dilemma with the bank diplomatically. Unfortunately for Monsieur Huxley, the threat was not taken seriously."

"How do you know this?"

"Remnants of a note addressed to me were found by my brother-in-law, a member of the investigating team looking into the unfortunate occurrence. It only suggested that Percival was in grave danger. If Monsieur Fuquay's name had been mentioned in it, I doubt very much I'd be here today. However, when Fuquay could not find Huxley's letter in Dantes's possession, he naturally thought I might have it in mine."

"Then why didn't Dantes come straight to me with Huxley's letter?"

"Because, Your Majesty, Dantes's son, Jacques Lafitte, had also been borrowing large sums of money from the banque, and he didn't want anyone to know about the promissory notes until the matter was resolved."

"Monsieur Fuquay told me he had been gathering evidence against Jacques Lafitte for that very reason and that his father was an accomplice," Charles retaliated. "I have a letter in my possession from Monsieur Huxley verifying what I just said."

"Your Majesty, closely examine the letter Monsieur Huxley had written to you; the one Monsieur Fuquay had delivered to your attention. Then match it with the handwriting of this letter." Montclair removed a sealed letter from his coat and continued to say, "If you still have Monsieur Huxley's first letter, compare the two chirographies. Surely you can't help but notice the painful influence exerted upon him by Agular in forcing him to write exactly what he had been told."

"Have you read the letter Huxley wrote me?"

"No, Your Highness, indeed I have not read it."

"If you haven't read the letter, what makes you so certain the handwritings will differ?"

"Because, Your Majesty, Monsieur Huxley would never betray a friend, unless, that is, he was put to a test he could not endure."

"Monsieur Montclair, do you have any inclination as to why either Dantes or Jacques Lafitte would borrow such large sums of promissory notes?"

"I believe it was the only way Your Majesty's ship could be built in time."

"My ship, what has my ship have to do with anything?"

"I believe you will have to ask the Queen of France for the answer to that question."

The wheels in the king's head began to churn. Charles had wondered about the many innuendoes Catherine had made in reference to a magnificent galleon she thought he ought to have. Fearful it would spoil her surprise, when he discovered what she was up to, Charles deliberately pretended not to know anything about it. However, at the present, he had a gentleman before him who apparently knew more about the affair than he did. Right now Charles needed to probe the curio shopkeeper a bit further.

"When Pierre Fuquay approached you about Huxley's letter, tell me what happened."

"He demanded that I hand it over to him immediately. When I inquired to what he was talking about, he slapped me hard in the face. I told him that I had no such letter. 'If that's your final word,' he said, and then all hell broke loose."

"Go on." Charles seemed to be captivated by Gilbert's fascinating disclosure of events.

"That big brute of a fellow, whom Fuquay addressed as Agular, roughed me up a bit. I thought my day of judgment had arrived. At first, only a few of my most expensive pieces were destroyed. The irreplaceable fourteenth-century Ming porcelain plate clinging to its pedestal was blatantly thrown to the floor. Agular then picked up the colonial Jacobean chair that was in his reach and hacked it to oblivion with his sword. He crushed several other artifacts with the weight of his foot.

"I was infuriated by what had just transpired, the total lack of respect for antiquity. 'The king shall hear of this,' I protested vehemently. Ignoring me, as though my words fell on deaf ears, Fuquay responded with 'The letter, Monsieur Gilbert, or would you rather Agular continue his buffoonery? It'd be a pity if every last item in your shop, shall we say, lost its attractive appeal to the aesthetic eye?' I thought my heart was going to give out.

"I was in a panic. 'What letter? I don't know what you're talking about. I don't have any such letter. Stop what you're doing at once,' I insisted. It was no use. Agular kept breaking things up, while Fuquay forced me to open my safe."

"Monsieur Huxley's letter wasn't in your safe?" inquired Charles.

"No, Your Majesty, if it had been, I think the despicable monk would have taken me for another of my Gregorian trophies he had just destroyed."

Charles paced back and forth twice before he asked, "It's been eight months since you possessed the letter. Why didn't you come forth with this information much sooner, Gilbert? Surely you must know withholding vital information is a treasonous offense against the crown? The consequences are quite severe, Monsieur."

Gilbert Montclair wiped his brow with a handkerchief he kept tucked in his sleeve. "Monsieur Fuquay threatened me, Your Majesty."

"In what way, Gilbert, tell me, how did he threaten you?"

"He emphatically warned me that he'd have my wife and two children disemboweled if Monsieur Huxley's letter ever surfaced, that I would naturally witness the entire spectacle before I too received the same fate. 'If you know what's good for you, Monsieur Montclair,' he said, 'what transpired here never occurred.' Then he laughed and said, 'Who do you think the King of France will actually believe in the event you dared to approach him about any of this, a mere sentimental shopkeeper seeking attention or his personal Treasury minister?' Fuquay then scoffed at me when I pleaded on my knees to have mercy and that I didn't possess the letter to which he was referring. I was still shuddering at the things he threatened to do, long hours after he left."

"You must have been very convincing, Gilbert. Monsieur Fuquay is very clairvoyant when interrogating those who come under his scrutiny. He's had plenty of practice in abstracting information from even the most obstinate criminals. I've never known him to fail in eliciting the truth from anyone attempting to conceal it. However did you deceive him? If the letter you hold in your hand is indeed Monsieur Huxley's, wherever did you hide it?"

"I didn't hide it, Your Majesty."

"Then who did, Monsieur Dantes?"

"Not exactly, Your Majesty."

"Not exactly? Then who did, if I may be so curious to ask?" Charles was determined not to lose control of his usual short-fused, arrogant temper.

"Why, you did, Your Majesty."

"Me? Don't be absurd. You have it just now cradled in your hand."

"I don't mean to be contradictory, Your Majesty, but I'm not being absurd. You see, when Dantes came into my shop that afternoon with the letter, he did not give it to me. Instead, he went directly to an exact location where he placed it."

"Get to the point, Gilbert, just exactly where did he place it?"

"Monsieur Dantes removed Huxley's letter from his pocket and hid it behind one of the portraits I had on display."

"A portrait, whose portrait?"

"Your portrait. 'Fuquay will never think of looking for it here' were his precise words, Your Majesty. And he secured it in a fold behind the frame."

Charles did not at all appear flattered. "So why the change of heart? What suddenly inspired you to bring Monsieur Huxley's letter to my attention?"

"An associate of mine who happened to be in Versailles at the time the *Vera Cruz* set sail nearly eight months ago informed me in routine conversation that Monsieur Fuquay and Agular had been aboard. At least, for the moment, I thought it would be reasonably safe for me to bring Monsieur Huxley's letter to Your Lordship's attention."

"You said you did not read the letter you have in your hand, Monsieur Montclair?" Charles inquired.

"No, Your Majesty, I did not read it."

"Why not?"

"It wasn't addressed to me, Your Majesty. It's addressed to you."

"Good. One more question, Monsieur Montclair."

"Yes, Your Majesty?"

"Do you happen to know who it was that interred Monsieur Dantes Lafitte's remains? Under the circumstances, as I recall, his son was preoccupied at the time with looting the Bastille of my prisoners for the purpose of sailing off with my ship."

"Since the good Lord had given me the necessary strength to stave off my ordeal with Monsieur Fuquay, I sincerely believed in my heart He would be my standard bearer in that which I had to do next. Shortly after Fuquay and his wretched cohort left my shop, word reached me that Dantes lay slain in a carriage on the Bourbon Street Bridge. Despite my shaken condition, it was not a chore for me to recruit a few friends to tend to the task at hand. Once the authorities concluded their preliminary investigation at the crime scene, they released the body in my custody. Today, Monsieur Dantes Lafitte lies peacefully at rest next to his wife, Elizabeth, in le Grand Cemetery de Paris."

"Gilbert, I believe we're finished here. I deem you to be a loyal subject. Be assured, you and your family have nothing to fear." Tinkling the small bell on his escritoire, Claude Truffaut entered the room. "See to it that a twenty-four-hour guard is placed at Monsieur Montclair's disposal."

"It shall be done immediately, Your Grace."

"You may put the letter on my table, Monsieur Gilbert, and take your leave." The elderly gentleman did as he was requested and bowed gracefully before withdrawing. He was speechless.

*   *   *

Charles found himself standing alone in the room. He did not open the letter immediately. Instead, he reflected for a moment on Monsieur Montclair's testimony. There was no apparent reason for him to have lied about anything he said. It was clear that Gilbert hadn't come to defend Dantes Lafitte's reputation or to assist his adopted son at this late hour on matters that transpired nearly a year ago. It made perfect sense, however, that Monsieur Montclair's singular motive for having an audience with the king was to implore protection for his family. What's to prevent what happened to Huxley from happening to him?

Charles unlocked his escritoire and removed the three letters that he had read and reread several times. The first thing he decided he would do was to compare the two Huxley letters, the one just now presented to him by Monsieur Gilbert Montclair and the one that had been given to him by Monsieur Pierre Fuquay. The others he would be inclined to read as well—Jacques Lafitte's letter that had been obviously filtered to his attention by the meddlesome Bevier, and Catherine's, the one Monsieur Truffaut found under the king's pillow the morning after she curiously stowed away on the *Vera Cruz* to Martinique.

Upon noticing the queen's letter, Charles set Huxley's aside and thought back to when he and Catherine spent what was to be their last private moments together. They were alone in the Rose Garden, after the large shipment of treasure had left the palace for Versailles. Catherine was obviously distraught. She couldn't understand why the tiara Charles gave her on the day she became Queen of France had to be sent off to a far and distant place called Martinique. Politics and pirates should not have been in the mix with the one possession she prized more than anything else. This she told Charles more than once. He distinctly recalled Catherine speaking in a manner as though she wanted to say something but didn't quite know how to express it. If she'd only given him the opportunity to speak first, perhaps his precious princess wouldn't have run off the way she did. The queen did not appear to be her usual self.

*   *   *

"Charles, after what has just transpired, I finally realized that you and I are really not alike at all."

"What on earth are you talking about, Catherine?"

"We're really different, aren't we?"

"How are we different, cheri?"

"You assess things from a royal point of view, whereas I see things as they are."

"Obviously you're distraught, and understandably so. You'll soon get over your melancholy, my lovely princess, perhaps sooner than you may anticipate."

"No, my husband, you're not listening to what I'm saying. You see, I really haven't given it much thought until now. Charles, you look at things objectively, in a way they may suit your fancy. I see each thing for what it really is, not for the pleasures of personal amusement."

"Don't be ridiculous, Catherine. Flowers are the same, regardless who it is that looks at them."

"Tell me, Charles, what do you see in the garden of roses before you?"

"All right, my pet, I'll play your amusing little charade. Before me I see a bed of pink roses. They remind me of the color of your supple skin. Then there's the reds, they remind me of the fire in your eyes at such times you engage your temper in a feisty exchange of words. Now, in the yellow roses I see—"

"Stop it, Charles. Don't placate me."

"You simply asked me what I saw, and I told you. Supposing you tell me what exactly it is that you see in what I have just described to you? How could it be otherwise?"

"Charles, where you see color I see life. I see a reflection of God's inner spirit reaching out to you and to me, to everyone, cheri. Life, Charles, nothing else matters."

"It's him, isn't it?" The king's voice reverberated louder than he had anticipated.

"Lower your voice, Charles. The servants will hear."

"The devil with the servants! Tell me, Catherine, do you still love him?"

"I don't know. There are times I think I do, yet he seems so far away. It's difficult to love someone who is," she hesitated for a moment and then said, "unreachable."

Charles said in a much lower voice, "Tell me, Catherine, I must know. How many times have you slept with Jacques Lafitte? It is his baby you're carrying, isn't it? I'll not have a bastard child inherit the throne of France. Get rid of it. I want the thing destroyed."

"Charles, have you lost your senses? The child I'm about to . . . we're about to have is yours and mine. It must be."

"God, if it were only true. How many times, Catherine, how often did Jacques Lafitte make love to you?"

Catherine paused and then said, "Charles, it's true there were times Jacques and I were alone in the garden together. You are fully aware of my occasional fantasies. I can remember only one time when I was with him that I lost complete control of my emotions. I must have been hallucinating. The one time, I recall, we passionately embraced; but I never intended for it to happen. You must believe me, Charles, it was only a fantasy. Won't you find it in your heart to forgive me, my husband?"

"I think I'm going to be ill." Charles clutched his stomach with both hands, as though an acute virus was tearing at his insides.

"I know I wronged you, Charles. It was the woman in me that betrayed you, not the queen." The king waved her off, as if what she just said made no sense to him.

"Can't you give me an affirmative answer, Catherine? Is the child his?"

"By God's honest truth, I don't know, Charles. For all the times we slept together, you and I, the baby must be yours."

"So then why Louie, if you're so certain the child is not his? Surely Lafitte told you everything about himself."

"It's true we discussed possible names for a child, at such time I was to conceive one. When he suggested Louie, I readily thought fondly of the name. That's why I heavily leaned toward it, in the event our firstborn was to be a prince. Charles, what did you mean by Jacques telling me everything about himself?"

"It really doesn't matter now, does it, my pet?"

"Charles, when I married you, from the start I knew my life was condemned to—"

"Condemned? Is that what's being married to me has done, condemned you? Am I that despicable?"

"Of course you're not despicable, cheri. You didn't let me finish." Catherine approached Charles and held him to her bosom. He wept profusely. "What I intended to say was that being married to a king confines a woman to a restricted sort of life. She's obligated to uphold and remain faithful to him. There's little room for anything else. Charles, you must believe me. I never intended to betray you, not for an instant."

Charles lifted his head and said quite earnestly, "I wish to God I can believe you."

"You can, Charles. If you could just put your shame for me aside until you've heard the rest." Catherine turned from him and looked toward the Seine. "Try to understand, my prince, at the time of our prearranged marriage, and even before I learned about it, I knew in my heart that I could never relinquish my fantasies. You see, ever since I was a small girl, they became almost real to me, secretive thoughts that kept me from going insane. My father was too busy being a king to give Henry and me the affection we sorely needed. Only a child who lost its mother could possibly understand the constant haunting pain and loneliness that routinely accompanies such a tragedy."

Looking at Charles again, she said, "My love, I don't expect you to forgive me, but I beg you, cast aside your doubts about my relationship with Lafitte. You needn't think for a moment I once ever considered you less than satisfactory, especially when we shared our bed together."

"It's true your ecstasy was obtained in thinking of him during our lovemaking, Catherine?"

"It may seem so, Charles, but if it means anything, anything at all, it was in you, and only you whom I as your queen consummated my love."

The king collapsed in Catherine's arms and wept rivulets of tears that streamed down the sides of his cheeks, but Charles remembered them being combined droplets of sadness and joy. He wanted to tell her the complete truth of the matter. If he had, however, the pain would have been too much for him to endure.

*   *   *

Charles tinkled his bell, and Monsieur Truffaut appeared almost instantly. Before he could ask His Majesty what it was that he wanted, Charles said, "See to it that I am not disturbed unless it is of the utmost importance."

"Yes, Your Majesty. Is there anything else? Would you like me to pour you a cup of wine?"

"Not right now, Truffaut, perhaps later. There are a couple of letters that I must first scrutinize."

"Scrutinize, Your Majesty?"

"Yes, Claude, someone has lied to me, and I'm most curious to find out who it is. And when I do, God help whoever that poor soul may be."

Charles's valet de chambre bowed and withdrew. Closing the doors behind him, Monsieur Truffaut, timid in his ways, wondered whether he inadvertantly misinformed Charles about anything, anything at all.

Discretionary Precaution

After her two seizures, the Queen of France appeared to be resting comfortably. Captain De Villefort assured Catherine that the arduous journey was in its final stages and that she needed to focus on elevating her weakened condition. If she expected her unborn baby to survive, it was absolutely necessary for an atmosphere of tranquility to dominate her inner spirit. According to the *Vera Cruz* physician's diagnosis, quiet repose was a fundamental prescription she could ill afford to ignore. Dr. Bernard Trousseau had emphatically forewarned Catherine, "Martinique is only a horizon away. Your Majesty, if you do not heed my professional advice to the letter, I dare say, you may be placing yourself and the child in grave danger."

Philippe explained to Catherine how Agular assisted her after she had swooned under the mizzenmast and that Monsieur Fuquay, upon removing her outer garment, alerted De Villefort she was pregnant. "Be assured, Your Majesty, you were treated with the utmost dignity in every respect."

"Thank you, Captain. I shan't have thought otherwise. I'm feeling much better now. It was foolish of me not to have told you that I am with child. Everything happened so suddenly. I didn't forecast this occurrence as being part of the journey."

"Nonsense, now that you are stabilized, it's all anyone can ask. Monsieur Fuquay, incidentally, was at your side during the worst part of your ordeal. I don't know what I would have done without him. He's asked Francois to bring you some libation. It's what the doctor ordered."

A loud knock interrupted De Villefort. "Ah, just as I speak. Entre!" Francois entered with a tray that held a pot steaming with the scent of ginseng. Clouds of vapor mushroomed from its spout.

Monsieur Beauford was directly behind him. He said, "Captain, may I have a word with you, right away, sir?"

"I was just leaving." Turning to Catherine, Philippe spoke in a kindly tone of voice, "I must confer with my navigator. Francois will see to your needs."

"Thank you, Philippe, a cup of tea will do me good, I should think."

Once outside the cabin, Captain De Villefort said, "What is it, Monsieur Beauford? You sounded a bit apprehensive just now."

"Look there, toward the stern, Captain."

De Villefort turned to where he was pointing. Along the southeastern horizon dark ominous clouds blackened the skies. The flagship, *Calcutta*, had already signaled the fleet to trim its sails. To avoid the approaching storm, orders had been given to steer due north. It was the prudent thing to do.

"This maneuver will obviously delay our port of call."

"Aye, Captain, for at least a day or two."

"Very well, anything else?"

"Yes, Captain, Governor Dupree alerted all ships to use discretionary precaution until the storm has passed. It's too soon, however, to determine its apparent trajectory or wind velocity."

"Try to get a fix on its movements, and inform me of any change."

"Aye, Captain."

Discretionary precaution was not a good omen. It meant each vessel in the fleet had to avoid being entrapped within the perimeter of the storm's outstretched tentacles. After the squall had passed, the fleet would then regroup and assume its original formation. Captain Philippe De Villefort, though surrounded by a network of heavily armed brigantines, felt vulnerable. He suddenly realized that not only the *Vera Cruz's* cargo of riches was in harm's way, but France's queen and future prince were in jeopardy as well. Though neither of his gloves had a blemish, he first removed the one and then the other. Tossing them simultaneously into the sea, he spoke to the wind that was now whipping into the sails above his head, "Accept this humble offering, oh, turbulent master of the sea. Quell your fury in our midst. Shed ye tranquil spirit upon us. Be ever so merciful in your ways."

*   *   *

The tea was refreshing. Catherine felt, at least for the time being, her abdominal discomfort had passed. Perhaps the "little prince" was getting impatient within the constant darkness of her womb. She inwardly encouraged him to wait at least until they were on solid ground before making his grand entrance into the New World. The queen replaced her fearful thoughts with the jubilant notion that her newborn son will one day bring peace and prosperity, not only to France but to every nation that embraces his vision in bringing human dignity to all mankind.

A bowl of rainwater sat on a small table next to her bed. Catherine first sponged the sides of her face and forehead. She then patted down her chin and neck. Unbuttoning the top part of her tunic, the queen proceeded to bathe each of her slender shoulders. She noticed the chain and key, the one Jacques had given her, was missing.

There'd be no reason to panic. It obviously broke away during the restless moments of turmoil she recently encountered. Lifting herself gently, Catherine threw aside the covers and alighted from her couch. She searched the folds of her underclothes and the linens that were strewn over her cot. Looking under the bed, she noticed only a few cobwebs that had gathered there. It had to be found before—then it struck her. What if—A gentle tap on the cabin door aroused Catherine from her revelry. "Who is it?"

"It's only I, Pierre Fuquay, Your Highness. May I enter?"

Catherine's heart palpitated. "Just a moment, Pierre, I'm not quite ready."

"I can come back later, Catherine, I just wanted to see if you needed anything."

"No, no, Pierre, I'll just be a moment longer."

*   *   *

"Thank you for waiting, Pierre. I just finished making myself presentable. Please sit down. I truly want to thank you for assisting me during my unexpected attack."

"There's no need to thank me, Your Majesty. It just so happened Agular and I were close by in your time of need."

"I must remember to thank Agular when I next see him."

"Any acknowledgment from you will be humbly received, Your Majesty. Catherine, is there anything you need right now?"

"Why, no, Pierre, I'm feeling much better. Have we nearly reached our destination?"

"Apparently there is a storm moving in our direction, Your Highness. The sea, I'm afraid, is going to increase its turbulence."

"Just what I don't need at the moment."

"Fortunately, the force of the wind is behind us and further south. The *Vera Cruz* is altering its course to avert its full impact. Captain De Villefort asked me to assure you that the ship is in no serious danger. Is there anything else, Your Majesty?"

"I still haven't had a chance to discuss the itinerary of forthcoming events with Captain De Villefort."

"If I may strongly suggest, madame, this would not be an opportune time for the captain to leave his post, with the raging winds playing havoc with the fleet."

"Of course, Pierre, how thoughtless of me, my problems are so small compared to his."

"Not at all, Your Majesty, I'll inform Philippe that you would like to see him at his earliest convenience."

* * *

Catherine had been used to being in control, having things her own way. Spoiled for as long as she could remember, England's enchanting princess wondered if her obstinate ways would cause a rift in her prearranged marriage. Catherine recalled how vulnerable she felt when Edward approached her. "For the good of England," he said, "would you consider being the next Queen of France?" She hardly knew what to say. The thought of marriage had not even entertained her imagination. Princess Catherine had been contented with just being her father's daughter. Traversing to France and having to live there for the rest of her life seemed less appealing to her than most pretentious damsels would be willing to admit.

When it was explained how important it was for Edward to seal an alliance with Charles, she immediately made up her mind to fulfill her father's wishes. Though the King of France, upon meeting him, seemed much older than she had anticipated him to be, he appeared cheerful and gracious in his ways.

The more Catherine thought about it, being the Queen of France couldn't be such a bad thing, after all. She would simply use her charm to get whatever she wanted, as she had always done in the past.

A sudden crashing wave against the portside of the ship gave Catherine a fright. "Not even the Queen of France, I suppose, can do very much about that which is beyond her endowment," Catherine quipped to the unborn prince who had just given her a jolt. "Right now we must rest, you and I. The little key must be somewhere in our midst. We'll look for it later, cheri, just the two of us."

XXI

A Measure of Fate

Lafitte's small fleet of five ships, *Dantes's Revenge*, *Sea Witch*, *Adventurer*, *Seascape*, and the *Royale*, saw the same approaching storm that coerced Governor Jean Dupree's armada of fifty-three seafaring vessels to disperse for cover. While the larger force was in the process of going around the hurricane's trajectory by first sailing in a northerly direction and then turning toward Martinique in a southwesterly swerve, the pirate schooners were on a course heading eastward. The odds of their convergence narrowed considerably.

Jacques had conferred with the captains of the four other vessels in his fleet before they had set sail for their intended destination. Several vantage points along Martinique's northern coast provided adequate concealment for an unsuspecting surprise attack. If they reached the island prior to the massive flotilla's arrival, three of Lafitte's vessels would swiftly interpose themselves between the fleet and treasure-laden ships. Since the Queen of France was reportedly aboard the French brigantine, if such an aggressive incursion took place, a rather precarious situation faced both its captain and military escort. Who would dare retaliate against the invaders and risk Her Majesty's safety by hailing a barrage of cannon shot upon the audacious pirates that placed themselves in Catherine's line of fire?

In the event the treasure ships had completed their journey before they could be intercepted on the high seas, Lafitte's task force faced a dilemma. It'd be suicidal for Jacques's paltry convoy to enter the confines of Saint-Pierre's harbor. Once entrapped, there would be no means of escape. However, upon the fleet's return to France, after the colonization had been concluded, a daring attempt to capture the queen's ship, as it exited the harbor, seemed plausible. A nonexpectant onslaught by the pirate ships would give them the leverage they needed in employing a salient bold attack before the prestigious larger navy could ready itself for a counterassault.

Ironically, a twist of fate precipitated by nature played melodrama with both fleets. The wind and sea simultaneously engineered a catastrophe that would alter a page in history, as an earthquake might likewise change the shape of a prominent land mass.

*   *   *

Captain Jacques Lafitte had been upheld. Only a handful of men opted to take their share of the accumulated treasure that belonged to the brotherhood and remain on the isle of Tortuga. Though they were protected by steep cliffs surrounding Dolphin Cove, the platoon of dissenters lacked the necessary manpower to fend off an invasion of greedy bounty hunters. Shortly after Lafitte's small navy evacuated the island, a swarm of privateers stormed the lagoon and massacred every last buccaneer who had severed his tie with the brotherhood. Ile de la Tortue, after the bloodbath had been trumpeted throughout the Caribbean, was no longer considered a safe haven for wanton pirates.

*   *   *

It had been decided that the *Seascape*, commanded by Captain Benitez Chavez, be the designated ship to bear all confiscated treasures. Whatever booty it contained would be joined by the payloads abstracted from the *Vera Cruz* and her accompanying sister ships, the *Calcutta* and *King Richard*. Quicksand and Yates approached Lafitte at an opportune moment, when they were away from the others, to discuss his decision in appointing Captain Chavez as caretaker of the pillaged swag.

"He can't be trusted, Captain," the first mate protested alarmingly.

Just as concerned, the boatswain chimed in, "We know so little about him."

"Think for a moment, mateys. Would either of you sail off with the treasures we've captured thus far, if you were in Benitez's position? Where can he go, and how far do you think he'll get? Besides, a portion of the contraband will remain with us, after we have confiscated it from the *Vera Cruz*. Relax, you two; we must have more fervent faith in our brothers, especially at such times as these."

Captain Victor Puente's *Adventurer* was assigned to shadow the *Seascape* and assist Chavez in the event bounty hunters suddenly appeared from out of nowhere. The *Dantes's Revenge* and the two remaining heavily armed frigates, *Sea Witch* and *Royale*, would attempt a swift surprise attack from the north before the contingency of precious cargo ships were able to seek refuge within the perimeter of their escort's safety net. The interception could easily be made somewhere along the Martinique Passage that flowed between Dominica and the isle of Martinique. Once the Queen of France had been taken hostage, negotiations could prevail without a single cannon shot being fired.

King Charles was known to be a man of his word. He lauded those who portrayed strength of character, fearlessness, and adroit candor. If an audacious band of expatriates put themselves at risk for the sole purpose of reconciling themselves with their native homeland, how could he ignore such gallantry? So long as his queen and treasures were unharmed, Charles may even consider amusing himself by elevating the entire fraternity of renegades to a prestigious rank in his French admiralty. All, that is, for the exception of Jacques Lafitte who he inwardly despised.

Whether it was for reasons of revenge or jealousy, or an intermingling of the two that angered the King of France, Charles wanted Jacques Lafitte wiped clean from the face of the earth. Pierre Fuquay's future depended upon it. Before the magistrate left France for Martinique, Charles gave him an ultimatum. *"Bring the bastard to me, dead or alive,"* he had bitterly demanded, *"and I will acclaim you before all France. However, lest you fail me in this, Monsieur Pierre Fuquay, you will regret, so help me God, the day you were born."*

*   *   *

Benitez Chavez had fled from Spain after killing one of King Ferdinand's sentinels during a scuffle over a woman while transporting slaves to Portugal. Barely escaping the scene of the crime with his life, Chavez was providentially given passage to the New World by the captain of a merchant ship who needed experienced volunteers at low wages to make the arduous journey. While in

Hispaniola, he met up with a band of disenchanted Spaniards who decided to engage themselves in the lucrative business of piracy. They commandeered a ship and renamed it the *Seascape*.

Later, Benitez hooked up with Captain John Brough's *Sea Witch*. Two other brigantines, the *Adventurer* and *Royale*, had joined forces with them before the four captains formulated an alliance with the *Dante's Revenge*. "Sevin's a lukee numer," Brough once told Jacques Lafitte, "but fie's lukee too."

Chavez was a risk taker. He solidified a partnership with Captains Victor Puente of the *Adventurer* and Delorae Faunce who commanded the *Royale*. At an opportune point in time, they'd carry out a nefarious plan of skullduggery by betraying Lafitte and Brough. The three loathsome captains longed for a life of power and luxury. Their small band of unscrupulous buccaneers conspired to abscond with the cache of accumulated treasures. The caper was destined to occur when the *Dante's Revenge* and *Sea Witch* were engaged in securing the *Vera Cruz* as a hostage ship to be used in negotiating freedom for the brotherhood.

It had been settled at a meeting on the isle of Tortuga that the *Seascape* was to fortify all the treasure thus far amassed. Though Captain John Brough vehemently objected, he was outvoted four to one. Captain Chavez argued that with Puente and Faunce protecting his bow and stern, the booty would be adequately protected, while the *Revenge* and *Sea Witch* aggressively intercepted the *Vera Cruz*.

Although the logical pathway of escape was to sail in a southerly direction, the three rogue ships anticipated in following a course that'd take them northward, away from the hub of commercial activity. There were numerous tributaries along the vast continent's vast meandering coastline that could easily provide suitable camouflage for anyone attempting an escape to places rarely traversed. Although Chavez, Puente, and Faunce often shared their dreams in private of embracing wealth and prosperity, none of them would actually live long enough to savor the reality.

*   *   *

A collision course was inevitable. While every seafaring vessel along the Windward chain of islands scattered to seek shelter from the fast-approaching storm, Governor Jean Dupree gave the order to his fleet to disperse as well. If they maintained their present heading, none of the ships could hardly survive the typhoon's backlash of torrential winds and monstrous sea swells. There was still time to avoid a total disaster. The signal was deployed for all captains to change course, away from the storm's southwesterly projected path. Before the ensuing turbulence passed, however, the entire armada would find itself in complete disarray.

*　　*　　*

In the midst of it all, intermittent cries carried by the wind announced the presence of a newborn prince. Louie's small but audible voice echoed his arrival into the New World. Catherine, though initially uncertain as to who fathered her child, gently pressed the baby to her bosom with a glad and exuberant heart. She looked quizzically at her newborn infant. Its subtle eyes and pursed lips seemed to reflect Jacques's unmistakable adoring features. However, the suckling prince's clenched fists and precariously grasping arm motions gave Catherine the distinct notion that Charles could very well be the indisputable sire. Whatever the case may be, Her Majesty's extremely weakened condition did not deter the Queen of France from shedding multiple tears of joy.

XXII

Letters of Concern

Before Charles peeled away the seal of Percival Huxley's letter, the one that had just been handed to him by Monsieur Gilbert Montclair, he first read one of two notes that accompanied it. Dantes Lafitte, after having read a memo from Huxley regarding his letter to the king, had included it in a Manila envelope with his own personal note addressed to His Majesty. "Perhaps I should have been a cogitator of letters instead of a king," Charles amusingly mumbled as he began to read Dantes's brief dispatch. It began:

22 November—12:10 PM

His Majesty, King Charles of France,
    The attached letter from Monsieur Percival Huxley, la president el Banque de Paris, has been delivered to me a few moments ago at my residence by his secretary, Monsieur Andreas Fallon. According to his verbal instructions, I am to present this letter to you, as is, in the event of Monsieur Huxley's death.

Your humble servant,
Monsieur Dantes Lafitte

The second note had been addressed to Dantes Lafitte. It began:

22 November—11:05 AM

Monsieur Dantes Lafitte, my noble and trusted associate,

In asking the following favor, I am placing you and your son in grave danger. There is no one else for me to entrust. In the event of my unforeseen death, I urge you to deliver the sealed dispatch to His Majesty, King Charles, without delay. I pray to God that Monsieur Andreas Fallon gets this to you before Monsieur Fuquay intercepts him. Believing the letter would protect me from bodily harm, I informed Monsieur Fuquay of its existence when he stopped by my office earlier today. He flew into a tantrum at the mention of it. The thought that I would write such a letter, incriminating the king's loyal magistrate of embezzling funds from the treasury, infuriated him beyond rectification. Though I will never divulge the letter's precise location to him, Pierre Fuquay may have surmised, being that you and I are closest of friends, it has already been referenced to your attention. Dantes, be ever vigilant, and may God keep you safe.

Your loyal and humble friend,
Percival Huxley

Placing the two notes in a tray, Charles carefully peeled away the seal of Percival Huxley's letter that had been forthwith delivered to him by Monsieur Gilbert Montclair. It began:

20 November—10:15 AM

His Majesty, King Charles of France,

Though my life has been dedicated to King and Country, it is not beyond reproach. One's reputation defines an individual. Because of a singular lapse of poor judgment in using improper etiquette, my reputation has become sullied beyond repair.

Monsieur Pierre Fuquay, chief solicitor to the king's court, ascertained that I used indiscretion whilst seeking to assist a youthful apprentice in procuring a lucrative position in le Banque de Paris. To my dismay, the gentleman in question, Monsieur Gerard Garret, believing he could propitiously advance his status, informed Monsieur Fuquay of my lascivious indecent proposals toward him.

Your Highness, for the past year I've been held hostage to the extortive measures exacted upon me by Monsieur Fuquay. He threatened to publicly expose my uncomely behavior if I didn't fully submit to whatever he insisted I do. (You see, I foolishly incriminated myself by writing an amorous note to Monsieur Garret at such a vulnerable moment when I thought he could be held trustworthy of keeping my deepest affection for him a personal affair.) Ever since the incident occurred, Monsieur Fuquay has been embezzling funds from le Banque de Paris with my silence being the passkey to his misdeeds.

In a manner of speaking, to add kindling to the fire, Monsieur Fuquay learned from an inside source that my venerable friend Dantes Lafitte and his son had solicited five hundred thousand francs from the banque without sufficient collateral. Having obtained the reassurance the debt would be paid in full, I honored their promissory notes which were to be used to finance Your Majesty's ship, the King Charles. *The arrangements of collateral were duly approved by Her Majesty, Catherine, Queen of France.*

She agreed to surrender her illustrious tiara in exchange of the debt incurred by Jacques Lafitte, had it been necessary to do so. In an attempt to dishonor the good names of Dantes and Jacques Lafitte, knowing full well neither of them would divulge the principal source for which the King Charles *was being funded, Pierre Fuquay falsified documents to implicate Jacques and his father of injudicious fraud and embezzlement.*

It was about the same time the banque was to be audited that I confronted Fuquay with an ultimatum. He must return whatever he withdrew from the depository or answer to you personally for his improprieties. Fearing for what Monsieur Fuquay might do in response to my demand, I assured him that such a letter as this did exist and that if he dared exact any harm to me, it would be forwarded to your attention without delay. I hope to God it never comes down to your ever having to read it. Please be advised I am entrusting this memorandum to Monsieur Dantes Lafitte.

I have instructed him to deliver it to you in the event the above matter has not been resolved in a fruitful and expedient time frame.

As God is my judge, all that I have written is the truth. Forgive me,
Your Majesty, for whatever pain my indiscretions have caused you.
May God have mercy on my soul.

Your loyal and humble servant,
Monsieur Percival Huxley
(le Banque President de Paris)

The king could not believe what he just read. He'd have to read the letter several more times before contemplating the many connotations it implied. As he examined the epistle carefully, Charles noticed that Percival's every word was written with a firm and steady hand. He placed it aside and took up the one Pierre Fuquay had said he received from Huxley's courier, Monsieur Gerard Garret, moments after Dantes Lafitte allegedly murdered the esteemed banker. To refresh his memory, Charles decided to first read it before closely comparing the graphologies of both missives. It began:

22 November—11:45 AM

His Majesty, King Charles of France,
I can no longer in conscience uphold my long-standing friend and confidant, Monsieur Dantes Lafitte. It dismays me to inform you that he and his son, Monsieur Jacques Lafitte, secretary Treasury minister of France, have misused their privilege of office by extorting large sums of francs from le Banque de Paris.
After warning them repeatedly, that if they didn't return what they had embezzled in a propitious and timely manner, I'd have no other recourse but to bring the issue to Your Majesty's attention. No sooner had I said it than I was threatened by them with my life.
This has given me sufficient cause for concern in prompting to write this letter. Monsieur Pierre Fuquay has been informed of the circumstances and will hopefully rescue me from my plight before it is too late. Monsieur Gerard Garret, my esteemed colleague, upon my completing this letter, will make every effort in seeing to it that it is delivered to you expeditiously.
Long live the king!
Monsieur Percival Huxley
(le Banque President de Paris)

Without further ado, Charles placed both Huxley's contradictory letters side by side. The one he just received was written with a free and confident bold stroke of the pen. The letter Fuquay had given him appeared to be hastily written, as Gilbert had suggested it might be. The *y* in the signature also lacked the flamboyant flare that noticeably tailed across the entire length of his surname, as it did in the first letter.

The closings of the two letters also differed. Huxley's sentiments were much the same in his note to Dantes, as they were in his letter to the king, *your loyal and humble, servant. Long live the king* sounded more what Fuquay might presume to think proper protocol, as indicated in the letter proclaiming his dearest friend to be a betrayer and a thief.

Charles studied the times and dates each of the memorandums were scripted. In less than an hour on the twenty-second of November, Monsieur Huxley contradicted himself blatantly in characterizing Dantes Lafitte. He also made paradoxical statements concerning Monsieurs Gerard Garret and Andreas Fallon. In Percival's note to Dantes, he specifically stated that Andreas was entrusted with a letter of utmost importance, that he hoped his friend would receive it before Fuquay managed to intercept it. Why then was Gerard killed before he reached the palace gates? Did Pierre want it to look as though Dantes and Jacques Lafitte in attempting to intercept the letter were the purveyors of the deed?

For the first time since she left Paris, Charles feared Catherine was in grave danger. The king was not so very much concerned with what the sea might do to her. It was Pierre Fuquay who raised the tension in his veins.

Endeavoring to make sense of all the writings strewn upon his desk, Charles picked up the one addressed to him by Jacques Lafitte. It began:

22 November

His Majesty, Sir Charles of France,
 Though I write this in haste and my faculties are wrought with grief, because of reasons by now have manifested themselves to Your Worship's attention, I hereby swear upon the blood of Dantes Lafitte, that his son's solemn words are truthful.
 It was my father, may he rest in peace, who cautioned me not to use the powers entrusted to my authority with indiscretion, as I did. Whatever has been told to you, or however you may perceive things to

be, I acted alone and take full responsibility for commandeering Your Majesty's illustrious brigantine, the intended gift to you from the people of France who wished to pay homage to Your Lordship on the occasion of your fifteenth coronation ceremony.

Though my father and I have been falsely accused of committing treasonous acts against the crown, certain evidence does exist that will prove our innocence of any wrongdoing. It is with great regret that I am unable to produce specific written documents to affirm this truth.

Dantes, before he was murdered in the streets of Paris, had obtained sworn statements that incriminated Monsieur Pierre Fuquay of orchestrating the very seditious acts he has accused my father and me of perpetrating. Before its contents could come to light, explaining the entire truth of the matter, Dantes was killed by order of Monsieur Pierre Fuquay. I know this to be true because my father lived long enough to identify his assailants. By now you must realize it was in Fuquay's best interests to malign Dantes's character and dedicative spirit to the throne of France, and to publicly denounce me as a malevolent traitor.

For reasons I have little time to explain, the ship that all France proclaimed for you to have will not be returned to Your Majesty anytime soon. It is within my heart to ultimately surrender myself to you for any such improprieties that may deem me unworthy of your forgiveness. Before I do so, however, Pierre Fuquay must first pay for his dastardly crimes against Dantes Lafitte.

Jacques Lafitte

Charles cringed at what he just read. Why no mention of Catherine and his frequent interludes of fornication with her in the palace gardens? To hell with the other improprieties. The king wanted to know the precise despicable nuances that transpired between Jacques Lafitte and his wife, however loathsome they may have been. He could forgive her for anything else, but not this. "Damn you, Jacques Lafitte, you haven't told me anything I already didn't know," Charles blurted toward the letter he just read.

Calming his frustrations, Charles picked up the fourth and final letter he was savoring for last and opened it. Catherine's words began:

3 July

Charles, My King and Adoring Husband,

I do not write this in fear or trepidation. It is because of the unique relationship you and I share that I am able to loosen the shackles that have bound my silence.

Won't you, my prince, set your crown aside just long enough to view your queen objectively, as a woman who has fancied herself for the sake of her father to share in your royal splendor?

As your wife, I have always endeared you, but as a woman, when at times I needed to escape from the mundane cloistered life I inherited when I became Queen, my heart betrayed us both. You see, ever since I could remember, I had to escape into a world of fantasy to protect myself from the haunts of loneliness. It's true my heart reached out to someone other than you, whose affections momentarily satisfied the contemptuous void that constantly plagued me in my dreary existence.

Charles, I solemnly swear to you the child I bear is yours. Though I have broken my vow to you only once, for all the times we have bedded down together, in all certainty the babe I'm carrying within is the rightful heir and successor to your throne. Upon my return from Martinique, I will abandon myself to whatever just punishment you deem fit to bestow for the crime I have committed against my king and the people of France.

My husband, though I obviously did not act alone in this matter of betrayal, I accept full responsibility for its occurrence. The last thing either of us wanted to do was to dishonor our king. Perhaps your firstborn son will help you to one day suave the hurt that lingers in your heart. Forgive me, cheri, forgive me.

+ Catherine +

Not a mention of his name. Jacques Lafitte is all she needed to say. Charles wanted desperately to believe that Catherine was unfaithful to him just the one time. However, only one other person could testify to what she had said, as being the truth. There were ways to extract the veracity from Jacques Lafitte, painful ways that would precede his execution.

Monsieur Fuquay, should he have anything to say about it, would certainly know which proper devices to use in persuading the pirate to divulge whatever information Charles wanted to hear. Then maybe, just maybe, His Majesty's horrific recurring visions of seeing Catherine and Lafitte together might bring to an abrupt halt the torments of his inner spirit.

Exasperated, Charles stood up from his desk and walked to the courtyard window. He drew the curtain aside and peered through the casement. Looking downward, he observed a gentleman whose surname momentarily slipped his mind. The king could hear Monsieur Joseph spouting orders to a handful of laborers. They were in the process of constructing something of a surprise, that the inventor promised would amuse His Majesty for the duration of his reign. Whatever delights the contraption promised to bequeath, the spectacle did not quite seem ready to whet Charles's curious appetite, as its unassembled pieces were in disarray and concocted little evidence of anything spectacular in the realm of mirthful amusement.

A Common Enemy

Catherine managed to temporarily deceive herself that the missing key and chain had obviously fallen away from her neck during the restless seizures she experienced earlier. However, upon awakening from a brief rest, the Queen of France confronted here worst fear. She was fully convinced Pierre Fuquay had found the duplicate key to his, rather, Dantes Lafitte's timepiece. But why didn't his curiosity prompt him to probe Catherine, as to how she happened to have obtained the object? He surely must have recognized it?

Without hesitation, Catherine threw her cape about her shoulders and gathered Louie in her arms. She quickly found herself on the quarterdeck. The entire eastern sky was frought with dark billowy clouds. Though the ship appeared to be in a continuous swerving motion, Catherine managed to remain steadfast on her feet. Luck seemed to be with her. She could see a large assemblage gathered near the bow of the *Vera Cruz*. The ship's safety was their obvious concern. Fuquay and Agular had their backs toward her. Upon finding Pierre's sleeping quarters, Her Majesty entered it and shut the door behind her. How clean and orderly everything looked!

Catherine first searched the escritoire. The key wasn't there. Then she felt inside a few of the jacket and pantalon pockets that were carefully folded at the foot of the bed; still no key. Noticing a small travel bag clinging to a hook on the other side of the cabin, the queen quickly went to it and started rummaging through its contents. "Please, God, let it be here," she whispered to Louie.

"Is this what you're looking for, Your Majesty?" It was Pierre Fuquay. In his hand, the small key and chain she was seeking swayed this way and that. If Captain De Villefort hadn't entered the room when he did, Catherine thought she and the newly born Prince of France would not live to see another day.

"Your Majesty," Captain De Villefort said alarmingly, "you and the young prince must get back to your cabin at once. The storm is nearly full blown. We've nearly enough time to prepare you for the worst."

*   *   *

Catherine and her baby were strapped to her bed. If they were to die, they would die together. The fleet was unable to outdistance the now-raging tempest. The three treasure ships seemed to be caught up in a vortex. Like ducks on a tumultuous pond, they bobbed and gyrated haphazardly in the ocean's swirling current. At times the expanse between the arc of a wave's crest and trough superceded twenty feet. The motion of the sea seemed to have the entire fleet in its watery grasp. Catherine was terrified. Her troubled mind began to hallucinate.

If, my precious Lord, you would only admonish the wind.
Tell it to be still and quiet, so my tranquil spirit may rest peacefully in your bosom.
If, dear God, you would only spare my son.
He must grow tall and strong to one day proclaim your unending glory.
If, oh Lord, you would only assist Charles to see things as they really are.
Bestow upon him the compassion he needs to see the truth of thy wisdom.
If, merciful Lord, you would only permit me to embrace Jacques one more time.
I need him now, as never before.
If, Almighty One, You would cast Fuquay into the sea.
Have mercy on me for speaking what I just . . .
If pigs were piglets . . .
If, if . . .

XXIV

Tropical Surge

here would be no forthcoming colonization ceremony on the isle of Martinique or lavish spectacle of France's crown jewels. Hispaniola's anticipated extravaganza in bolstering an austere fanfare in the Caribbean would similarly be denied. Spain's intended efforts to display her superiority and prestige in the New World had been predicated on the assumption the *Calcutta*'s journey would not end in tragedy. England too would fail in making a fanciful impression of its opulent exhibition of the *King Richard*'s elaborate cargo of exorbitant merchandise. The ship's itinerate ports of call, Saint Lucia, Anguilla, and Saint Kitts of the Lesser Antilles, would later learn of its failure to complete its journey. Had the expedition been terminated by an act of God, people would wonder, or had the fleet succumbed to renegade pirates?

While the ravenous storm steered the treasure ships northward, Lafitte's schooners sailed easterly in a right angle head-on collision.

"Cap'n, straight ahead, I see them." Quicksand had his spyglass trained on the whirlwind's erratic movements. "I can recognize the lead ship. It's the *Vera Cruz*, Jacques."

"How can you be sure?" Lafitte yelled into the blustering wind. His heart pulsated at the thought of Catherine being only moments away.

"She proudly displays her coat of arms atop her fore topgallant mast. The vessel's in trouble, Jacques. She's caught in a whirlpool, and its aft sails have collapsed."

There was little time to signal the brotherhood's four sister ships in conjunction to what he planned on doing without delay. While Catherine's safety filled his thoughts, Captain Lafitte navigated the *Dantes's Revenge* directly toward the queen's ship. He had to reach her before it was too late. Engaging in a skirmish with the *Vera Cruz* was not an option. At the moment, negotiating nature's fury was Jacques's immediate concern.

Aside from the three treasure ships, only two others were in sight. The fleur-de-lis markings on its sails indicated that one of the brigantines was French. It managed to evade the storm by sailing northeast, away from the lashing wind's impending force. Desperately trying to remain afloat, the second vessel, a Spanish galleon, was spiraling in circles. With its sails nearly parallel with the sea, the frigate precariously listed dangerously close to the water's edge.

Noticing the five pirate ships with their flags of intimidating skull bones whipping in the wind, the *King Richard*, unable to right itself for battle, hoisted the flag of surrender. The *Calcutta*, however, under the fleet command of Governor Jean Dupree of France, fired several rounds of cannon shot in the wake of the *Revenge*'s swift approach. Being in a constant seesaw motion caused by enormous wave swells, none of the missiles found its mark. Realizing it could not adequately retaliate in the event it was fired upon, the Spanish galleon quickly abandoned its attempt to wage war with the enemy.

*   *   *

Captain De Villefort was amazed at the five-mast schooner's agility and swiftness, as it spearheaded each of the crashing waves that pummeled the ship's exquisitely crafted bow. Never before had he laid eyes on such an elite, unrivalled vessel of such magnitude. Its many cannons could annihilate an entire fleet, but what impressed him more than anything else was the *Revenge*'s graceful tact in negotiating the turbulence of the sea. Realizing it was futile to engage the enemy in combat, he said to Pierre Fuquay who was standing by his side, "We have no other recourse but to surrender. We've lost our cover, and Her Majesty's safety cannot be compromised." Captain De Villefort's words were emphatic.

"Think, Philippe, if we capitulate now, all will have been for naught. Lafitte will never place Catherine in jeopardy by doing anything unconscionable. She's our assurance he will not endanger this ship."

"This ship, as you call it, happens to be in the command of its captain. If the dastardly rogues insist on confiscating the treasure, let them have it. Of that much, Charles will not hold us responsible."

"Don't be a fool, De Villefort. We must stand our ground and fight. You don't know Charles as well as I do. He'll hang us both for showing cowardice to a traitor he totally despises."

"It's no use, Pierre, I've little choice. We must concede to surrender; all odds are against us. It's the sensible thing to do."

De Villefort rushed briskly by Fuquay to inform the flagman of his decision. Before he was able to give the alert, Pierre retrieved a dagger from inside his jacket. With a quick twist of his arm and wrist, it sped through the air, finding its mark between Philippe's shoulder blades. Throwing up his arms, Philippe staggered toward the side of the ship. Agular, who was in close proximity and in full complement of battle armor, clumsily lunged to grab hold of De Villefort. It was too late. The captain painfully twisted around facing Fuquay before stumbling backward. Losing his balance, he plunged into the sea whose rigorous motion began to subside.

The last thing to disappear beneath the surface of the water was Philippe's two white gloves still firmly attached to his hands. The key to the treasure chest, the one he had been commanded by the King of France never to remove before the mandated time, would cling to his neck forevermore as a memento of his undying fealty.

Sequence of Events

Moments after Captain De Villefort entered his watery grave, the winds subsided almost instantly. It was as though Queen Hera, having one of her jousts with Zeus, convinced him it was her turn to be the puppeteer of human events. Rain, thunder, and lightning should have nothing to do with the way this particular episode concluded. Besides, Poseidon owed her a favor. The sea right now ought to be calm and tranquil, as it should in such climactic times as these.

With the ocean being still and the wind hovering like a furry cat along the inner wall of the hurricane's eye, the *Revenge* effortlessly pulled alongside the *Vera Cruz*. Jacques and several of his crew, clinging to ropes tethered to the five masts, boldly swung like trapeze artists to gain a foothold on the inflicted ship. Though he was eager to locate Catherine, Lafitte had to first contend with the fight that confronted him.

The battle commenced. There were aerial combatants holding on to rope lines with one arm, as they brandished cutlasses with the other. Hand-to-hand clashes permeated the decks, while the sound of rattling sabers and exploding pistols created a din. Riotous brawling broke out everywhere. The foray soon reached full intensity. During the skirmish, several sequence of events ensued.

*   *   *

Captain Chavez wasted little time in alleviating the *King Richard* of its valuable cargo. The escort vessels that were to protect it were nowhere in sight. They appeared to have vanished from the sea. The treasure ships were in a predicament, especially after the storm had taken its toll on several of their crew and armed mercenaries. Upon boarding the schooner, Benitez ordered his men to lock the English captives in the ship's hold. Securing the booty on the deck of the *Seascape*, Chavez quickly ventured his way toward the *Calcutta*. He had it in his mind to seal the fate of England's prestigious schooner by blasting holes in her hull, but he'd wait until first confiscating the treasures from the other two ships.

Benitez knew he had to be careful not to arouse Lafitte's suspicions as to his true intentions. Sinking the *King Richard* would ostracize him immediately for breaking the brotherhood's ludicrous code, "Sanctity of life before death."

*   *   *

The *Calcutta* was similarly in no condition to do battle. Its captain had no other option but to surrender. Governor Jean Dupree, however, accosted his assailants with a vehement protest. "In the names of the sovereign kings of England, Spain, and France, I command you to leave this ship at once!"

"When a ship surrenders," Chavez retorted, "the fight is over. But evidently, sir, your quarrel with us has not ended." Unsheathing his sword, Benitez unhesitatingly pierced Dupree in the heart. Cries of outrage filled the bridge. "If anyone else wishes to retract the ship's surrender, step forward now and defend its honor." No one stirred an iota.

In close proximity of France's most admired statesmen, in the presence of his slain body that lay strewn beneath the main topsail, the *Calcutta*'s illustrious cargo was promptly transferred to the *Seascape*'s foredeck by several pirates whose allegiance to the brotherhood had been forfeited by greed. Prior to leaving the ravaged ship, Chavez growled, "If anyone here wishes to join us, now is the time to speak up."

Six of *Calcutta*'s sailors shouted aye and stepped forward.

"What makes me think I can trust any of you," Benitez chided amusingly, "being you just now betrayed your own countrymen?" At Chavez's command, several of his buccaneers drew their cutlasses. The six sailors that were about to be executed turned and jumped overboard. Their chances for survival were slim, but perceptibly better than no chance at all. Satisfied with the outcome of his workmanship, the rueful captain said gleefully, "Let us not tarry, two down and one to go."

Locking everyone in the hold, as he did to the crew of the *King Richard*, Captain Chavez, this time, broke open a keg of gunpowder that had been retrieved from the *Calcutta*'s storehouse. Sprinkling it over the deck, he told his men to stand clear. He then walked over to the quartermaster's cabin and crashed a lighted lantern to the floor. Watching it for a moment flare up in flames, he said, "We'll be long gone before she catches up to the gunpowder."

As the *Seascape* sailed away from the burning *Calcutta* toward the skirmish taking place on the *Vera Cruz*, Captain Chavez remarked to his first mate, "Two shares of mine to one of yours, I wager the flames will sink her before we rendezvous with number three."

"Win or lose, I reckon there'll be enough shares to last me for ten lifetimes. Two of yours to one of mine it is, Captain."

* * *

After Pierre Fuquay had harpooned Captain De Villefort in the back with his knife, he conferred with the gentleman who appeared to be his identical twin and Agular. They had a mission and one mission only: kill Jacques Lafitte. Pierre then scurried directly to Catherine's cabin where she was still tethered to her berth. Locking the door behind him, he noticed the queen attempting to undo the ropes that held her in bondage. She clutched her baby in one arm, while struggling to break loose with the other. Upon seeing Fuquay, she said, "Pierre, what's happening? Where are we? Untie me. Please, please untie me."

"Don't exert yourself, Your Majesty. You'll need all your strength to ingest the latest turn of events, but first I must inquire about the key."

"What key, Pierre?"

"Come, come now. Catherine, there's precious little time to play childish games. For the sake of your newborn, I warn you, no more bantering. Let's cut to the heart of the matter, shall we?"

"Pierre! What did you mean by that, for the sake of my newborn? Tell me, Pierre, you're frightening me."

"For the last time, Catherine, the key, where did you get it?"

"Captain De Villefort shall hear of this, Monsieur Fuquay. Perhaps you've forgotten who I am."

"No, Your Majesty, I haven't forgotten. I've run out of patience, Catherine. The key, tell me, who gave it to you?"

"I demand you send for Philippe, at once!"

"Captain De Villefort is dead. I killed him a few minutes ago."

"You can't be serious, Pierre. How terrible!"

"The word *terrible* will soon have new meaning for you, Catherine, since you've delayed me long enough. Answer my question. Who gave you the key?"

Fearing Fuquay meant to harm Louie, if she procrastinated any longer in telling him the truth about the key, the queen said unhesitatingly, "The key was given to me by Jacques Lafitte, as a token of his affection for me."

"It amazes me, Catherine, how nothing seems to ever stand in the way of your telling the truth. At least we're finally getting somewhere. However, Your Highness, I need for you to delve a little deeper."

"Ask anything, Pierre, but do not harm my child."

"The fate of the prince lies completely in your hands, Catherine. Now, tell me all you know about this key." Pierre removed the same key with the familiar chain, for which she'd been desperately searching, from his pocket.

Catherine had to tell him the truth, but not the entire truth. She knew Fuquay was an artful interrogator. One slip of the tongue could mean disaster for her and Louie. She said, "I believe the key was used to wind a timepiece that once belonged to Jacques's father, Monsieur Dantes Lafitte. It was given to me by Jacques one moonlit evening in the Rose Garden. I wear it for sentimental reasons. Honestly, Pierre, what's all the fuss about this particular key? If you must have it, by all means keep it. It's just a memento. I attach no real value to it."

"On two separate occasions, Your Majesty, I recall your being present whilst the key's function was either being discussed or demonstrated."

"Don't, Pierre. Whatever it is you are alluding to, I have no recall of ever seeing the key anywhere, excepting the time Jacques Lafitte gave it to me in the palace Rose Garden, as I just told you. After all, Monsieur Fuquay, a queen has more important remembrances to contemplate than any momentous occasions this insignificant key may suggest to you. What's happening out there, Pierre? Why have you killed Captain De Villefort?"

"You are a very clever woman, Catherine. Before we move on to other matters, allow me to first untie your fetters. Perhaps a small glass of sherry will help to improve your imperceptible memory." With his back facing her, Fuquay poured a small vile of crimson liquid into a goblet and gave it to the wearisome queen. "Drink this," he said forcefully. "It'll do you good. Besides,

Catherine, you will need every ounce of strength for what lies ahead. Surely you won't mind if I join you?"

"No, of course not, Pierre," the queen's voice was soft and subdued.

Fuquay was determined to link Catherine's key with the one he had taken from Dantes Lafitte after he had murdered him. She knew Pierre prided himself on extracting information from captured prisoners. The Queen of France felt as though she were a detainee in the Bastille, that she could not convince him of anything, especially the truth. At this juncture she had no other recourse but to give Fuquay the satisfaction of tearing away the veil that thus far protected her baby. As to why he killed Captain De Villefort, and for whatever the bedlam was occurring on the *Vera Cruz*, Catherine doubted very much she'd live to learn the answer to either question. Without thinking twice about it, she sipped the drink Fuquay had just given her. It tasted somewhat bitter, nothing like the fine sherry she'd been accustomed to.

*   *   *

Jacques maintained his composure in battle. Spilling another man's blood detested his innate principles. Schooled by France's finest swordsmen, Lafitte was a skilled fencer. Exhibiting masterful dexterity, he repelled one challenger after another without delivering a fatal thrust of his blade.

No wonder Jacques Lafitte was admired by his supporters. The handsome privateer exuded an enviable portrait of what a true buccaneer ought to be. One can imagine how the precision of his chivalrous agility seemed to overwhelm his opponents in battle. In comparison, Agular was his antithesis. Upon spying Captain Lafitte making his way to the forecastle, he took firm hold of his ball and chain. Securing a shield to his forearm, the burly helmeted predator approached his prey. Jacques did not hesitate to engage Goliath. He knew that if he trusted his sacred beliefs instilled in him by Leticia and Dantes, his ideologies would uphold him in battle, as they have always done in the past.

"Lay down your weapons, and you will live," Jacques boldly exclaimed to the crazed monk who already lashed out at him with the spiked metal ball attached to a three-foot chain. Sidestepping behind the center mast pole, Lafitte avoided making contact with the lethal weapon. He managed to counterattack with a glancing blow of his sword which harmlessly recoiled from Agular's steel neck brace. The giant was completely protected from the head to his insulated shoes. Desperately searching for his Achilles' heel, Jacques could find not a single flaw in his armor.

Perhaps by luring Agular toward the bulwark's waist rail, he could manage to trip him up on the loose rigging. If he fell prone to the deck, Jacques might be able to render him helpless by throwing strands of netting over his cumbersome, heavily plated body.

It all happened so quickly. Backing toward the starboard side of the *Vera Cruz*, it was Jacques who entangled his footing in loose debris that had fallen to the deck from one of the shattered sails. Looking up, he saw Pierre Fuquay coming straight at him with a two-edged sword. Lafitte grappled for the weapon he had momentarily released from his grip in order to free himself from the muddled ropes. Regaining his composure, Jacques narrowly escaped a fatal blow from Agular's overpowering weapon. Simultaneously, he warded off Fuquay's impelling drive of the sword by interposing his own to defray it from its piercing thrust to the heart. The deflection broke Captain Lafitte's sword at the curvature of its hilt.

Though unafraid and sensing the end was near, the words for which he commanded the utmost respect and valued above all others, came to him in a rush. Preparing to die, Jacques stood up and, true to form, shouted in a voice that penetrated the din, "The Lord is my Shepherd, I shall not want!" Catherine did not know whether she was hallucinating or that the voice she just heard was real. Saying nothing, she held Louie tightly to her chest, hoping to God her senses had not gone awry.

As Agular hesitated to savor the moment, he slowly lifted the ball and chain to one side. Bringing it around over his head, the murderous fiend said, "Those same words were uttered by your father, just before I killed him. *Au revoir*, bastard son of Dantes Lafitte."

Clinging to a rope tied to the main topsail, John Brough managed to win his feisty contest with a French naval officer who unwisely chased him up the center mast. Spying Agular, who was about to finish off Lafitte, Brough quickly untied the string and swooped down toward the monk. Like a huge pendulum, John collided with the heavily armored adversary while interlocking both his legs beneath the would-be killer's raised arms. As the swinging motion completed its arc, the momentous force of impact uplifted the entangled men into the air. At the apex of the upward movement of the pendulum swing, the rope tied to the masthead snapped, causing Agular and Captain Brough to disappear beneath the surface of the sea.

Looking on in dismay, Jacques could not help but wonder. He had managed to answer all Captain Brough's inquisitive questions in the past. Right now he hoped the one that had concerned John the most, the one Lafitte could not honestly answer, the one pertaining to whether there was life after death, had finally been resolved in accordance with John Brough's wholehearted approval.

The distraction that had just occurred gave Jacques Lafitte just enough time to grab a discarded sword and lunge for a hold above his head. Catapulting onto a rope ladder, he adroitly avoided Pierre Fuquay's thrashing rapier. His strokes were bold and fierce. Jacques wondered in amazement how Fuquay, who had never been considered a legitimate swordsman, handled himself so skillfully with a blade. Though exhausted from his bout with Agular, as long as he was above his assailant, Lafitte felt he had a fair chance in avoiding his pursuer's sword that repeatedly lashed at the lower part of his legs.

While momentarily looking away to secure a more stable position, Jacques felt a sharp sting below his knee. In a catlike motion, Fuquay had maneuvered to the opposite side of the rope ladder and was nearly level with him. Noticing spurts of red trickling from its wound, thoughts of Dantes lying in a pool of blood sparked Lafitte from his lethargic weariness. As Pierre's sword was about to be thrust into Jacques's back, he swerved to parry the blow. Missing its mark, Fuquay's sword crossed between two strands of rope that formed one of the ladder's steps. Losing his balance, Pierre plunged thirty feet below. Unbeknown to Jacques, the dead man who had just broken his neck and lay lifeless on the mizzen deck, the man responsible for his father's death and who falsely accused Lafitte of betraying his king and country, the individual who forced him to flee France and his beloved queen, was indeed not who he thought it was, the villainous Treasury minister to the court and personal friend of the king, Pierre Fuquay.

*   *   *

Having checked to see the door was locked, Fuquay stood before Catherine who was sitting in a chair beside the empty cot. Louie, lying in a makeshift crib, remained remarkably quiet despite the tumult and commotion happening around him.

"All right, Pierre, if you insist upon playing this supercilious game of charades, for whatever end you may have in mind, I'll cooperate; but there is a salient question or two of my own I'd like for you to answer as well."

"Your Highness, that's a fair request. However, I cannot promise that the outcome of our bantering will provide a favorable compromise to either of our ends, unless, of course, we are both inclined to make concessions on the other's behalf." Catherine thought about what Fuquay just said and was somewhat perplexed by what he meant. "Shall we begin, Your Majesty?"

"Yes, Monsieur Fuquay. I'm ready to tell you anything you wish to know, especially if it will help resolve whatever it is on your mind that seems to be troubling you."

Unsheathing a sword from his scabbard, Pierre's demeanor changed. He appeared to unmask a wholly different personality that Catherine till now had never before witnessed. Though a pair of horns did not conspicuously protrude from his head and a devilish trident tail was nowhere to be seen, at what he said next gave the Queen of France the distinct impression that she was in the presence of Satan himself.

"If you invoke the slightest falsehood, Your Majesty, you condemn your firstborn to the thrust of my sword."

Splitting at the seams, Catherine managed to bite her tongue. It was imperative she controlled her emotions and did not appear to speak irrationally. The demon before her was obviously incensed with inner rage, and she had to quell it with responses that could not be disputed. First gazing down at Louie, she then lifted her head and said to Fuquay in a tranquil and almost acquiescent tone of voice, "Pierre, help me recall the first occasion when I was supposed to have witnessed the key being explained away or fulfilling its function, as you say I did."

"Certainly, Your Majesty. Think back to the time when you were introduced to Monsieur Jacques Lafitte. It was during one of your husband's gala celebrations. Allow me to jar your recollection. You see, I was standing only a few feet away. Charles had his back toward the three of you. His quota of wine expired, but the boredom continued into the night. Monsieur Dantes Lafitte was in the process of whisking you and Jacques onto a balcony before Charles inadvertently saw the two of you making a spectacle of yourselves."

*   *   *

Given the chance to escape the incessant babbling of Governor Jean Dupree, I seized the moment to gather a breath of fresh air and found myself standing on an unlighted balcony adjacent to where the three of you were gathered. I saw and heard everything. You see, the shadows provided me adequate shelter from being noticed by anyone. It was then Monsieur Dantes showed you his timepiece, and you invariably commented upon its quaint uniqueness.

"Monsieur Dantes," I recall you explicitly saying, "your timepiece, may I ask where you obtained it? Perhaps Charles would fancy one just like it. He never seems to arrive wherever it is he's supposed to be . . . A king should be punctual . . . don't you think?"

Then moments later, when you were exhibiting your infatuation for Monsieur Lafitte, you said, "Why it's a key, quite unusual to be sure."

He then said to you, "The key is a duplicate. There is only one other like it. You see, it fits in the back of my father's timepiece . . ."

*   *   *

"Tell me you do not recall the incident I just described." Fuquay's voice reflected the anger of a frustrated interrogator. Catherine did remember the incident, as though it occurred yesterday. She hoped, however, by asking a question or two, it might help convince Fuquay that what appeared to be a moment of importance was nothing more than a trifling passage of time.

"Pierre, if ever Charles finds out about this, I'll deny it. Now that you mentioned it, I can't very well hide the truth. I remember very clearly what transpired that evening. Do you really believe that my focus of attention was riveted to a silly old key and chronometer when my chief interest at the time obviously was in the dashing statesman that swept me off my feet? Can I help it if you left your watch tower before witnessing my lascivious advances toward young Lafitte?"

"I saw it to the last, sadly enough. And I must say, if Charles hadn't been so inebriated, Jacques Lafitte would this very minute be spending the rest of his life with the Bastille's most prevalent guests: the rodents. I believe you have had your share of them by now, Your Majesty? They tend to have an insatiable appetite, particularly among those who no longer maintain a desire to live."

Ignoring his remarks, Catherine said, "I'm not proud of my dubious behavior during such times as the one you have personally witnessed, but I assure you, Monsieur Fuquay, the Queen of France must answer to Charles and only Charles for any improprieties she egregiously committed against him. I do not wish to subject His Majesty to any further unnecessary embarrassment. If you give me your word of honor to allow the matter, say, remain just between the two of us, I'll give you mine that upon our immediate return to France you will receive a handsome reward. Now, I believe there is something else you insist upon me remembering?"

Catherine felt confident that her story was convincing enough. If she were to succeed in besting Fuquay in a duel of wits, she had to mince fact with fiction. The queen could not under any circumstance give Pierre Fuquay the slightest impression that she knew he was a fraud, a murderer, and a traitor to his country. It did not so much matter what Pierre would do to her. Perhaps she truly deserved to die for her unfaithfulness to Charles; Louie, however, for reasons only a mother could fathom, had to survive this insanity and live to be the next King of France.

God help her to keep from faltering in responding to his obnoxious inquiries. Whatever the outcome of Catherine's testimony, for the sake of her child, she had to reassure Fuquay that the woman before him was telling the truth. If the half-crazed, demented interrogator did not elicit from Her Majesty precisely what he wanted to hear, it would be as though she were executing her own child.

Pierre Fuquay went on to say, "It was halfway into our journey when you received me into your cabin. We were discussing Monsieur Dantes Lafitte's honor or dishonor, however you wish to phrase it."

*   *   *

Upon retrieving a key from my vest pocket, identical to the one you've been wearing around your pretty little neck, I then proceeded to wind my chronometer with the key. Though I didn't think anything of it then, you nearly swooned to unconsciousness. "What appears to be ailing you, Your Majesty? Have my words made you feel ill at ease?" is what I distinctly recall asking you.

"No, no, Pierre, quite the contrary. You have enlightened me considerably. The ship's incessant bobbing makes me nauseous at times" is how you responded.

*   *   *

"Might I remind you, Catherine, you contributed your faintheartedness to the ship's motion when, in fact, the sea was positively going through a maritime phenomenon known as the doldrums. The *Vera Cruz* was as still as still could be. Tell me, Your Majesty, do you recall the incident I just recounted?"

"Why, yes, Pierre, I believe I do."

"Well?"

"I'm thinking. What was it that caught my attention?"

"You obviously recognized them, the key and chronometer, hadn't you?"

"Recognized? No, Pierre, however they did remind me of Monsieur Dantes Lafitte's timepiece. You see, since you were there the entire time, when we were on the balcony, I mean, you should recall he hadn't inserted any type of key into his chronometer, as you had done a few weeks ago. While on the ship, however, I was naturally curious in learning how the two separate entities interacted.

"And as you said, I did swoon. It was stupid of me to use the motion of the sea as an excuse for my sudden in disposal, but I was desperately attempting to keep anyone from knowing I was about to bear a child. As I recall, it was the young prince behaving quite rambunctiously within my womb which caused me to falter. In regard to the key I've been wearing about my pretty little neck, as you put it, Pierre, if it serves as a match to your timepiece, by all means keep it. The shops of Paris undoubtedly are inundated with such fine curios.

"Really, Monsieur Fuquay, there are far more important things you ought to be concerned about than threatening the firstborn child to the King and Queen of France. I give you my solemn word, so long as you say nothing to Charles of my flirtatious behavior with Monsieur Jacques Lafitte, I'll say nothing of what happened here. Don't you think, for the moment, at least, your undivided attention is needed elsewhere?"

The tension pent up in Pierre Fuquay diminished considerably. Satisfied Catherine did not equate her key with the chronometer he held in his possession, the one he had taken from Dantes Lafitte and intended to toss overboard at his earliest opportunity, Pierre Fuquay was convinced there was no longer any reason for him to be threatened. And hadn't the queen just promised she'd never mention to Charles the subject of Pierre's blasphemous interrogative tactics?

"I believe this belongs to you, Your Majesty." In saying that, Fuquay handed Catherine back her key. "As for Captain De Villefort and the din taking place outside these walls, I'm afraid the answers to those queries will have to wait until I return." Pierre Fuquay then exited Catherine's cabin, promptly locking the door behind him.

XXVI

Betrayal

everal of Captain Lafitte's shipmates had assisted him down from the center mast rope ladder. After binding his wound, they applied a tourniquet above the deep laceration on his leg. The *Seascape* drew parallel to the starboard side of the *Vera Cruz* and adjacent to the *Sea Witch* whose crew mourned for their captain who had heroically sacrificed his life for Lafitte. Brough, indeed, had laid down his life for his friend. As the tropical storm turned slightly northward, brisk winds once again began to stir the air.

Benitez reported to Lafitte that he had successfully captured the contraband he was ordered to confiscate from the *King Richard* and *Calcutta*. All had proceeded according to plan, but the *Calcutta* seemed to have caught fire moments after the *Seascape* left the scene. Unbeknown to Jacques Lafitte, none of the ship's occupants survived because they had been chained within the vessel's cargo hold before Benitez had torched it.

"Break down every door if necessary, but find her!" Jacques hollered adamantly. "Catherine is somewhere on this ship!"

"You heard the captain," Chavez retorted. "When you locate the queen, you'll find the treasure, mateys."

Quicksand, before joining the search, said to Lafitte, "If she's aboard ship, Jacques, we'll find her."

*   *   *

Whether it was a vile of poison that had been administered to Catherine by Pierre Fuquay or a drug to render her unconscious, no one could be sure. The cradled baby in the queen's arms appeared to be alive and well. Several buccaneers clumsily maneuvered the heavy treasure chest found in the anteroom of Catherine's cabin to the foredeck. Pierre Fuquay managed to find a secure hiding place among one of the aft cannon carriages to avoid being detected. Realizing his look-alike, Monsieur Henri Colbert, an accomplished swordsman and impersonator, had been slain, and Agular, his protector, no longer appeared to be among the living, Fuquay acted quickly.

While everyone converged like flies around the queen's quarters to ascertain what all the commotion was about, Pierre, believing Catherine and the treasure chest would invariably be transferred to the *Dantes's Revenge*, found an opportune moment to sneak aboard the five-mast brigantine. Like the mole he was, Fuquay wedged his lean body between two planks located inside the cargo hold.

Noticing France's treasure chest was being carefully hoisted by ropes to the *Seascape's* foredeck, Quicksand vented a protest to Chavez. "Captain Lafitte wants the cargo from this ship transported to the *Dantes's Revenge*."

"That's not what he just told me, matey. The booty is to be stored on the *Seascape*, at least for now anyway. The queen, she's real sick. Maybe she's dying. Jacques's been asking for you, Quicksand."

What Chavez said contradicted Lafitte's earlier plan. However, this was not the time to raise questions. If Benitez had an ulterior motive regarding the treasures stored on his ship, the rogue would be foolish to take a chance in making a run for it. The *Revenge* could easily overtake him, and in the end Chavez had much more to lose than to gain. Quicksand waved him on.

As the drug administered to her by Fuquay was losing its potency, Catherine gradually began to stir. Opening her eyes, she saw Jacques looking down on her. She had been in his thoughts since he left France. Holding each other's hand tightly, neither of them spoke. The wetness on Lafitte's face was tears of joy and gratitude.

"I'm all right now, Jacques. I knew I'd find you. Louie has your eyes, don't you think?" Catherine's words were barely audible.

After knocking on the cabin door, but not waiting for a reply, Quicksand entered the queen's quarters and said, "Jacques, you wanted to see me?"

*   *   *

Several sails popped up out of nowhere. The escort that had been separated from the three treasure ships had waited out the storm. Chavez's outlook spotted them from the crow's nest. "Captain, ten, maybe twelve ships are on the horizon to our starboard."

"It's now or never. Signal the *Adventurer* and *Royale*, full sail astern!"

"We're too heavy, Captain. The *Revenge* will bridge the gap."

"There are more important things right now on his mind." Sarcastically, he added, "Captain Lafitte's thinking between his legs, I reckon. She's a real beauty, even in her sickly condition. While he's busy with the queen, we'll head toward those dark yonder clouds. They'll give us the cover we need, sure as I know the sea. Put a few holes in the *Vera Cruz*. It'll give our righteous brothers something else to think about, aside from us. Full ahead!"

Before anyone realized Chavez's intentions, the *Seascape* unfurled its sails and quickly responded to a favorable breeze. The backlash of the storm was beginning to make its presence felt. As Benitez made his retreat, he idly watched his crew fire upon the *Vera Cruz*. One of the cannonballs struck the center mast and brought it crashing to the deck. "That'll hold 'em, mateys!" shouted Captain Chavez who already outdistanced the *Adventurer* and *Royale*. Both ships had been turned about the wrong way and got caught up in a wind current that was blowing them adrift from their intended course.

Ordering Quicksand to find out what was happening outside, Lafitte remained with Catherine and her infant prince. Chavez, believing he could elude the *Dantes's Revenge*, made a do-or-die decision. The skirmish gave Benitez the impetus to slip away from the chaotic scene and sail in a zigzag direction toward the northeast. Several scattered convoy ships that had temporarily evaded the storm were fast approaching the *Vera Cruz*. As for the *Adventurer* and *Royale*, once their captains began firing at the queen's ship, they took a pummeling from the *Sea Witch* and *Revenge*.

As the *Seascape* disappeared under the cover of darkening clouds, Benitez Chavez wondered to himself if there was such a thing as honor among thieves. While taking one last glimpse of his sister ships burning up in flames, he came to an abrupt conclusion that the notion was entirely preposterous.

XXVII

Heart to Heart

aptain Benitez Chavez had been correct in his assumption that the *Dantes's Revenge* would not pursue him. Lafitte's preoccupation with the Queen of France, as predicted, proved to be the infatuated pirate's foremost priority. However, the *Seascape's* captain made a serious miscalculation. He omitted to sink the *King Richard*, as he had earlier planned to do. The navigator of the English barkentine, Sergeant Pierson Roberts, after the hostages busted their way out of the ship's hold, managed to record a navigational fix on the *Seascape's* heading. His line of perception had not been impaired by the veil of smoke and flames created by the fiery encounter that had just taken place off the port bow.

After directing the *Revenge's* long-range cannons on the *Adventurer* and *Royale*, Quicksand, who assumed command of the ship, seriously crippled both frigates and watched them slowly dissolve into the sea. It was the *Dantes's Revenge* that hoisted a flag of surrender, so it would not be fired upon by the converging reassembled fleet. The *Sea Witch* quickly followed suit.

Since Lafitte's schooner was the swiftest sailing ship among those that remained afloat and had not been afflicted by the storm or damaged in an exchange of gunfire, it was settled that the *Dantes's Revenge* would immediately escort the queen and her newborn son back to France. If they did not receive proper medical attention for all they've been through, the possibility remained that neither of them would survive.

Admiral Duvall, commander of the French contingency assigned to the fleet, had been asked by his queen to chase down Chavez before he found safe haven in some remote corner of the world. After conferring with the survivors of the *King Richard*, the decision was confirmed to locate and capture the rogue pirate ship before half the wealth of Europe faded into oblivion. It was upon Catherine's insistence that Admiral Duvall bowed to her convictions and permitted Jacques Lafitte to escort her back to France.

"Might I remind you, Your Highness, Captain Lafitte is a wanted criminal by the king's own edict," he felt obligated to say.

"Right now I'm sure you'll agree, His Majesty's main concern would be none other than for the safety of his royal family. Admiral Duvall, I order you in the name of King Charles to pursue those responsible for plundering his cache of jewels. Go in God's name and without delay."

"What of the other vessel, the *Sea Witch*?"

"We'd like to go back with you to France, Your Majesty," a crewman of Brough's ship spoke freely. "It was our captain's decision, afore he's been taken by the sea, Your Grace, that we give our allegiance to Captain Lafitte."

Jacques stepped forward and raised his voice for all to hear. "For what has happened here, I release anyone under my command to take privilege in deciding his own fate. Mateys of the *Sea Witch*, you know these waters more than anyone in our midst. Charles will honor those among you who will assist Admiral Duvall in recapturing the king's treasure. I believe too, it is how Captain John Brough would have wanted you to respond, if indeed he were here to tell you himself."

"Aye, Captain. Who are with me, men?" The cheers were unanimous, and the *Sea Witches'* flagman lowered each of the three pennants bearing a skull and cross bones. The weather-beaten frigate would now serve the very sovereign powers it had been dodging, after her crew had unscrupulously looted so many of Europe's richly laden cargo ships.

*   *   *

For the first time, since Jacques left France nearly nine months ago, Catherine felt contentment in her heart. Though the wind had picked up again, she was unafraid. Fear stems from a broken spirit that has lost faith in God. If she only had surrendered herself to Him unconditionally, perhaps the awful grief she experienced thus far could have been avoided. The only real control any of us has is the direction in which each individual takes the next step. Catherine had been compelled to follow her heart. Whether she was right or wrong in traipsing after her lover, it would have been an easier trek, if trusting in the way of the Lord had first been her foremost concern, so she believed.

After a few hours of rough seafaring, the *Dantes's Revenge* cleared the storm's outermost perimeter. The setting sun and tinctured clouds gave the sky a picturesque splendor of peace and harmony. Jacques was at Catherine's side. Looking toward the distant skies, she saw nothing but loveliness. The twilit firmament sparkled with radiant colors, and the ocean waters reflected a kaleidoscope of shimmering beauty.

Catherine felt relieved. Her thoughts indeed did not betray her heart. As the queen blissfully inhaled the freshness of the sea, her breasts gave shape and form to the scarlet bodice she was wearing. If Lafitte hadn't interrupted her thoughts, Catherine could have sworn she had been experiencing a momentary vision of heaven.

Jacques drew Catherine into his arms where she gently laid her head on his bosom. The queen was fully aware that this was not another one of her dreams. She was not hallucinating.

"Catherine," he said, "Charles will be elated when he learns you have honored him with a newborn prince."

"And what makes you so sure Louie is not yours?"

"I'd like for him to be, but my father taught me well about probability and chance. What I'm thinking falls into the realm of just you and Charles."

Catherine smiled and turning away said, "Jacques, believe me, Louie is ours, yours and mine."

"You sound so unmistakably certain, Catherine. After all, cheri, we only consummated our love just the one ti—"

"Shhh, my love," Catherine had quickly turned to face him so she could place a finger to his lips. "A woman, I think your mother would agree, knows more about these things than—"

"Than who?" Lafitte interrupted.

"Than a pirate," Catherine retorted.

Drawing the queen closer, Jacques kissed her passionately. He then whispered in her ear endearingly. "I can never stop feeling the way I do, nor do I want to, Catherine, my love. If only the future will provide a way of escape for the two of us."

"You mean the three of us."

"Catherine, how can it be otherwise? Regardless of how you may wish to perceive things, Prince Louie is the son of Charles, who's been your affectionate husband for nearly a year."

Not wishing to prolong the present topic of conversation, Catherine said, "Jacques, the ocean seems endless. I've always wondered how ships navigated their way to an exact location without getting lost. I was amazed when the lookout informed everyone he had spotted Martinique. It seemed for a while we'd never reach our destination, that we were just going around in circles."

"Occasionally, a ship does get turned about in the vast sea. Some brigantines never reach their destination. Wind change, and sudden shifts of ocean currents are unpredictable at times."

"But how does a navigator know which way is east, or north, or wherever it is his ship is destined?"

Jacques laughed lightheartedly and said, "Catherine, you should have been a sea captain. Though your ship will most likely not get to where it's going directly, eventually it will find its way."

"Honestly, Captain Lafitte, I'm quite serious. When Louie grows up to be tall and strong, he's bound to ask me questions about my adventures of the sea. I'd like to be the sort of mother who knows what she's talking about."

Pretending to be an expert in nautical lore, as he was, Jacques responded, "Your Majesty, you have come a long way to ask the right person for the answer to that serious and, might I add, very profound question. You see, on a clear day, all you need to do is look toward the sun. When it is directly overhead, it is noon; and a navigator, such as me, can fix an approximate position of latitude, a distance north or south of the equator by referring to his astrolabe."

"His what?'

"I knew you were going to ask that. An astrolabe, my lovely apprentice, is an important instrument that is designed to enable a seaman to pilot his ship by the sun during the day and the North Star by night. It has something to do with measuring altitude along an imaginary line above the horizon."

"What are the fixed points he uses to determine east and west, if that's where the ship is heading?"

"Longitude is an entirely different set of circumstances. Unfortunately, there are no fixed heavenly beacons that will assist a navigator with an east-west coordinate. He usually has a good idea of his whereabouts by comparing familiar land masses with his charts."

"And if there aren't any land masses in sight, what does he do then?"

"On second thought, maybe you ought to let Louie's tutors answer whatever further inquires he or you may conjure up about the sea." Failing to elicit a response from Catherine, he continued to say, "A navigator has many instinctive decisions to make, based upon his knowledge of the trade. It takes many years to master the sea's compass points."

"Jacques, right now, I'm not concerned in the least with any of the compass points. I just wish we can sail into oblivion."

"That is my wish too, cheri."

Catherine did not waver in the slightest when he asked, "Your crown, could you give it up?"

"The crown of which you speak, I've come to see what it truly is, my dearest. During the past few months, for all that has transpired, I fully realize now that my crown is nothing more than a shallow disk."

Looking up into his eyes, she said, "Jacques, I loath it with all my heart. When I'm with you, my sweet, I can clearly discern that it is an ornament around my head that speaks of all the things I ought not to be. It's a mask that hides me from who I really am. For you, my love, yes, I would gladly give it up. If it were with me now, I would cast it into the sea. Oh, how in an instant I would exchange my tiara for the strength and happiness that enlivens me when your arms hold me tightly."

Catherine placed her hand gently upon his cheek. "And you, Jacques, can you do the same for me? Do you love me enough to cast aside your revenge for Fuquay?"

"He's already been avenged. What has he to do with any of this?"

"Everything!"

It was Pierre Fuquay's voice that penetrated Jacques Lafitte's heart like a piercing dagger. The dead man had come back from the grave and was holding a loaded pistol in his hand. It was pointing slightly toward the left of Catherine, directly at her lover's heart.

XXVIII

Tallyho

Superstition is a combination of one's beliefs that places an unreasonable fear of the unknown in awe. Captain Chavez was a person who adhered to this principle. Though rats, fish, and various types of birds were often associated with good and bad luck, so too did weather play an important role in the life of a sailor. To ward off dangerous water spouts and tumultuous waves, the *Seascape's* prow, like most ships, was adorned with a bare-breasted woman carved in its wood. The figurehead was believed to possess a power that would appease the gods that ruled the seas of any possible wrath they might conceivably incur upon a ship that had been involved in an unholy, despicable act.

When Captain Chavez fired upon the *Vera Cruz* knowing the Queen of France was aboard, the blasphemous act, according to pirate lore, deserved a rigorous retaliation by forces that governed the ocean. Benitez, at his earliest opportunity, would disassociate himself from the dastardly deed, hoping his heavily laden ship might skirt nature's abhorrence for what he had done. The contraband he was carrying, however, did not fall within the realm of wrongdoing, since all was fair in love and war.

"Captain," it was one of Chavez's crew that spotted several sharks following the *Seascape*. "Lookie there!"

The anticipated omen showed its face sooner than expected. Someone was about to die, but who?

"An eye fer an eye," Benitez growled determinedly to ward off the evil spell.

Three of his men had been incapacitated for different reasons. One was bitten by a scrawny rat while retrieving food supplies from the cargo storehouse. The fever he incurred lingered for days. Another had fallen from a masthead during the previous storm and broke an arm and a leg. The third sailor who had been sidelined was caught stealing property that belonged to another matey. His punishment was standard procedure. Both his thumbs and forefingers were broken by the captain's crew chief.

Anyone who died at sea was routinely consigned to a watery grave. Having little use for the three rogues who no longer appeared healthy enough to be of assistance to the crew, Chavez gave the order to have their throats cut before casting them into the Seascape's shark-infested wake. This gesture of appeasement to the gods had been displayed in hopes of avoiding whatever reprisals they might have sanctioned against Benitez and his brigands.

For days and days, as it journeyed northward, the Seascape began to feel the impact of howling winds and lashing currents. Luckily, the ship had managed to escape the wrath of the storm and the omen's subtle curse. Everything appeared to suddenly change at once. An albatross had been sighted. This particular premonition indicated good luck. The large bird was considered to inhabit the restless spirit of a dead seaman who, if given food and treated respectfully, would have compassion on a lost ship and its crew by leading them to safety. The sighting of the albatross also meant something else. Land could not be far away.

Since the adventure began, Chavez had a distinct look of satisfaction on his bearded face. His dreams where milk and honey incessantly flowed were nigh on being fulfilled. Whatever else it was that tickled his fancy, Benitez possessed enough gold and silver to sustain him for the rest of his life.

Whether it was a newly formed tropical storm that was providing a northwesterly surge of air, or favorable trade winds stemming from the south, the Seascape angled its way toward the meandering North American coastline. Unbeknown to Captain Chavez, Admiral Duvall had gotten an accurate reading of the pirate's course from Sergeant Roberts of the King Richard and was in close pursuit. His fleet now consisted of twenty vessels. Eight more schooners, five Spanish galleons and three English naval frigates, had made it safely through the storm and rejoined the twelve warships engaged in tracking Chavez. Hoping to entrap the enemy, Admiral Duvall aligned the ships under his command in a pincer-type formation, similar to an inverted arrowhead.

Realizing he was sailing in unfamiliar territory, Benitez referred to some maps strewn about his cabin. They were confusing and made little sense to him, so he relied on his gut instincts. An enormous continental land mass, according to everything he'd been told, ought to be in line with the *Seascape*'s projected path. However, while the ship was sandwiched between the wind-driven Labrador Current pushing toward it from the northeast and Gulf Stream currents sweeping up from the southwest, the vessel tended to stall in its forward progress. Admiral Duvall's fleet, on the other hand, caught a favorable oceanic circulation of air that brought the armada closer to its prey.

Chavez's insatiable lust for earthly treasures temporarily clouded his mind. Though the ocean seemed to be in rapid motion, the *Seascape* was at a near standstill. "Captain, we're being harried by a crosswind," cried a sailor whose navigational skills were in tune with the sea. "The coast is our only chance."

"Steady she goes. Be patient, mateys. Soon we'll be clear. Soon, I say."

A cry rang out from the crow's nest. "Ahoy, Captain, the fleet, they're emerging from our stern's cloud cover." The sails looked like small cotton balls against the grayish skies, but the mariner knew they were enemy ships forging toward them, desperately attempting to reclaim their stolen treasures.

Another voice yelled, "We're approaching a squall, Captain!"

"If anybody's seen us, they won't be seeing us for long!" hollered Benitez to his crew.

"Land ho, Captain!" snapped a sailor pointing a spyglass toward the coastline.

Captain Chavez shouted, "Cast ye eyes forward, lads! I likes our chances with the squall, being we're about to be trod upon!"

XXIX

A Dream Come True

Since there was no longer a bountiful treasure to negotiate, the King of France would undoubtedly have a dim view in granting the brotherhood's plea for amnesty. This is what Quicksand and several of the crew had been thinking. To quell the fears of his shipmates, he needed to review the matter with Lafitte.

As he approached his captain, the *Revenge*'s first mate noticed Jacques with his arms curiously raised in the air. Catherine was there too, but a third person appeared to be menacing them with a lethal weapon of some sort. Without hesitation, Quicksand unsheathed his dirk and whisked it at the unknown stranger. The thrust found its mark. Fuquay's pistol harmlessly discharged and fell abruptly to the deck. Several buccaneers quickly converged around Pierre with brandished swords and cutlasses.

"Don't kill him!" It was Catherine who shouted. "Please, Jacques, no more killing."

"Relax your arms, mateys." Turning to his assailant, Lafitte continued to say, "With my own eyes, I have seen your lifeless corpse consigned to the sea. Is it possible? Have you come back from the dead, Fuquay, to rekindle my haunts?"

"Jacques, I saw two of him on the *Vera Cruz*. You're not imagining things."

"Quite correct, Your Majesty, the gentleman who suffered a most unfortunate mishap at the hands of your dashing captain was Monsieur Henri Colbert. It's a pity his adept swordsmanship had not prevailed in living up to its impeccable reputation, as did Henri's ingenious ability to disguise and impersonate." Turning to Jacques, he added, "To satisfy your quizzical disbelief, Monsieur Lafitte, you can be certain that it is I, Pierre Fuquay, that stands before you and not some imaginary specter. The haunts, as you call them, will pale in comparison to what Charles has in store for you upon our return to France."

"Pierre, whatever needs to be said will be aired in the presence of your king. Try as we may, nothing can be resolved here." Catherine's words evoked a response from Fuquay.

"Your Majesty, let me remind you of the terms of our tête-à-tête, lest you lose heart at the eleventh hour."

"Bind his wound and take him to the brig, Quicksand. Do it now before I run him through with my sword."

As Pierre was led away, Lafitte asked Catherine, "What did Fuquay mean by 'lest you lose heart at the eleventh hour,' cheri?"

"It was nothing, Jacques, nothing either of us should be concerned about. We discussed so many things during our journey. It's difficult right now to recall exactly what he was referring to."

Fuquay's parting words to Catherine were intimidating. It was unlike her to have dismissed them lightly. At an appropriate time, Lafitte would have his own tête-à-tête with the Queen of France. He'd glean from her every last detail she and Pierre discussed during their long ocean adventure to nowhere. What Jacques couldn't possibly have imagined, however, was that the unforeseen future dictated otherwise. For Catherine, his heart of hearts, life's last few hours of expended time raced unabashedly to its climax, as unimpeded granules of sand would similarly hurry through its final stage of an hourglass.

*   *   *

After conferring with his crew, it was settled that the Queen of France would stand by the brotherhood in upholding each member before Charles. The late afternoon sun seemed to be basking above the sea like a colossal orange orb balanced on the horizon. Lafitte was standing on the main deck next to Catherine, as she lovingly held Louie in her arms.

"Jacques, if I asked you to do something for me, could you find it within yourself to say yes without asking why?"

Smiling at what she said, in the manner she uttered her words, Lafitte answered, "Your Highness, behold your humble servant. Ask anything, and if it is within my power to do so, upon my oath of allegiance, it shall be granted."

"It's something I've dreamt about often, Jacques. There were the two of us then, but now there are three."

"And if we sail into oblivion, there'll be four, five, and several more of us."

"I'm serious, Jacques. You must promise me."

"I have already given you my promise. Tell me, cheri, what is your request?"

"Have you ever dreamed dreams that were only just that—dreams? What I mean to say is that a dream is often just a fool's paradise and nothing more. Upon waking from a dream, after thinking about it for a while, you come to the realization it's only a fantasy, and not something that could ever be true."

"I've often experienced such dreams, as you just described, thinking they could never become a reality, especially when thinking about us—but I was wrong. I'm not dreaming now. It is you that I can see, and it is you I can hold in my arms."

"No, Jacques, you're not dreaming, and neither am I. Believe that what I'm about to implore is not trumpery. You see, it's something I wish to take with me into my next life, something that connects what I have often dreamed to that which I have actually experienced. I want to savor it with all my heart forevermore."

"What is it you desire for me to do, Catherine?"

"Not here, Jacques."

"Shall we go inside? No one will disturb us."

"No, Jacques, what I have to say, I want to say it up there—the crow's nest is what I think you call it."

*　　*　　*

Captain Lafitte informed Quicksand and Yates of Her Majesty's request to ascend the rope ladder with Louie swaddled in her arms, and that they were given the responsibility of finding a safe prescription for how the deed was to be executed. Although the sea was currently tranquil, a cool Arctic breeze filled the air. Catherine donned a greatcoat similar to the one Dantes Lafitte wore when young Louis Grapier first encountered his future namesake on the *Orgueil de France* many years ago. The Queen of France was in no condition to exert her strength. A makeshift hoist included an armchair secured to several ropes attached to wooden pulleys. At least two dozen buccaneers aligned themselves at intervals on either side of the conveyance. Jubilantly, Her Majesty's recurrent dream, being near to it as possible, was about to become a reality.

Catherine took a deep breath and relaxed. She and her prince child was strapped to an elegant settee and cautiously lifted upward. Being in close proximity to her assent, Jacques gave Catherine reassurance. He would be there in the event she suddenly became frightened or lost hope in fulfilling her heartfelt desire. Never in his life did Captain Lafitte observe his crew work with such tiptoe precision.

When the queen was in her desired position atop the crow's nest, Quicksand handed her a bell to signal the entourage at which time she wished to descend. As the crew left them to their bizarre affair, Jacques said to Catherine, "I never could have imagined that two people could share the same dream."

Tears welled in her eyes. The queen's platform gently swayed, as though she were rocking in her chair. Had she seen dolphins skipping on the water, or was she just hallucinating? She was ecstatic by what Jacques had just said, about never imagining how two people could share the same dream. Despite all her earthly transgressions, how good God had been to her! Wiping the mist away, Catherine eyed the picturesque splendor surrounding Jacques, Louie, and her. She was indeed experiencing a dream come true.

Upon basking in nature's vast abyss of color and majestic grandeur for several minutes, she unbuttoned her tunic and pressed the key that was around her neck to Louie's forehead. Softly, she said, "Cherish this, my son, as a memento of my love. It was given to me by your father whose father cherished him, as I cherish you. Someday, my gallant prince, when you find someone special to love, well, fear not, your heart will ring true. Oh, how I love you so."

Then turning to Jacques, Catherine said, "Cheri, for either of us to survive a life together, we must begin anew. Whatever mistakes we made in the past, they can be made straight. Since first we met, you and I have had our share of demons. In letting mine go, I have found an indescribable peace, and so must you."

"What is it you're trying to say, cheri?"

"Jacques, whatever anger, hatred, or revenge might still linger within either of our hearts, if we don't expel them, they will one day rise up and tear us apart."

"Nothing can ever come between us, Catherine."

"Don't you see, Jacques, our love is real—and it's strong. The love we share is giving us a second chance. Let's not allow anyone or anything to stand in its way."

"It's Fuquay, isn't it? Are you forgetting he's responsible for my father's death?"

"No, Jacques, Pierre Fuquay has a lot to answer for, but not to us. We are merely victims of his crimes. Just as you and I must answer for our transgressions, so must he be accountable for his. You see, something beautiful is happening right now, before our very eyes. Can't you see it?"

"I'm listening."

"If what we mean to one another is real, and I believe it is, we must, the two of us, make a supreme sacrifice. Let the misdeeds of the past flow from us, Jacques. I'd gladly relinquish my crown to the sea, if I were wearing it now. Promise me you will cast your revenge there as well. It's a perfect resting place for them both, my prideful attachment for worldly acclaim and your bitter vengeance, don't you think?"

"What of Charles, do you no longer love him?"

"I never loved Charles. England needed an ally; France needed a queen. Whenever he touched me, I thought only of you. How else do you think I could survive his . . . Jacques, your promise, please, I must have it."

"I can promise you anything, Catherine, but not this. There was a time, when you were absorbed in my thoughts, and I was standing where you are now, that I believed I could actually forgive Fuquay for his betrayals. But in essence, my spirit can never rest until my father's death has been avenged. What of my dreams? What peace will my restless spirit have, if it is not avenged?"

Kissing his hand that caressed her shoulder, Catherine said, "It's not where we allow our dreams to take us, Jacques; it's where we have the faith and courage to take our dreams that's important. Don' you see? We must bury the past."

There was a momentary pause, and then Lafitte said, "Ring the bell, Catherine, I see many ships. They're French. It's Charles. He's come looking for you. He's come looking for you and Louie."

Catherine just stared into the horizon. Taking the bell into his hand, Lafitte leaned over to one side of the perch and rang it vigorously. While he watched his men scamper up the ropes, Catherine turned and gazed at him with renewed tears in her eyes. "Jacques, my dearest, I desperately need to hear your promise. Don't fail me now. I'm no longer afraid of him. We can face Charles together."

The queen's last utterances fell upon deaf ears, as the clamor of hoots and commands diverted Lafitte's attention from Catherine's incoherent, mournful plea.

The Chase

To be this far north gave Benitez Chavez consternation. The unfamiliar shoreline seemed void of the many protective lagoons and inlets immersed in the Caribbean. So, too, the *Seascape* ceased to make substantial forward progress, and the ever-present flotilla of naval vessels continued to bridge the gap between them. His only chance was to find a place of hiding before the squall behind him dissipated, but where? Chavez had to take a chance. To be surrounded in open waters by an armada of ships meant total disaster.

Taking everything into consideration, Benitez pondered the likelihood of making a deal with his pursuers. The possibility remained that if the *Seascape* surrendered its vast treasure, the commander of the fleet would allow the pirate ship to go free. Wouldn't those terms seem acceptable enough? How could the capture of a handful of worthless pirates be compared to a cache worth a fortune beyond belief? It seemed plausible. The pirates would give up the treasure in return for their lives. If a battle ensued, and the *Seascape* went down with the crown jewels, the mission would be deemed a failure.

Chavez's thoughts were interrupted by one of the crew. "She's lapin' too much water, Cap'n." The bilge began to give up its rodent-infested inhabitants.

Drenched and panic stricken, they spilled onto the deck. The *Seascape* began to list. "What say ye, Cap'n?"

"Steady as she goes," he retorted. "We're not done fer yet."

Encircling the base of the center mast, several laden chests of untold riches were strapped to the deck. Crest after crest, the *Seascape* forged its way through the ocean chop. The heavily weighted ship began to sink lower into the sea, as waves pelted her bow spilling water profusely in every direction. It was merely a matter of time before the ill-fated frigate gave up its ghost.

Chavez eyed the treasure. He knew what his men were thinking. *Get rid of it. Throw it overboard.* Their thoughts were ringing in his head. The ravages of war could plainly be seen in the sentries appointed to watch over the contraband. They guarded it intently, as if one or the other of them was bent on pillaging the plunder for himself. The men's appearances seemed somewhat bizarre to their captain.

Yager's peg leg, for instance, was more to be feared than pitied. A sharp instrument of death had been attached within its wooden frame. The patch covering Deek's eye made others somehow feel doubly leery of his deceit and sly cunning. While Flint's scar-smitten face could intimidate the fiercest buccaneer, it was his hardened heart of steel that made the hairs on one's arms stand on end. Aldo, too, though he looked harmless enough, rarely spoke an utterance. His silence created a din louder than a tavern of drunken sailors.

With his back to the treasure, each of these vigilant sentinels stood fast, facing toward a different compass point. Yager looked to the starboard, while Deek's one eye scanned the port. Flint canvassed the bow, and Aldo concentrated his silence to the stern. Each of the four pirates bore a cutlass at his side and had been ordered by Chavez to kill anyone attempting to intermingle with the booty. No one seemed bothered by this, because every man's portion of the spoils was to be fairly divided, according to the pirate code of ethics. To resolve any disputes, an olive-bound ledger would duly record each buccaneer's allotted share. At any rate, it appeared that the sea was first in line to claim the invaluable treasure, every last doubloon.

The alternative Chavez alluded to earlier crept back into his thoughts. To surrender would actually be fatal. First, there'd be no sure guarantee that a truce would be honored. An acknowledgment of defeat and ridicule was likely to follow. Finally, in the end, after much inflicted pain and suffering by vengeful sovereign magistrates, the hangman would gleefully send everyone to Hades. Another cry interrupted the captain's thoughts.

"Land ho!" The lookout's bellicose cry reverberated in the afternoon air.

Like an echo in a belfry steeple, the answer to what he must do resounded clearly within. Benitez's eyes were entranced. Everyone watched for what sign he might give next. An eerie pall shrouded the ship, excepting for the outgoing tide that swooshed against the portside of the waning vessel. Perched on slackened ropes and buckling sails, whitened gulls looked on in amusement. They appeared to be paying homage to the spectacle enfolding before them, as though they half understood what was transpiring on the decks below. Instinctively the birds gave up their vigil. They filled the sky like a flurry of wind scattered snowflakes. Deckhands pulled the sails taut.

"'Tis an omen, I say!" cried Chavez. "Follow the fledglings!"

"Many protruding rocks, Cap'n, what say ye now?"

Ignoring the first mate's query, Benitez steadied his gaze upon the coastal cliffs that loomed in sight. His thoughts deepened. Countless had been his close escapes. Impending doom lay ahead. What to do? A fleet of warships was about to sail into the clearing from behind the cloud cover. Then he saw a narrow opening.

Clutching a spyglass in his calloused hands, Chavez concentrated his instrument on a tree line that formed a ridge behind some low-lying cliffs. A distance further to the north, he focused his gaze on a peculiar configuration protruding from high atop the escarpment, an overhanging wedge of stone resembling a bony finger. To the west, clouds were breaking up, giving the sun a spectacular golden hue.

*　　*　　*

Admiral Ashley Duvall's primary orders were to capture the rogue ship, *Dantes's Revenge*, and whatever treasures it may have contained, if the five-mast vessel indeed had been spotted. The King of France was adamant about having his ship returned to him without so much as a scratch inflicted upon it, unless it proved irrefutably impossible to do otherwise. The crew and captain should also be captured, but if every last one of them were killed, it was fine with Charles. The safe return of Catherine's gift to him had been the king's chief concern. Whatever the case may be, however, at no point during the ship's siege should the Queen of France be placed in a posture of compromise.

Now that the course of events had changed and a totally new scenario was pending, Duvall wondered what he should do. He had been commissioned for this assignment because of his dexterous naval expertise. Realizing that an enormous cache of treasure crammed the storage compartments and decks of the *Seascape*, he had to use extreme precaution in engaging the enemy.

Satisfied Lafitte's sincerity for the royal family's safety had manifested itself, Duvall now had to find a way to reassure the *Seascape's* captain that he and his men would receive amnesty if, after its capture, they surrendered peacefully. In the event he returned to France empty handed, Ashley believed the mission would be deemed a complete disaster, to say the least. The consequences weighed heavily on his mind, how Charles would react to Duvall's inability to protect the king's treasure.

Once the enemy ship was spotted, Admiral Duvall would signal for the fleet to close in tightly. Under no circumstance must a shot be fired directly at the *Seascape*. A warning volley across the bow seemed the most efficient approach to stop the chase and ensure the treasure's safety. Captain Chavez had little choice. He'd be more than happy to negotiate a truce, his life and the lives of his crew in exchange for the contraband he held in his possession.

Duvall had it all figured out. He'd allow the pirates to go unharmed. They'd receive adequate provisions and even enough gold to see their way to wherever they wished to begin a new life. Though the *Calcutta* and *Vera Cruz* had been sunk and several lives had been lost at the hands of Chavez, none of this would stand in the way of a fair and equitable settlement. Right now the treasure was all that mattered.

The pirates would only lose the treasure, but not their lives. It was a fair bargain, more than they deserved. Duvall envisioned himself being highly acclaimed before all France. So what if Benitez and his dastardly crew lived to see another day? It'd only be a matter of time before a huge reward for the capture of Captain Chavez and his insipid gang of cutthroats would flush them out from wherever they decided to mask themselves.

Things, however, did not work out for Admiral Ashley Duvall as he had hoped. He'd later wonder if Charles of France would understand that the fleet did all it could to rescue his jewels before the *Seascape* had been swallowed up in the wake of the same storm that sank more than a dozen other ships.

* * *

The craggy shoreline was strewn with a minefield of rocks and giant boulders. Beyond them, a barrier reef protected a crescent-shaped cove. It was though an inexplicable force took control of the Seascape's steerage, pummeling it toward impending disaster. Gusts of wind filled the sails.

White puffs of smoke pervaded the escarpment high above the water's edge. Indians! Benitez would assume taking his chances with them over the French. If he got through the maze of hazardous rocks safely, there'd be enough trinkets with which to bargain until the end of time.

Tirelessly the crew worked in tandem. Crashing against the hazardous boulders, the cresting tide spewed water everywhere. It was difficult to know which direction was safest to maneuver. It didn't matter. The rocks had no orderliness to their pattern. "We have one chance in ten," Chavez's voice resounded optimistically. "Pull, pull, I say!"

The men tugged on the ropes until their brawny shoulders ached. Though a rock's jagged edge tore a gashing hole in the *Seascape*'s bow, the ship persisted to lunge closer to shore. No one uttered a word. The crew's weather-beaten faces gave no sign of what they were feeling or thinking. Each man knew full well that the *Seascape* was heading toward its final resting place. The question remained whether the buccaneers were going to share the same inevitable fate. As long as the ship responded to their efforts in keeping it afloat, a ray of hope prevailed—much like a flickering candle about to be extinguished still burns.

Alas! Though it was threading its way through what seemed a pathway to hell, the crippled vessel gyrated every which way, barely colliding with the treacherous shoals. Three men were swept overboard, their bodies engulfed by the choppy waters. Death was instantaneous. An overhanging wedge of stone marked the location. To the southwest trees were in a line. A little to the north, a hideous-looking sea cave appeared to be gazing at the enfolding phenomenon with an evil stare.

In utter haste, the treasure chests were lowered in the *Seascape*'s two shore boats. They'd make several hazardous trips to the sparsely scattered pristine sandy beach before all the booty had been extracted from the failing ship. Chavez summoned the navigator. Using his sextant, he plotted measurements and coordinates as best he could. The notations were inscribed with a stylus on parchment. Dubious symbols represented particular landmarks in close proximity to where the treasure was to be buried. The mapmaker checked and rechecked his figures. Triangulating the treasure's proposed hideaway with the setting sun's exact position in the western sky, relative to a conspicuous geological fixed land coordinate, the able seaman completed his task.

"I've noted the exact time and date here, Captain."

"It may be years afore we return, matey, make certain of no mistakes."

"Aye, Captain."

"Too late for that, lookee there, it's the fleet. Me thinks they haven't spied us yet."

Chavez quickly completed his immediate task. An X, indicating the buried treasure's location, had been placed on the cryptic piece of parchment. Benitez was reasonably certain he could later decipher the code. Once the massive treasure was laid to rest and shrouded from a search party's detection, he was convinced it would remain safely undisturbed. For however long it would take him to return, Chavez knew, with the map's assistance, he could readily locate the treasure's position. His only doubts centered on the possibility that a band of heathens might be spy watching from the bluffs while the enormous treasure was being hurriedly concealed in its huge crater. An LT was inscribed on the lower left-hand corner of the map. When asked what it meant by the mapmaker, Benitez totally ignored him.

"Trim the sails, what's left of them, and break up the masts. Punch holes in the kegs so they'll drown in the sea. Camouflage the shore boats and stay out of sight." Chavez's every command was adhered to, in fear that his final order would indeed be fulfilled. "Run yer cutlass through any lackey that shirks his duty. Hurry, lads, they'll take it we zigzagged round yonder cape."

"Cap'n, look! It's a bad omen, I tell ya. It's the devil hisself. He's coughin' up everything he's a swallerin'. 'Tis the devil's own cave, I tells ya."

Unbeknown to the first mate, he had just christened the hellhole that would be remembered for ages to come by the name he just called it. The ominous cavity loomed menacingly at the base of a huge granite precipice that jutted into the sea. Its hellish manifestation looked quite beastly, almost alive, as it were. The cave appeared to have a reproachful sneering stare. Beleaguered by tempestuous waves, the cavernous jaws rhythmically coughed up a foamy backwash. Bubbling eddies and lurid whirlpools monotonously lapped at the imposing sight. Years of erosion had etched a hideous stalactite toothy grimace upon the mouth-shaped granite face.

"Quit yer fool hollering and help the others, or I'll put an extra eye in yer belly." With its trigger cocked, Chavez pointed his pistol at the perplexed pirate.

Fearing his captain would not hesitate to carry out what he said he'd do, the buccaneer replied ever so softly, "'Tis his lair, I tells ya. I knows it. Bless my soul. I seen his face. 'Tis the Devil's Cave."

XXXI

It Is in Forgiving

By the time France's prominent peninsula loomed into sight, two things caught Jacques's attention. One of the *Revenge's* lookouts spotted a familiar vessel. It was the *Sea Witch*. Since John's crew had expressed a desire to sail along with Lafitte, Admiral Duvall decided to use the frigate as a hospice for the infirmed. A contingency of his men joined Brough's buccaneers in escorting the storm-injured sailors back to the homeland. The second thing that captured Lafitte's mindfulness was Catherine's whitened complexion. Her fair skin took on a frightful ghostly appearance.

"It's nothing, Jacques. I'm just a little tired. That's all."

"Catherine, I'd give anything to undo all the anguish and heartache you had to endure."

"Be still, my love. It is you who have made my adventure palatable, everything I hoped it would be. For this and the son you have given me, I thank God with every breath I take. Jacques, one must always remember to take the bad with the good. If you really think about it, the good strokes of fate far outweigh the bad ones. Take time to notice, cheri. It should be staring you in the face. I see it so clearly."

Whether it was Louie's incessant craving to suckle Her Majesty's milk that drained the queen of her strength or the sudden chill that attacked what little immunity lingered within, one thing is for certain—Catherine ordinarily would never have succumbed to adversity so precipitously. She loved life to its fullest, and the newborn prince gave her an abundance of insurmountable joy.

Whether it was the long, tedious journey that took its toll on Catherine's weakened constitution or Pierre Fuquay's malevolent threats that deflated her combative spirit, whatever the reason may have been, the Queen of France slipped into a coma. Jacques removed Louie from her bedside chamber and thanked God that Charles was close at hand. In all probability, the king's personal physician was aboard his ship and could give Catherine the proper medical attention she desperately needed.

Lafitte had noticed it in his previous two encounters with Catherine, the one earlier atop the crow's nest and in the conversation he had with her on the aft deck. Though she never complained of being ill, the Queen of France looked forlorn and tired. Her God-centered thoughts seemed to inebriate Catherine's innermost reflections. Life and death were powerful forces, but life was stronger than death.

Had she envisioned her time on earth was about to expire? *"Each person has two lives,"* Lafitte remembered her saying, *"and one death. First, you are born, and then you die. But then you are given a second lifetime. A clue to the second life's quality of existence very much depends upon how one embraces the first life. It's a kind of direction an individual feels most compelled to travel. The pathway leads to a sanctuary where one's heart yearns to be—in accordance with the sticks he or she has chosen to live by in the first life."*

Had Catherine been invoking a plea for mercy and reconciliation so that God might grant her and Jacques the wisdom to choose the right sticks, as she called them—sticks of moral righteousness that would catapult them into an endless love for all eternity? And what was in the note she had just written to Charles? Couldn't Catherine simply say whatever she had on her mind to his face? His ship was well-nigh two hours away.

Tears blurred Lafitte's vision, as he recalled Catherine's last words while descending the rope ladder. *"Jacques, in clinging to anger and revenge, and having only these to present before Him as one's final tribute, will it not fall short, very short of His expectations? It's in forgiving others, cheri, as He has so nobly taught us to forgive, that one can render Him equitable satisfaction."*

"I do forgive him, Catherine." Jacques was near to trembling. "Please, God, let Catherine live, that she may hear me speak the words she so much wanted for me to say. Please, God, I do forgive him for all he's done. I forgive. Dear God. Dear Catherine. I know now what you meant. Fuquay, he's no less important to Him than the least of any of His brethren."

Though there was still time to flee Charles's impending wrath for all the things that had gone awry, no one dared approach Lafitte to exhort that the *Dantes's Revenge* be turned about. The ship's captain was obviously overwrought and clearly unable to respond to any affirmative action. As fate would have it, what was to be was to be.

XXXII

Dream Catcher

After years of plundering, debauchery, open war, and fleeing bounty hunters, the *Seascape* foundered and sank along the rocky shores of what is known today as the state of Maine. Somewhere below the granite cliffs that continuously turn back the onslaught of rushing ocean waves, a vast treasure had been buried, but not before ample shares of gold and silver were distributed to the ship's twelve survivors. Oaths had been cast. It was agreed under penalty of death that none of the men would utter a word about the hidden cache's existence. They'd return to divide the spoils at a time disenchanted treasure seekers grew weary of the hunt and ruefully abandoned their search.

According to the articles of pirate lore, Chavez was to receive a share and a half of the total accrued treasure. His first mate, boatswain, and navigator were to receive a share and a quarter of the spoils. Since his "gunner in charge" had been swept overboard, his allotment of shares reverted back to the common pool, as did anyone else's who may have perished prior to the final distribution of accumulated wealth. Benitez and his crew were careful to make certain the treasure could not be detected by seasoned scavengers who were familiar with the usual traceable signs of masked concealment.

Aside from those who buried it, the cryptic map remained the only source of evidence to the hoard's precise location.

As it were, things turned out quite favorably for Chavez. With the freshly etched parchment in his possession, and the massive treasure chests safely stored away, he pondered his next move. Handfuls of gold sovereigns were deliberately scattered where a vast storage of chests might likely be buried. If the remains of the *Seascape* were located, Benitez had cogitated, a full-scale search for the booty would undergo severe scrutiny. In discovering a trail that seemingly pointed to the treasure's exact location, the fortune seekers would undoubtedly probe the vicinity until they found it. However, after having little success, the frustrated gold seekers in the end would eventually abandon their quest believing the false trail of contraband was meant to deceive them.

Before the band dispersed, Chavez and his small troupe had one last order of business to finalize. They followed a steep vertical trail strewn with pine needles and broken twigs. The ascent was slow and cumbersome. Why hadn't the savages shown their faces? They must have seen the treasure being lowered into its entombment. Whatever the case may be, Chavez was not about to leave the arena before completing a final task he felt compelled to execute.

The party of adventurers finally reached an opening to the narrow footpath where an aroma of cooked venison, dancing to the beat of drums, and unfamiliar chants greeted their senses. Strange-looking tree-carved structures basked in a semicircle along the camp's western perimeter. Plumes of grayish smoke continued to rise above a stretch of trees that caught the last rays of the evening sunset. Chavez and his men were pleasantly surprised that the natives who wore leather leggings and moccasins of soft doeskin were friendly in their greeting. They soon learned the indigenous tribe of Indians called themselves Algonquians.

Though the heathens did seem cordial enough, Chavez was adamant in his decision to carry out his original plan. It was necessary to temporarily remain close to the treasure so he and his men could keep a trained eye on the coastal waters, just in case the fleet doubled back to probe the area. Lastly, the possibility did exist that the Indians managed to get a glimpse of the contraband being buried. To resolve the problem, the natives had to die, all of them.

Ironically, in knowing what they must later do, the band of cutthroats accepted the hospitality of the villagers. The unscrupulous pirates also seized the opportunity to satisfy their libidinous cravings. It was easy to inveigle the tribe of infidels by offering them curious objects that aroused their primitive inquisitiveness. The needle of a compass that always pointed north, for example, and a weapon that felled a deer with a single clap of thunder, mystified these ignorant creatures with intense fascination.

Strange as it may seem, the one thing that captivated Chavez's attention, a particular artifact he found amusing, did not deter him from carrying out his abhorrent deed. The dream catcher, as it'd been called, was believed to catch the bad dreams of a child or warrior and allow only the good dreams to make their way through the weblike netting that hovered over the dreamer's nocturnal blankets. Since recurring nightmares often haunted him, Benitez contemplated on acquiring one of these contrivances to thwart off the many ghostly visitations that often interrupted his nightly slumber. If only there hadn't been the treasure to consider, he and his motley crew could have lingered among the savages for as long as they wished. However, it was imperative they move on and distance themselves from the vicinity, in the event their trackers spotted the *Seascape*'s wreckage or plume of smoke that unabashedly pervaded the darkening sky.

*　　*　　*

Benitez gave the order to kill every last one of them. He couldn't risk the possibility that any of the natives had secretly observed the treasure being salted away. During the carnage, however, four of Chavez's men were killed by tribesmen of an adjoining village who happened to be paddling the river in search for food. Among those who received fatal wounds during the intermittent battle of flying arrows, clashing iron, and echoes of gunfire, were Deek, whose eye patch had been embedded inside his head by a spear, and Aldo, who never uttered a word when an arrow pierced his hardened heart. Though he planned on taking a dream catcher with him, being that a third of his party lay in a pool of blood, Benitez couldn't be sure if the omen was a good one or a bad one; therefore, he decided against it.

*　　*　　*

Eight men stealthily pulled away in the two shore boats that had been hidden in nearby reeds. The crafts hugged the shoreline and paddled southward. The pirates held faithful to their oaths; but when the rum in them loosened their tongues, tales of plunder, buried treasure, and a hastily sketched map escaped their lips. As the eight remaining buccaneers forged their way toward warmer climate, they left a trail of rippling waves of interest that encouraged inquisitors to follow in their wake.

One of the stories that induced opportunists to wonder and believe stemmed from Indigo. He had been one of the crewmen who was fearless enough to break through the toothy gap of Devil's Cave. You could hear a pin drop while he spoke.

*　　*　　*

"It's a smelly hellhole, foul and stinking. It churns up and spits out everything it sucks in. It got Dirk. He got tossed out of the shore boat by a crashing wave and snatched up by the devil hisself. I reckon he was not all that ornery a person, Dirk wasn't, 'cause he got spit right out again—torn to bits, he was. The cavern churns and spits up most anything that enters its foul belly. It's the devil, I tells ya. He's mean, meaner than anything I ever did see. Poor Dirk, we reached out for him, his mateys and me, but it was no use. The devil hisself snatched him up and swallowed him whole. But he didn't want him, I say. We just got clear of the second thundering wave when I seen what was left of Dirk come popping out in bits and pieces. It was God awful, I tells ya. Lucky for us Dirk, our navigator, didn't have the map. He'd just given it to the captain, I tells ya."

*　　*　　*

On another occasion, the oldest of the surviving *Seascape's* crew, Poppy, they called him, spewed this account. *"One of the mateys, a youngin, who frequented the cap'n's quarters, I tell ya, turned an oar loose."* The old seaman looked back over his shoulder to see if anyone who shouldn't be was listening. He leaned forward and searched the eyes of his beholders. Though half inebriated, they were glued to every word Poppy uttered. With his eyes squinting in the dimness of the ale house, he solemnly whispered, *"The devil hisself, I swear to ya, mateys, tore the paddle from its turnbuckle. We called the youngin Hands. He had the prettiest pair of hands ya ever did see. I called to Hands, 'Leave it be! Boy, leave it be!' I reckon it was too late. They were silky hands, smooth and soft. The cap'n saw to that. Afore Hands could retrieve the oar, an unsavory wave turned us clear about and tossed him overboard. He went straight into the devil's mouth and never did come out again. It was his hands he wanted. I knows it. 'Tis the truth, I tell ya, every last word of it."*

*   *   *

Oddly enough, as fate would prescribe it to be, none of the *Seascape*'s voyagers would ever unearth the treasure. Chavez was the first to die. His throat was cut while in the midst of one of his nightmares. The map had been carefully removed from where he always kept it, beneath his mangy jacket, close to his heart. It doesn't really matter when or how the remaining seven *Seascape*'s crew died, but one thing is for certain: only the map survived. Through the years, it had changed possession frequently; but when the parchment became lost in antiquity, the killings ceased. It wasn't until the legendary map was discovered centuries later in a Key West antique depository that the murderous slaughters once again resumed, wreaking havoc more than ever.

XXXIII

Charles Confronts Lafitte

fter spending nearly an hour next to Catherine's beside, Charles left her cabin and stoically walked over to where Jacques Lafitte stood under close guard by the portside of what had formally been dubbed the *Dantes's Revenge*. The *King Charles*, which had not yet been christened such, was now in the possession of its rightful owner, the sovereign ruler of France. His physicians were powerless against the malignancy that plagued his beloved queen. Despite their efforts to revive her, Catherine remained in a deep, dreamless sleep.

Fuquay joined Charles, and they conferred privately on the foredeck. Pierre had a victory smirk written about his face. A recorded recollection of all that had transpired since the voyage began was clasped under his arm. As much as it detested Jacques, the two of them joined Lafitte. He spoke first.

"Congratulations, Monsieur Fuquay. You've won."

"Won? What have I won, Monsieur Lafitte? I assure you, I've won nothing. I merely upheld my duty to serve His Majesty, Lord Charles, as all loyal subjects should do."

"Pierre, you could have come to terms with my father. He was a just man. You didn't have to dishonor his name and then have him killed." Amazingly, there wasn't a shred of bitterness in Jacques's voice.

"Your innuendos will do you no good here, Monsieur Louie Grapier. That is your rightful name, isn't it? I shall produce the necessary evidence which will prove that you are not who you claim to be, but a mere imposter. His Majesty has in his possession certain documents that will exonerate me completely of any false accusations with which you wish to slander me."

Charles, upon hearing enough, said, "Monsieur Fuquay, leave us. I wish to have a word with Monsieur Lafitte, alone." The king totally ignored Pierre's reference to Lafitte's former name which was obviously voiced to embarrass him.

"But, Your Majesty, he disdains you almost as much as he despises me."

"To be sure, and, Pierre, take them with you." Charles was alluding to his personal gendarmes whom he dismissed with a limp wave of his hand.

"Certainly, Your Majesty, if that's your final word." As he was turning to leave, Fuquay gave Lafitte a menacing stare. Jacques did not acknowledge it.

"I see you didn't do away with Monsieur Fuquay. I hardly thought you were of the squeamish variety. Pray tell me, I'm excitedly curious, what prevented you from wringing my Treasury minister's neck?"

"If she were able to, Catherine could explain."

"I see. She mystified you too."

"Do with me as you wish, Charles. You have all that you came for."

"To see you hang would be my deepest pleasure; but that will only anger Catherine's spirit, whether, in fact, she lives or dies. No, I've witnessed enough ghostly dreams to last a hundred years, and then some."

Charles walked toward the stern of the ship, as though he were inspecting it for the very first time. "Such an exquisite gift, don't you think, Monsieur Lafitte?"

"It was Her Majesty's most ardent desire to make the facsimile in Monsieur Montclair's novelty shop a reality."

"Ah, yes, Monsieur Gilbert Montclair. I've had the unique pleasure of meeting the gentleman. He'd say positively anything to assure me that you and Dantes are innocent of whatever treasonous acts may have been sanctioned against you."

"Not anything, Your Majesty. Gilbert, I assure you, would never fabricate a lie, especially to his king."

"I stand corrected. Of course, he's as loyal to you, as he is to me, is what I meant to say. How foolish of me to imply otherwise!"

Looking at Lafitte, Charles said somewhat sarcastically, "I think you have just enough time to kill me before anyone has a chance to intervene."

"Why should I want to kill my king?" Jacques said soberly.

Having confirmed what he suspected all along, that Jacques Lafitte held no personal grudge toward Charles, he answered, "Because what I have to ask requires an answer that will most certainly hang you." Of the many unanswered questions that still lingered in his mind, Charles had a burning desire to have one in particular resolved without further ado. Perhaps then, and only then, the pent-up ghostly dreams that continuously plagued him might just find a nightmarish exit from his beleaguered soul.

"Your Majesty, what is it you wish to ask?"

Without hesitation, Charles came out with it. "How many times did you sleep with her?"

"Your Highness!"

"Don't you dare impugn the issue, Monsieur Lafitte! I am your king. Tell me. How many times did you and Catherine commit adultery?"

Jacques turned his head, as though uncomfortable in speaking to Charles directly. "Just the one time, Your Majesty." To lie about it would be worse than telling the truth.

The words rattled in the king's head, as though what Lafitte just said couldn't possibly be true. He had envisioned Catherine having almost daily illicit affairs with the man before him, the once-debonair statesman who had wrenched his beloved queen from the depths of his heart. Could Charles have possibly been wrong about Catherine?

"If I am to endure even one more day, Jacques Lafitte, I must know the sordid details of her unfaithfulness to me and the conditions of its relevancy. Again, how many times did you conjoin with her, and which of you encouraged the other?"

The King of France was obviously shaken in hearing his own words. It would do no good to deceive him or even remain silent. Charles must have been distraught all these months. Why else would he leave France to find Catherine? He needed to know everything that occurred between his adoring wife and her lover. Jacques looked straight at Charles and said, "As God is my witness, Your Majesty, Catherine and I conspired in love only once. We were in the Rose Garden. I stopped by to let her know that your ship was nearing completion. So excited she was in the prospect of pleasing you; Catherine wanted me to keep her informed of its progress on a daily basis . . ."

*   *   *

Catherine was sitting at her easel. We were quite alone. "Jacques," she said, "what do you think of my painting?" She was still perched on her bench, so I had to come around and look over her shoulder. The scent of her perfume completely dazzled me. Being so near to the woman I secretly loved inebriated me. There was no forewarning. Catherine suddenly turned, and without provocation our lips touched. We caressed.

Neither of us said a word. I drew her into my arms, and we embraced. Almost as though we were drawn to the nearby secluded hedge against our will, it was there we consummated our love.

*　　*　　*

Lafitte looked into the sea and said, "If anyone's responsible for what happened that evening in the garden, it is I, Your Majesty. Catherine is innocent of any wrongdoing. I swear to it."

Charles did not seem convinced. "You dare expect me to believe that you conjoined with Catherine only once? Is it possible that you lost track? Could you maybe have slept with my wife perhaps twice, or thrice? Could it have been a dozen times, ten dozen?"

"Stop it, Charles." Lafitte was perturbed. "No, Your Majesty, for whatever it means to you, Catherine and I yielded to our emotions only once."

Without truly being amused, Charles said, "It amuses me to think how convinced you are of what you just said."

"And why shouldn't I be? I've told you what you wanted to hear. Can't we just leave it at that?"

Charles paused. Then he said, "What do you expect me to do with the child? Louie, I believe, is his name."

"Your Majesty!" Lafitte was caught off guard by the remark. "He's your son. Louie is yours and Catherine's. How can you ask such a thing?"

"Are you so certain he's not your son?"

"Those near-exact words, I recall Catherine saying to me the other day!"

"And you didn't believe her?"

"No, Your Majesty, I didn't then, and I don't now."

"You seem so sure of yourself, Monsieur Lafitte. Pray tell me why?"

"In all due respect, Charles, whatever Catherine and I shared in private or felt for one another, it was nothing more than what I related to you just now. It is my sincerest and deepest conviction that Louie is unequivocally your child. I lay no claim to him and pray to God he never once learns of my existence."

Charles reflected for a moment and then said, "Please step this way, Monsieur Lafitte." The king walked to where one of the exits of the ship was clasped shut by a secured latch fastened to the gate. Disengaging the tether, he shifted the barrier to one side which exposed him to the open sea. "Come closer, Jacques." It was the first time Chares addressed Lafitte by his first name. "Surely you're not afraid?"

"No, Your Majesty, I'm not afraid."

Seeing that the king left himself in an extremely vulnerable position, several armed soldiers instantly made a motion toward him. Charles raised his arm and said vehemently, "Nay, go back!" As though they had been smitten by the hand of God, the armed guards retreated instantly.

Looking at Lafitte, Charles said quite emphatically, "If I can prove to you the child of which we speak is yours and not mine, will you give me your solemn word that without further ado, you will plunge yourself into the depths before you?"

"Your Majesty, what are you inferring?"

"I'm saying the Queen of France mothered a bastard child, and you are its father."

"You're absolutely mad. Since when has God Almighty endowed you, of all people, with Solomon's wisdom, that you too can determine the lawful parent of a child?"

"I think not, Jacques Lafitte, I'm sorry to disappoint you. Jehovah has in no way elevated my perceptiveness to such magnanimous proportions."

"Then how can you know the truth of the matter?"

"Will you take the plunge?" Charles insisted. "Or perhaps you would rather throw me overboard? Jacques, my heavily sequined garments will pull me straight down to hell before anyone could avail themselves to assist me. Why don't you?"

"Why, you ask? Charles, it is I who ought to be cast into hell. Not because of what I still feel for Catherine, but for my betrayal to you, my king."

Lafitte turned to jump but halted for a moment. Without turning toward Charles, he said, "Your Majesty, how is it that you're so certain the child is mine?"

"Look at me, Jacques."

Lafitte turned to look at Charles. "Yes, Your Majesty?"

"I may be obsessed, but I'm not mad. The child indeed does not stem from my loins. You see, Jacques Lafitte, I'm impotent and have been so all my life."

*   *   *

Lafitte had remained frozen for what appeared an interminably long time. Coming to his senses, Jacques said to Charles, "Does anyone else know of this?"

"Not even Catherine."

"And Fuquay?"

"If I thought for a moment Pierre knew anything of my plight, I would have had him hanged long ago."

"Then perhaps there is a possible solution to all this, Your Majesty."

"I'm listening."

"My father is dead. Catherine, God help her, may soon be as well. I no longer desire to live."

"And what of Louie? Are you forgetting he's your child, yours and Catherine's?"

"No, Your Majesty, I have not forgotten. I was just coming to that. From what you said, only you and I know this to be true. The matter need not concern anyone else. You have my word on it." What Jacques said next stemmed from the depths of his heart. "Perhaps, Charles, what I'm about to suggest is not all that delusional, incomprehensive as it may sound."

Revealing his impatience, Charles said, "This is hardly the time for riddles, Monsieur Lafitte, exactly what is it you have to say?"

"Louie's still a prince of royal blood, Catherine's blood. Has not God in His wisdom found a way for you to bear the son you've always longed to have? Accept him into your heart, Charles, and reign in peace. Surely Catherine would have wanted you to nurture her son."

"Not love her son?"

"Unrequited love stems from the heart and must be given freely. One cannot cajole love, though it was something that can be obtained by mincing words."

Charles, wishing to change the subject, said, "Catherine never did know Edward passed away in his sleep?"

"No, Your Majesty, nor did I until this very moment."

"I should think his son, the former Prince Henry, had something to do with it. He'll burn in hell before he gets any recognition from me."

Caring very little about political implications, Jacques went on to say, "I beg from you only this, Charles. Spare my brethren from the gallows. Cast not your anger upon them for what I may have done to provoke your indignation. It was they who assisted Her Majesty in returning to France."

"Before you released them, most of your crew were prisoners of the Bastille."

"And Fuquay put them there."

"Do you think me a fool? I signed the admittance papers."

"Yes, you signed the papers, but only because Fuquay lied to you. These men were friends of Dantes Lafitte, the man who was about to expose Pierre Fuquay for what he really is, a despicable thief and murderer, not to leave unsaid, a traitor to his king and country."

Charles already believed that much of what Lafitte just said was true. The letters he held under lock and key verified his every word. Pierre Fuquay, the king's most trusted Treasury minister, used his ministerial position for his own ambitious ends. What the king said next was quite extraordinary.

"Monsieur Lafitte."

"Yes, Your Majesty."

"Would you care to see Catherine one last time?"

"With all my heart, Charles."

"Which do you prefer, seeing her before or after the lashing?"

*   *   *

Catherine looked beautiful as ever. Though she seemed far, far away, Jacques sensed his beloved knew he was kneeling before her. If he hadn't been teary eyed himself, Lafitte would have noticed a trace of moisture forming along the crevices of her ashen lids. "Farewell, my love," he said. "The peace you talked so much about is nigh upon us. I've done what you asked. Be patient, cheri, soon, very soon. Till then, my love, au revoir."

Charles had ordered Louie to be brought forth. Lafitte rose and took the child into his arms. Softly, he whispered, "I pray to God, my prince, that one day you will be a good king. Your mother and I love you, son. Serve your king well, but surrender your spirit only to God."

*   *   *

Charles held a scourge in his hand. Lafitte was stripped to the waist. His hands were tied above his head and attached to the center masthead. Jacques's muscles quivered in anticipation of what was about to occur. "I must do this, you understand, if I am to let you and the others go free," he whispered softly to Jacques. "I can't have all France actually believe I've gone soft. My reputation must be upheld."

The King of France drew the whip over and around his head.

Swoosh.	Not a sound from Lafitte.
Swoosh.	Rivulets of blood oozed freely.
Swoosh.	Louie muffled a cry.
Swoosh.	The *Sea Witch* drew closer.
Swoosh.	A cloud shrouded the sun.
Swoosh.	Fuquay nudged a smile.
Swoosh.	Welts and bruises came to life.
Swoosh.	Charles began to tire.
Swoosh.	Catherine drifted deeper and deeper.
Swoosh.	It was finished.

Discarding the whip, Charles turned for all bystanders to hear, "Monsieur Lafitte has taken His Majesty's ship without my consent for the past eight months. I gave him ten lashes for his indiscretions. As most of you know, France, Spain, and England have lost a wealth of treasure. Monsieur Lafitte and his crew know the waters of the Caribbean far better than any among you. Under the penalty of death I forbid him to return to France until the looted contraband is recovered. This is my final word, and it will not go well for anyone who repeats any of what I said to friend or foe."

Signaling to his guard, Charles said, "Cut him down and have the shore boats take Captain Lafitte and his crew to yonder vessel." The *Sea Witch* was close at hand and readying itself to take on the banished crew in exchange for the wounded sailors it had on board. Jacques noticed a slight bow of the king's head as he looked back before descending the *Dantes's Revenge*'s rope ladder for the last time. Lafitte returned the gesture and thought to himself that perhaps there was a trace of Solomon's wisdom in Charles of France, after all.

XXXIV

Fuquay's Recollections

ierre Fuquay was satisfied his interview with Charles went better than expected. All the principal players were either dead or far removed from the prospect of implicating Fuquay in any wrong doing. According to the king's physicians, Catherine would never regain consciousness. Pierre felt secure in relating to His Majesty the following account:

- Catherine stowed away on the *Vera Cruz* without Pierre's knowledge until they were four days into the journey.
- It was Captain De Villefort's authority that rendered Fuquay helpless. Pierre insisted Catherine be returned to France immediately when he discovered the queen was aboard ship.
- All three treasure ships were attacked by five pirate brigantines, including the *Dantes's Revenge*, in the midst of a fierce sea storm. The *Vera Cruz* and *Calcutta* sank, while the *King Richard* was escorted back to England empty handed by a small contingent of British naval vessels. Captain De Villefort was killed in the siege by one of the marauders.
- All three treasure chests had been hauled aboard a ship called the *Seascape*. Admiral Ashley Duvall gave chase to the rogue vessel, but his

fleet of ten or twelve ships disappeared behind a storm cloud. It is not known whether he was successful in his mission to retrieve the crown jewels.

- Captain De Villefort's log mysteriously disappeared.
- Catherine endeavored to break off her relationship with Captain Lafitte, but the impertinent pirate persisted in taunting her in hopes she'd give way to his persuasive overtures.
- Pierre was present when Louie was born and assisted Captain De Villefort in the prince's delivery.
- Fuquay's compatriot, Monsieur Henri Colbert, an excellent swordsman and master of disguises, had been killed while in the process of bringing Jacques Lafitte to justice. In attempting to deceive Lafitte, Colbert was to appear as Fuquay's double. Needless to say, the scheme went awry, and Jacques Lafitte survived Henri's attack.
- Agular, Fuquay's personal priest, was killed while attempting to defend the Queen of France from Lafitte's unscrupulous marauders.
- During the confusion surrounding Catherine's unconscious state, Pierre had learned Catherine was to be taken back to France. He had the good fortune to conceal himself on the *Dantes's Revenge* before anyone detected his climbing aboard.
- Fuquay had overheard that Lafitte's main purpose in returning Catherine to France was to make peace with Charles and ask pardon for him and the compatriots he had earlier released from the Bastille.
- Governor Jean Dupree was on the *Calcutta* when it went up in flames before it sank.
- The storm is not to be blamed for the mission's failure. It was Jacques Lafitte and his renegades who took advantage of the fleet's immobile state of confusion to boldly attack the treasure ships and relieve them of its cargo.

"Finally, though not exactly as I had planned, in the end Jacques Lafitte was delivered to you, as promised. You were prudent in your decision to release him, Your Majesty. If anyone is in a position to recover the chest containing Her Majesty's tiara, it is he. However, I'm inclined to believe that should he indeed locate the treasure, his greed for gold and silver will most certainly deter him from returning to France."

"Pierre, did Catherine ever mention what possessed her to place her life in jeopardy by taking this voyage?"

Though he didn't want to hear it, Charles already knew the answer. "I asked her the very same question. She said, 'Wherever my tiara goes, there also I shall be,' Your Majesty."

"Is there anything else you wish to add, Pierre?"

"No, Your Majesty, my full report is before you. It explains everything of importance, since the voyage began nearly eight months ago."

"I promised you anything, my good and faithful servant. Since Governor Dupree is no longer among the living, I'd rather think you'd be a perfect replacement in filling his shoes. Very soon I will acclaim you before all of France."

"I'm overwhelmed, Your Majesty, I don't know what to say."

"I think the words *thank you* will be enough."

XXXV

Francois's Journal

Among the articles salvaged before the *Vera Cruz* sank off the northeastern coast of Martinique were the personal effects belonging to the ship's deceased. After the *King Charles*, formerly *Dantes's Revenge*, reached Versailles, unclaimed paraphernalia had been scrutinized by the port's cargo master, Monsieur Edmond Mercedes. One particular item that caught his fancy was a diary that belonged to a Francois Gallant, Pierre Fuquay's former cabin boy. Upon perusing a few of its entries, Edmond immediately brought the tattered bound encyclical to Charles.

"You came all the way from Versailles to give me this?"

"I was about to discard it, Your Majesty, when I noticed the queen's name had been written on one of the pages. Perhaps, I hoped, you'd find it relevant to whatever investigative queries may be taking place."

Charles thumbed through Francois's diary and said, "Has anyone else seen this?"

"No, Your Majesty, it's no one else's concern but yours is what I was thinking."

"You did the right thing in coming to me. Without saying, these gold sovereigns will be reward enough for your diligent service."

"If it is your wish, Your Majesty, but I assure you, it is not necessary for you to show such generosity. It is my duty to serve my king."

"And it will be my duty to hang you if you breathe a single word of this to anyone. Do you understand, Monsieur . . . Monsieur?"

"Monsieur Mercedes, Edmond Mercedes, Your Majesty, and I do understand perfectly what you've just said. My lips are sealed."

"Good, now get out. As you can see, I am extremely busy."

"Certainly, Your Lordship, I've already forgotten the reason for my visit. Good day, Your Majesty."

Charles sat at his escritoire and turned the pages slowly. He was extremely amused by what he read. Francois's words confirmed much of what the King of France already knew, but there were a few entries that captivated the monarch's undivided attention.

May 23—2:00 PM

How excited I am to be a part of this extraordinary adventure! From the many valets that applied for the position, Monsieur Pierre Fuquay selected me. How fortunate I am! I'll do everything I can to be the perfect servant master.

Same Day—7:30

I have just enough time to say that shortly before the Vera Cruz *left its berth in Versailles, I had the proud pleasure of spying the Queen of France in Monsieur Fuquay's cabin. She appeared to be traveling incognito, so I simply acknowledged her presence with a slight respectful bow. Even with her hood caressing her cheeks, I could tell that she was more beautiful than a flower.*

May 24—10:00 AM

The queen has taken over Monsieur Fuquay's cabin. No one must know she's aboard ship, I've been told. Captain De Villefort will be informed of her presence on his ship in due course, as explained to me by Monsieur Fuquay.

May 26—11:50 AM

Captain De Villefort was upset to learn that Queen Catherine was aboard his ship. He was extemely furious with Monsieur Fuquay. Though he wanted to return to France, the captain could not leave the protection of the fleet, so we continued on our journey. I miss you, Charlene Dubious. Perhaps you'll give me your hand in marriage after I've become a full-grown homme de mer.

May 30—3:45 PM

How is it possible that those who have taken an oath of allegiance to their god and king can bring themselves to abuse their authoritative stewardship? Are not His Majesty's subjects supposed to be protected by the moral code of ethics? For what Monsieur Fuquay forced me to do last evening, I feel completely ashamed. You must forget that I exist, Charlene Dubious, I'm no longer worthy of your affections. How can I be?

May 31—1:20 AM

Being on the verge of despair, I decided to end my life. It is despicable to be controlled by another man's lascivious whims. Viva la France.

May 31—2:40 AM

Thanks to Captain De Villefort, I am still among the living. He had just thrown one of his tarnished gloves overboard. He must have heard me attempting to climb the rope ladder. Realizing I was distraught, he brought me to his cabin, and we drank some warm tea. Philippe, he has granted me permission to call him that, should have been a clergyman. The captain in his kindly way ascertained all that was happening to me. This is what he suggested. He'd approach Monsieur Fuquay that I was needed for night duty to assist the surveillance officer in the crow's nest. Being that I aspire to be a naval officer one day, he strongly suggested that I spend my every moment with seasoned sailors to learn the trade, so to speak. Philippe also suggested that what we discussed be kept strictly between the two of us. He doesn't know about my journal.

June 4—10:00 AM

I feel much better now. Monsieur Fuquay must have more important things with which to preoccupy his time other than me. He nearly bowled me over earlier this morning and never as much lifted his head. I believe he had just left the queen's cabin. Monsieur Fuquay had a noticeable scowl on his face.

Charles noticed upon rummaging through several passages, the garcon's latter entries were sketchy, incomplete, and bore no dates. Two items in particular interested the king deeply.

— *I caught another glimpse of the queen. Practically every night, it seems, she strolls the deck alone. She must be thinking of her husband. I know from personal experience that it's lonely not being close to the one you love. I wish*

Her Majesty could climb the rope ladder so she can see how beautiful it is up here. Right now, I'm looking at her through my spyglass. She is lovely as ever.

— *The storm is subsiding. I believe the* Vera Cruz *is being attacked. I wish I were in the crow's nest, but I don't think it's safe anywhere. Is it possible? Have my eyes deceived me? Monsieur Fuquay just knifed Captain De Villefort in the back!*

Charles never did learn what happened to Francois Gallant. As it were, he was killed when one of the *Seascape's* cannon shots splintered the *Vera Cruz's* main mast, toppling it eighty feet below where the young man was tearfully clutching Captain De Villefort in his arms. Francois's bloodstained jacket and lifeless form was all that was left when the *Vera Cruz* listed toward the starboard before sinking to the bottom of the sea. His journal was one of the items among the remnants that had been salvaged before the ship had sunk.

Charles closed the tattered book and tinkled his bell. Truffaut entered the room. "Yes, Your Majesty?"

"Claude, I've decided on a replacement for Governor Dupree."

"Splendid, Your Excellency."

"Kindly inform Monsieur Fuquay that I would like to see him at once."

"Certainly, Your Majesty."

"And, Truffaut?"

"Yes, Your Majesty?"

"I'd like to see Bevier as well, the two of them, together."

"At once, Your Majesty."

XXXVI

Bevier, Fuquay, and Charles

"Bevier, do you realize that if you came to me in the first place, none of this would have happened? Catherine would not be in the state she's in today. Speak up. What have you to say for yourself?"

"Your Majesty, I cannot change the tides of time. I pray for her every hour that she will get well again. I assure you, Your Highness, I am completely devoted to my queen; and whatever I may have done, I did so because it was precisely as she wanted it to be."

"Then you do not deny that while serving the queen you were betraying me, your king."

"I don't deny anything, Your Majesty. However, if in serving the queen I did disobey you, for this I indeed apologize and beg your forgiveness. My offense was certainly not intentional."

"Bevier, you would beg for my forgiveness is what you said. Would you beg for my mercy as well?"

"No, Your Majesty, I will not beg for your mercy."

Fuquay looked at Charles, as if to say, "Why don't you just execute him and get it over with?" Pierre did not appear particularly interested in the king's line of interrogation.

"Tell me, Bevier, why won't you beg for mercy, if I may be of mind to show it?"

"Because, Your Majesty, what I did for Catherine, I would do again and again. You see, she placed her trust in me, and it gave me great joy in returning it."

"Monsieur Fuquay believes I should have you hanged. What do you say?"

"I say you should decide for yourself how I should be judged, but not because of anything Monsieur Fuquay has to say about it."

"And why not? He has served me well, ever since I can remember when."

"He has served himself well, Your Majesty. Pierre Fuquay is a traitor to you and his country."

Fuquay stood up and reached for a hand pistol he kept in his jacket.

"Calm yourself, Pierre. Let's not be so hasty. Allow Bevier to finish what he's saying. I haven't had such amusement in a long time." Looking at Catherine's coachman, Charles said, "Is there anything else you wish to add before I pronounce sentence upon you?"

"No, Your Majesty, I can't think of anything at the moment."

"Very well, Bevier, tomorrow you shall be executed at the break of dawn. There is nothing left to be said." Tinkling his bell, Claude Truffaut entered the chamber. Charles spoke indifferently. "Have Bevier remanded in his quarters under lock and key. Make sure he is well guarded. He's to have no visitors. Take him away. I wish to have a word in private with Monsieur Fuquay."

"Yes, Your Majesty." Truffaut's voice was noticeably somber.

*   *   *

"The physicians tell me it will only be a matter of a day or two before Catherine expires."

"I'm most disheartened to hear this sad news, Your Majesty. Has she shown any signs of regaining consciousness?"

"No, Pierre, not for an instant. I'm truly beside myself. I must find a replacement for the many hours of solace she gave me, before I go absolutely mad."

"Surely you don't intend to remarry so soon, assuming Catherine does not recover, that is?"

"No, no, Fuquay, Catherine instilled in me enough feminine affectation to last a lifetime. What I was thinking was an amusement of a different sort."

"If I can assist you in any way, Your Majesty."

"I can always count on you, Pierre. Now that you mention it, there is something you can perhaps do for me, after all."

"Anything, Your Majesty, there's nothing I shan't do for my king."

"While you were dodging storms and vulgar pirates in the Caribbean, things haven't been going ever so smoothly here either. When Edward died, the newly crowned King Henry decided to look unkindly upon France. He never cared all that much for Catherine, you know. Apparently she received most of her father's attention. I tend to sense there are more anarchists and traitors in our midst, thanks to Henry, than there have ever been before."

"What is it you would like for me to do, Your Majesty?"

"At the slightest sign of hostility emanating from across the channel, I wish to be informed."

"Without saying, Your Majesty."

"And just one more thing, Pierre, there's a gentleman, I don't believe you've ever met him, he's presently just completed an amusing device that I'd like for you to give me your candid opinion with regard to its functional use."

"I would be delighted, Your Majesty, what's the gentleman's name? Perhaps I've heard of him somewhere in my travels."

"His name escapes me, Pierre; it'll come to me in a moment. It's very good of you to assist me in this matter. You see, the device has never been tested before."

"Device, what sort of device, Your Majesty?"

"It's not like anything you've ever imagined. Trust me. It's quite unique, at least, that's what I've been told."

"You have elevated my curiosity beyond distraction, Your Majesty. I must see it at once."

"Oh, yes, now I remember. Pierre, do you happen to know a gentleman by the name of Monsieur Joseph-Ignace Guillotin?"

"The name is vaguely familiar. That's all, Your Majesty. Is he the gentleman whose device you would like for me to give my candid opinion?"

"So clairvoyant, Monsieur Fuquay, how will I ever manage without you?"

"Without me? I'm afraid you're very much mistaken, Your Majesty. You can count on my devoted service, for however long either of us shall live."

"Ah, if we only had the foresight of knowing the exact time and hour!"

"In this, Your Majesty, not even I can predict whatever longevity fate's future has prescribed for either of us."

"Splendidly spoken, Monsieur Fuquay, splendidly spoken."

"Is there anything else, Your Majesty?"

"Come to think of it, there is. Pierre, would you mind seeing to it personally that Bevier is delivered to the courtyard at the break of dawn? I see the people of France are already queuing up for his execution."

"I would be delighted, Your Majesty."

"Thank you, Pierre, that will be all."

Fuquay bowed profusely and started to take his leave.

"How many times have you acknowledged your loyalty to me, Pierre, as you just now did, since we have known each other?"

"A rather curious question, Your Majesty. I suppose many more than I can count. Why do you ask, My Liege?"

"Just wondering, Pierre, just wondering that if I had a gold sovereign for every time one of my subjects bowed his head in homage to me, I'd undoubtedly be richer than a king."

In trying to discern the meaning of what His Majesty just said, the previous notion, as to why Charles wanted him to accompany Bevier to the gallows, escaped his mind completely.

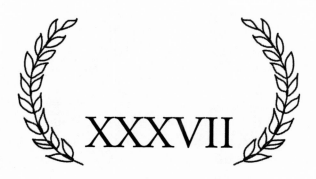

XXXVII

A Day of Reckoning

"**M**onsieur Fuquay, what is the purpose of execution?"

"To end one's life, naturally."

"Exactly! So what's the point of inflicting unnecessary pain on the victim to be executed? Why not treat everyone the same? This way none of the classes can proclaim foul when His Majesty sentences an individual to death. The device I wish for you to examine is swift and precise. Death is instantaneous."

"Continue, Monsieur Guillotin, your discourse intrigues me."

"As you can see, Monsieur Fuquay, the contrivance consists of an upright frame. At the top I've attached an oblique-edged knife. It is extremely sharp and weighted, to be sure. The instrument is meaningless unless it successfully slices through the neck of its intended victim. Let me show you. The individual to be executed lies on the platform in a prone position. Note the basket just below where the knife comes down."

"Basket?"

"Yes, to catch the severed head."

"Ingenious!"

"Yes, indeed, but unfortunately, Monsieur Fuquay, I can't take all the credit for creating this magnificent prototype. I merely added a few efficient details to perfect it."

"So much for the axe, hangman's noose, or burnings at the stake—such a pity, don't you think?"

"Exactly, Monsieur Fuquay, and this is why I need your candid opinion. You see, I do not wish to disenchant Charles. Monsieur Bevier's execution must be scintillating, to say the least. I'd hate for His Majesty to feel he's misjudged me. One never knows how he'll react to sheer disappointment."

"You needn't concern yourself, Monsieur Guillotin, Charles will be absolutely ecstatic."

"As you can see, Monsieur Fuquay, the blade is attached to a sturdy rope and will soon be raised by the executioner. At a given signal by His Majesty, he will release the rope's tension. In a split second or two—thud! Amusing, don't you agree?"

"Sensational, most ingenious. Charles will certainly ennoble you to govern one of his provinces."

"An undeserved honor, I am merely his humble servant. I've been meaning to ask, Pierre, is it all right if I call you Pierre? We barely met, and I feel I've known you all my life."

"Certainly, Joseph, I too feel that in this short while we have already become closest of friends."

"I agree. What I've been curious to ask, well, I am absolutely fascinated by your attire. Your costume is absolutely exquisite." Pierre Fuquay looked quite the courtly gentleman in his close-fitting doublet. Expensive lace adorned the long-sleeved cuffs, while a splash of jewels graced his ornate jacket. His feathered hat and buckled shoes gave Pierre an obvious touch of medieval splendor.

"It so happens, Joseph, that upon Bevier's execution, after his head has been decapitated, that is, I'm to be appointed France's newly ordained foreign minister. Charles just yesterday asked me to fill the shoes of Governor Jean Dupree. I'm certain you've already learned, how shall I put it, that he recently went down with his ship?"

"Unfortunate incidents usually have their bright side. Don't you agree, Pierre?"

"If all is in readiness, Joseph, I believe it's time for me to escort Monsieur Bevier to the threshold of his fate. Incidentally, do you have a proper name for your device?"

"Since it was I who perfected it, I thought it should be named after me, but with an *e* at the end."

"Very appropriate indeed, Joseph, the term *guillotine* has a ring of winsomeness to it."

"My exact sentiments, Pierre, how well you read my mind!"

*   *   *

The palace courtyard was crammed with onlookers. They came to see what was promised to be a spectacular event. A hush came over the boisterous crowd when Monsieur Pierre Fuquay stepped forward with Bevier in tethers. The two of them approached Monsieur Guillotin who was standing next to his insipid creation. Everyone's eyes were adhered to the strange device that exceeded twenty feet above the ground. The grotesque instrument of death captivated the throng's curiosity. Because it was a novelty, no one could anticipate how the assemblage would react to anything as bizarre as this.

Bevier was a friend of the people. Though he enjoyed the amenities of the royal palace, he never disenfranchised himself from the peasant class. In fact, whenever he could, Bevier assisted the impoverished. He was the chief intermediary of a secret network that provided a constant flow of food emanating from the king's stately kitchens to the ravaged streets of Paris. Bevier had been clever in his ways. Not once was he ever suspected of pilfering food from the regal pantry. Beatrice, the queen's handmaiden, assisted him; but it was Catherine who had orchestrated the project.

As Fuquay approached the guillotine with Bevier in tow, the crowd began to murmur groans of discontent. Their friend and ally was about to be executed, and there was nothing they could do to stop it. The executioner tugged on the rope, while everyone watched the blade ascend. Charles was standing by his upper chamber window and held a lace handkerchief in his hand.

"Are you positively certain it will work?" he remembered saying to Joseph-Ignace Guillotin.

"Absolutely, Your Majesty, without a doubt."

"Even if your own head depended on it?"

"Yes, Your Majesty, even if my own head depended on it."

Seeing that Charles was ready for the proceedings to begin, Fuquay ordered Bevier to be brought forth. Pierre approached the accused and asked him the customary question, "Monsieur Bevier Lamont, do you have anything you wish to say before your sentence of execution for high treason is administered?"

Bevier gave an affirmative nod to Fuquay and turned to face the populace. Charles looked on from his perch by the window.

"People of France, you know me well enough not to believe that the charges leveled against me are true. One can rightfully say I have not always agreed with all His Majesty's edicts and proposals, but I denounce anyone a liar who dares proclaim me a traitor to my king or country.

"My beloved citizens of France, have hope and do not despair. Know that I harbor no bitterness in my heart for anyone. Hold your heads high, and fight for what is right and just. Love one another, as Almighty God has loved each of us. One day, be assured, France will once again be the great nation she once was. Long live the king! God save the queen!"

Cheers spontaneously erupted from the bystanders. Turning toward the executioner, Bevier said, "I'm ready."

The hooded man dressed in black knelt before the condemned prisoner to implore his forgiveness. "You are merely doing your duty. For that I can forgive you, and my blessing I give to you as well—for soon you will deliver me to my Creator who has affixed for me a mansion where pain and suffering does not exist."

The executioner stood up and escorted Bevier to a nearby platform. Lying in a prone position, the queen's servant nestled his neck within the curvature of the block. Just below it, a receptacle waited forebodingly to catch his severed head.

Charles gave the signal. The king looked away. He could not bring himself to see the rest. It was the first time his stomach felt queasy in carrying out a death sentence. No matter what a person has done wrong, when you have known him for what seemed a lifetime, the difficult task in ending his life is revolting, to say the least.

The king suddenly froze. He heard the shuffling and outcry in the courtyard. Moments later a familiar voice pierced his eardrums. Charles caressed the embroidered cloth close to his heart. In the midst of the din, he heard it. Down came the blade. The horrifying sound of a thud shattered his thoughts. Cheers reverberated in unison. The king sadly glanced over his shoulder. Looking downward, he caught a glimpse of what he already knew was in store for his blurred vision.

The head was indeed severed, as Monsieur Guillotin had guaranteed it would be. The eyes of the victim appeared as though to be staring up at Charles, Pierre Fuquay's eyes. They would come to haunt Charles afterward, revisiting him on countless nightmarish occasions.

"Pierre, I did forewarn, you were next in line to fill his shoes, the 'deceased' Governor Dupree's shoes," Charles spoke resolutely to the victim's eyes that would not close.

The cheers continued. "God save the king! Long live the queen!" Truffaut approached Charles. Taking him gently by the elbow, he led the king away from the window.

"Your Majesty," he said, "Catherine often reminded him, time and time again, 'Be careful, Pierre, of what you sow, for in the end, it is indeed what ye shall reap.'"

Ignoring Truffaut's remark, with a renewed smirk on his face, Charles said, "I'm actually convinced the people of France approved my decision to dismiss Fuquay, as I did."

"Undoubtedly, Your Majesty, they most certainly approved. A proclamation denouncing Monsieur Fuquay as a traitor has already been posted. In fulfilling your wishes, Monsieur Dantes and Jacques Lafitte's names have been reinstated to His Majesty's good graces, as has Bevier's."

"Very good, Claude, perhaps now I'll have a moment's peace."

"You sound disheartened, Your Majesty. What's troubling you?"

"Catherine died not two hours ago."

"My sorrowful condolences, Your Majesty, the queen was loved by all France."

"I should think one month's duration should be sufficient for a king to mourn. Life must go on. There shall be a regal ball soon afterward. Be very selective in whom you invite. Louie needs a proper mother, not someone who's contented with leaving my son with a dozen squabbling nursemaids."

"Yes, Your Excellency, I will be most selective and discreet, in the usual manner."

"I've been meaning to say, Truffaut, you were right. The proletariat seems quite satisfied with this morning's performance. Perhaps the citizens of France will look upon me more kindly in the future."

"Indeed they will Your Majesty."

"Claude, I almost forgot to mention—Edward of France, before Henry did away with the poor fellow, sent in anticipation of Catherine's giving birth the finest stable of geldings you ever did see. It's never too early for my young prince to learn his equestrian skills. Do you think Bevier could possibly forgive me for temporarily proclaiming him a traitor? He's an excellent trainer of steeds, you know."

"Monsieur Bevier Lamont has always had a kindly, forgiving heart, Your Majesty. I'm confident he'll see to it that young Louie becomes the finest equestrian in all France."

"Just as I surmised, Claude, just as I surmised."

"Is there anything else, Your Majesty?"

"Come to think of it, there is. Inform Monsieur Guillotin that His Majesty is more than pleased for the way he gained Fuquay's confidence so quickly.

I never thought for a moment that Pierre would trod so close to his curious invention. It made the proceeding flow rather smoothly, and without saying, it conveniently helped me to resolve a rather sensitive issue."

"I'll see to it immediately, Your Majesty. Will that be all?"

"I believe I'll have a goblet of wine, Claude. Have it brought to the Rose Garden. As difficult it is for me to imagine, the day is perfectly gorgeous."

"Perfectly, Your Majesty, shall I give the order for the cathedral bells to chime? Catherine's admirers ought to be notified immediately that their beloved queen is no longer with us."

"Yes, of course, Truffaut, how insensitive of me not to have thought of it beforehand. Though I can't imagine he'll be concerned in the least, send a courier to Henry that his precious sister has gone to heaven, if there is such a place, to be with her father." Charles paused and then continued to say, as though he really meant it, "I wonder if either Henry or I will ever get to see them again."

"Certainly, Your Majesty."

"And don't forget the wine, Claude."

"To be brought to the Rose Garden, indeed, Your Majesty."

XXXVIII

Catherine and Charles

Charles had given explicit orders not to be disturbed. He looked upon Catherine for what was to be the last time. Several tall candles extending from elaborate brass holders burned brightly in the windowless alcove where the queen reposed in the quietude of the chamber. The king held a letter Catherine had left by her bedside moments after her descent from the rope ladder on the *Dantes's Revenge*. She had clearly foreseen her sojourn on earth had neared its completion. The undated inscription read,

> *Dearest Charles,*
>
> *Can you ever forgive me for my human frailty? My one regret in life is that I was unfaithful to you. Though I betrayed you only once, I feel I had forsaken you a thousand times. You must know that I am totally to blame for whatever has transpired between Monsieur Jacques Lafitte and me. Thank God you know me well enough to know that I speak the truth.*
>
> *Charles, I have already made my peace with God and would feel terribly remiss if I left this world without imparting to you, my noble king, these heartfelt sentiments. You see, a dying woman knows when*

her life is done, especially when she's the Queen of France. Shed not a single tear, my prince. Instead, take to heart these, our Lord's precious words.

Before I embarked on my journey, I left our wedding Bible on the settee in our boudoir. Let it be a companion to you. Therein you will find truth, love, forgiveness, and forever happiness. Heed the words, Charles. They will bring you much comfort. These are my favorite, because they sum up all that is required of a faithful servant of God.

"Love the Lord your God with all your heart, with all your soul, and with all your mind . . . Love your neighbor as you love yourself" (Matthew 22:37-39).

+ Catherine +

"They'll be here momentarily, Catherine. For all that has transpired, under the circumstances, I think you will agree that things were handled rather proficiently."

Speckles of reflected colors danced about in every direction. The diadem Catherine was wearing, the multifaceted tiara she had always prized from the very first moment she laid eyes on it, gave the queen's ghostly complexion a kaleidoscopic countenance. Looking upon her, Charles continued to say, "Catherine, my dearest Catherine, did you actually think for a single instant that I would let them display your crown jewels among heathen savages in some remote godforsaken archipelago? You often spoke of my remarkable ingenuity. I had it all planned from the very first moment Fuquay, God pity his wretched soul, divulged his ridiculous plan to the others. If only they hadn't unanimously agreed with him, the fools.

"Do you recall the din that took place in the courtyard, just before the container bearing your crown had been sealed shut? When I asked that the curtains be drawn to shed a bit of light on the dismal occasion, a disturbance had arisen in the patio below. I asked Pierre to see to the matter. It was effortless for me to switch the two cases. I removed your tiara and simply replaced it with an identical facsimile. No one noticed a thing because I had Truffaut stand in the way of what I was doing. You see, if I told you ahead of time what I had planned on doing, there would have been no suspenseful drama in the banter to follow.

"Forgive me, Catherine, if only I had been aware you'd react the way you did, I'd—" *Tap, tap, tap.* They had come for the queen. Charles touched

Catherine tenderly for one last time and delicately closed the lid to her casket. The dazzling colors emanating from the multifaceted tiara instantly vanished.

"All is in readiness, Your Highness," Truffaut's voice came through the closed door.

"Enter," Charles said, "it's unlocked."

*   *   *

The six-foot trench was supposed to be filled with stones from the quarry, so that a monument honoring Catherine would find a permanent home in the palace Rose Garden where the queen had spent much of her leisure time. At least, this is what the diggers had been told. When they returned the following morning to complete their task, the furrow had been filled in, and an array of freshly planted flowers had already replaced the hollowed site.

Charles thanked them for their meticulous adhesion to following his specific instructions the day before. It so happened he had a change of heart and thought the bed of flowers was more suitable for the occasion, since Catherine had always been partial to pink English rose. After dismissing the tillers, the king reminded Truffaut to make sure the archbishop was aware he was too grief stricken to attend the queen's funeral ceremony and that he was more than satisfied with the preparations the minister outlined in connection with the burial arrangements to follow.

*   *   *

The bells of St. Monica's Cathedral pealed loudly. Catherine's closed casket, which contained a hidden recessed lock, basked in the candlelit sanctuary. A velvety prie-dieu remained conspicuously void of the occasion's principal dignitary. High-ranking clergymen knelt ceremoniously before the queen's coffin. Hymns of praise were being chanted. They echoed throughout the vaulted knave of the gothic cathedral and beyond. People of all denominations came to pay their last respects. Multitudes assembled in droves along cobblestone avenues flanking the prestigious house of worship.

Whispers of "Where's the king?" rippled among the pews and spilled into the crowded vestibules where countless mourners had gathered.

"He's overwhelmingly distraught, and who can blame him?" voices hissed in response, as though the soothsayers had been privy to the king's inner, heartfelt emotions. More sacred hymns enveloped the cathedral; then, a brief melancholic homily reiterating the queen's dedicative spirit to France followed. A litany of requiem prayers indicated a closure to the proceedings was imminent—still, no Charles.

At the conclusion of the ceremony, pallbearers lifted the casket and started to parade their way to Catherine's final resting place. St. Monica's exclusive cemetery had been reserved for noble dignitaries of the highest rank. The adjacent hallowed grounds skirted a knoll that overlooked the grand palace. It was indeed a lovely spot. Poplar trees, hedge groves, and perennial gardens lavishly bloomed within the hallowed gates where Catherine's empty coffin was laid to rest.

*   *   *

"Several dignitaries are waiting to see you, Your Majesty. They wish to extend their sincerest condolences personally."

"You mean they want to procure their way into my good graces by acknowledging Catherine's departure with a generous stipend."

"More than generous, Your Majesty."

"Very well, Claude, delay them a while longer. Tell my sympathizers I'm in seclusion and will receive them after I've completed my meditations."

"Certainly, Your Majesty."

After Truffaut left the king, Charles stood up from where he was seated, set down his wine goblet, and walked over to the newly planted arrangement of flowers. He drew nearer and nearer to inhale the lavish scent of pinkish rose and yellow gardenia.

"Catherine," he said, "I understand your admirers are flocking to St. Monica's by the thousands in hopes of gathering a glimpse of your mausoleum. Though their intentions are well received, it's a pity they're merely paying homage to a barren sepulcher. Princess, I'm not yet convinced as you to what awaits me on the other side. Surely you don't mind my indulgence in keeping you close at hand? Your being here gives me great comfort, cheri. This way I can quite conveniently enjoy the repose of your company without having to make a public spectacle of myself. You may be pleased to know the bishop consecrated these very grounds earlier this morning. So rest in peace, my lovely queen, rest peacefully forevermore.

"Before I leave you for now, my precious, I make you this promise. Catherine, this very garden will be Louie's frequent playground. You'll have plenty of opportunities to encourage your son to be all that you had hoped for him to be. Someday, I imagine, if he has half the persistence of his mother, and the audacity of his father, we both know who that is, our young prince will indubitably settle the score with Henry whom I daresay never liked either of us.

"I see in the distance that even the heavens are shedding tears for you. However plentiful they may be, Catherine, without saying, it goes doubly for me."

*   *   *

To be precise, its exact location was 45 degrees 16' N and 38 degrees 22' W. Quicksand, Muslim Green, and Yates could not change his mind. To lock their captain in the cargo hold would only delay what he intended to do. The three of them were meloncholic as they lowered the shore boat in the waters of the Atlantic.

Each of the mateys embraced his captain and witnessed Lafitte descend the rope ladder. He took no provisions with him. Sadly, the trio watched Jacques steer the small craft toward the moonlit horizon until he disappeared from sight.

"Those three stars next to the bright one, they surely weren't there just the other night?" Yates noted to the others.

"You're right matey," answered Quicksand, "and if Captain Brough was correct all along in what he said, I suspect there'll be another one on the horizon in a day or two."

"What was it he said about the stars?" Muslim Green asked. "I plum forgot."

Quicksand replied, "He said that if the good Lord takes a likin' to you, you'll shine like one of those stars yer talkin' about."

"Then do ya reckon Jacques will be among 'em?" Muslim Green choked.

"Yep, he and Catherine both, I imagine," Yates answered with a distinct resonance in his voice. "Haven't ya figured it out yet? They're inseparable."

Epilogue

In the years that followed, Louie grew up to be Catherine's proud prince. It was a stranger bearing ten scars on his brawny back that assisted Bevier in grooming the next ruler of France to be all that his mother had hoped for him to be. Through the years the King of France loved him too, as though the garcon was his very own. Predictably, Henry and Charles became bitter enemies. Perhaps it is just as well we set aside, for the time being, at least, the segment of history that deals with how future events in this particular theater unfolded.

As for the treasure, the elusive papyrus that cryptically outlined its whereabouts surfaced nearly four hundred years later. Time has a habit of divulging well-kept secrets. The largest cache of stolen treasure is no exception. Eventually, it would be unearthed somewhere beneath the craggy shores of Maine in the obscure vicinity of Devil's Cave.

It was a young schoolboy, about the same age as Louis Grapier, when he stowed away on the *Orgueil de France*, who would find himself engulfed in the mystery and intrigue surrounding the newly discovered ancient treasure map. Perhaps it was destiny that suddenly jolted the young lad with a mystifying challenge to decipher the code—much the same as a charge of lightning in a thunderstorm might urge one to inquisitively investigate the principles of its origin.

So too, let us not be overly concerned as to how God will judge those who have imparted to others despicably heinous strokes of fate that would make an individual's soul cringe. Abhor the contemptible acts, rather than the creatures of sin who levied them. A moral being has enough with which to contend in making straight one's own path.

We must be ever mindful of bringing the fight to the proper enemy. Lust, gluttony, greed, sloth, wrath, envy, and pride are the true conspirators that plant seeds of malevolence in the minds and hearts of downtrodden and weakened spirits. Mankind cannot destroy ignorance if, in attempting to do good works, he or she ignores the fundamental truths of human decency.

Forgive me my sins, O Lord, Catherine's meditative prayer, is perhaps a worthy avenue of approach toward a healing process that no one—regardless of religion, race, creed, gender, color, or circumstance of life can lightly dismiss.

Praise be to God! May His healing power and eternal blessings be upon each and every one of us.

Author's Note

Nothing of this world is worthy of permanent immortality, not gold, money, jewels, paintings, coin, stamps, memorabilia, manuscripts, architectural grandeur, antiques, rare collector's items—nothing. The material splendor and ideas interwoven in human nature are subtle reflections of the Creator's genius who has chosen "time" to impart His magnificent artistry to those He saw fit to endow. According to popular concensus, the vast universe which is captured in this capsule of "creation" will pass. *Remember, brothers and sisters, we are dust, and unto dust we shall return.*

Religion must put aside its petty differences and concur that all human life is sacred. Since the Creator humbled His Son to become one of us, the dignity of all mankind must be recognized and upheld. Only after the sediments of avarice, injustice, and prejudice are purged away will the true Person of God be clearly manifested in the fabric of His disciples. Every individual must delve deeply within one's own heart to evaluate and discern the difference of what is essential compared to that which is fleeting.

If what we forge in life is consistent with the Creator's first two principles of love, it will render our stewardship reflective of His sacrificial Lamb. Let this premise be youth's guiding torch. Let it be the primary matter of all our concerns before each one of us has completed his or her timely journey through earth's celestial hourglass.